WHEN STARS
ALIGN

WHEN STARS ALIGN

E. K. McCoy

atmosphere press

For KP.

They say it's what you make,
I say it's up to fate
It's woven in my soul,
I need to let you go
Your eyes, they shine so bright,
I wanna save that light
I can't escape this now,
Unless you show me how

— *from "Demons" by Imagine Dragons*

Chapter 1

ELSIE MCCORMICK

In the utter darkness I hear slow, nearly inaudible gasps for air. It is the only thing of which I am aware—that is, until an overwhelming sensation rises inside me. Slowly my brain processes and then recognizes it as fear. Like a deer caught in the headlights, the fear paralyzes me. Lost somewhere between consciousness and unconsciousness, I realize these weak, pathetic gasps for air belong to me! They are my attempt to hold onto life—at least, I think I'm still alive. I'm not sure if my time on earth has expired, and the darkness is what awaits me as I leave this life, or if I'm holding on to whatever life I have in me. My gasps for air quicken as the overwhelming fear intensifies and I begin to panic.

I will myself to open my eyes—to look past the darkness that surrounds me. But no matter how hard I will myself to see, I am lost—lost in the darkness that is rapidly taking control. I am trapped, suffering, somewhere between life and death.

I try to remember what happened to me—how I ended up

here and, in this condition—but I'm incapable of even forming a coherent thought. My head pounds as bits and pieces of what could very well be the last memories of my life flash through my mind: Marie in a wedding dress, dancing, my maid of honor speech, bubbly champagne, wedding cake, laughing, waving goodbye as the newlyweds drive away, cleaning the reception hall, being the last one to leave while dodging the cold rain and carrying the last box of vases across the street to my car. And then . . . I remember. Out of nowhere, a car came at me faster than I could move—the blinding headlights, the screeching tires, my screams as I tried to leap out of the way. I thought I had cleared the car, but it clipped me in mid-air and sent me flying and spinning out of control into the darkness.

I'm trying to breathe, but it feels as if a hundred-pound weight is on my chest, preventing me from taking even the slightest breath. As my lungs plead for air, another sensation courses through my body. My mind decides to call this feeling pain. But it's nothing like any pain I've experienced before. It feels as if every inch of my body is burning from the inside out. The pain intensifies, making the darkness swirl and then suddenly explode into thousands of sparkling, multicolored dots.

The dots remind me of the fireworks I used to watch as a child while perched on top of my father's shoulders. "The fireworks are all for you, kiddo!" he'd tease as we'd watch the sky on the Fourth of July, and he'd loudly sing "Happy Birthday" to me over the noisy booms.

Suddenly, my happy memory is stolen from me as the pain reaches a level beyond my comprehension. The dots begin to swirl again—only this time at a pace that makes my stomach drop the way it does on one of those carnival rides that throws you straight up into the air then drops you without warning. I open my mouth to scream, but nothing comes out. I'm still trying to catch my breath from the sensation of free-falling. As soon as I do, I whimper in pain, but my whimper is muffled by bloody vomit. I gag as the metallic taste fills my mouth. Now I know I'm still alive—but also that I won't be for much longer. Surely, it's not humanly possible for anyone to live through the pain and agony I'm experiencing.

Then—before I can cry or yell for help—the pain subsides, and my body goes completely numb. I feel nothing. I no longer feel as if my lungs have grown fingernails that are frantically clawing holes in my chest seeking air. I no longer feel as if my body is burning from the inside out. I can't feel the cold rain falling on my face, making my body quiver.

Momentarily, I'm grateful the pain has stopped, but at the same time I'm terrified. Part of me knows the pain has stopped for no other reason than this: I am dying. I'm not ready to die! In my mind I'm pleading for more time, but I know there's no making deals. I learned this at a young age as I watched my dad bury my mom and my grandma bury my dad. My parents were taken from me far too soon; why should my life end any differently?

As I think of my family, my panic and terror begin to subside. My wheezing steadily decreases. My lungs are giving up the battle to expand. The swirling darkness grinds to a halt and becomes still. Like a silent, starless night, I am filled with nothing—nothing but steady, never-ending darkness. And suddenly I'm no longer afraid. I know my family awaits.

I am unaware that the rain has stopped falling onto my bloody body as I lie in the middle of the road. I can't hear the sirens from the approaching ambulance. I don't realize that one of the happiest days of my life just became one of the worst. Before I take my last gasp of air and let the darkness take my body, my mind recalls one last name: *Auggie*—the only man I ever loved.

The last word to escape my lifeless, purple lips was

"Why?" Instead of my life flashing before my eyes, or a bright light summoning me, it was his bright blue eyes that I saw as I let the darkness take me.

Chapter 2

AUGUSTUS OWENS

Another Saturday night spent working when I could be at home drinking some MadTree beer and catching up on my DVRed The Walking Dead. *Why did I decide to be an ER doctor? Better yet, why did I sign up for the night shift?* I asked myself these questions as I entered UC Hospital's Emergency Department holding my white lab coat over my head to keep from getting drenched. Thanks to the massive storms passing through the tri-state area, there were accidents everywhere. Both I-71 and I-75 may as well have been a parking lot. The traffic standstill had caused me to be fifteen minutes late for work and I despise being late for work.

I cursed myself upon entering the ER: *Why did I move back to Cincinnati when no one here knows how to drive—especially in the rain?* Once inside the waiting room, I removed my lab coat from my head and shook it several times attempting to remove some of the rain before putting it on over my scrubs. I took the opportunity to assess the room and get a feel for what I was walking into. Currently, only one patient was at the registration desk while a few people sat in chairs scattered throughout the room. In the corner of the room a middle-aged man was frantically pacing. I knew that pace; someone he cared about was sick or injured. *Waiting on an update,* I thought to myself as I walked past the registration desk and gave Andrea, the receptionist, a smile and a head nod before she buzzed me in through the doors that read "STAFF ONLY."

I walked through the doors and to the middle of the room where I expected to see everyone gathered in our quality control area. QC was where doctors and nurses did their patient charting, signed off at shift change, and hung out whenever we had a few minutes to spare. Currently, there were only two nurses there—one on the phone and one on the computer. As I glanced down the surrounding halls, I realized that all the examination room doors were shut, and no doctors were anywhere in sight. From the looks of it, no one would be leaving on time tonight; everyone was too busy.

To confirm my suspicion, I glanced up at the digital patient dashboard hanging above the nurses' station. The dashboard showed information about each patient in the rooms and kept track of how many patients were in the waiting room or coming in by ambulance. One look at the dashboard, and I knew the waiting room had deceived me. Almost all the rooms were full; I was in for a long night. Not only were we busy, but it was raining, which usually meant more accidents. And it was November, notorious for the start of the flu season. I braced myself for a hectic, eventful shift.

"Good evening, Dr. Owens." I looked down from the board to see Natalie standing right beside me, grinning ear to ear.

"Good evening, Natalie." I smiled back at her. "Glad you're here tonight." My smile began to fade as I immediately re-gretted my choice of words. I glanced back up at the board to avoid eye contact with her.

Natalie has had her eye on me ever since I started working

here six months ago. (Don't get me wrong; she was certainly easy on the eyes.) She had that classic "California girl" look—tall, skinny, busty, always tan, with sandy blonde hair and perfectly straight, white teeth. We'd been flirting back and forth for a while now, but girls like her just weren't doing it for me. Was she attractive? Hell, yeah! Would I hook up with her? Yes. But when it came to the "Natalies" in my life, I'd been there, done that too many times to count. Other than being single and working in the ER together, we had nothing else in common. Lately, I'd wanted something different, something more—something I used to have.

I shook my head to try and erase that last thought from my head. After all the daunting choices and sacrifices I'd made in the past, and my busy work life, maintaining a relationship was next to impossible. I had come to accept that an occasional fling every now and then was all I could handle. My life was dedicated to medicine now.

My thoughts were interrupted. "Well, I'll be here all night, Doctor," she said flirtatiously. "So if there's anything—and I do mean anything—that I can do for you, you just let me know," she said, flashing me that pearly white smile.

"Thanks," I said with a weary smile on my face and then added, "Looks like we'll have plenty of patients to keep us busy tonight." Her smile quickly faded. Helping me with patients was not what she was implying.

There was no time to get coffee or to check my email. After putting my wallet and keys in my locker, I returned to QC and glanced up at the dashboard to see that there were five new patients now waiting and a motor vehicle trauma patient (MVT) on the way via ambulance.

Within an hour, I was in full-on work mode, bouncing from room to room. Dehydration from the flu in room two; stitches in room three; suspected GI bug in room five; foreign body in the anus in room six. Wait, anus? (No matter how many years I've been practicing, I still can't figure out objects lodged in the anus. Show me bloody guts and mangled limbs and I'm fine, but just the thought of objects stuck where they shouldn't be makes me queasy.)

I will definitely be passing that one off to one of the residents, I thought to myself as I walked into room seven, where a man with chest pains awaited me.

It was midnight, and all our exam rooms were still full. We finally started to slow down after one o'clock in the morning, but it wasn't until close to two—six hours into my shift—that I finally was able to relax and take a quick break. After I checked my email, I headed to the break room to eat my "lunch." Upon entering, the aroma of pizza filled my nostrils, and my mouth began to water. I hadn't realized how hungry I was until now. Three large Dewey's Pizza boxes sat on the counter—leftovers from this afternoon's conference, I presumed. One of the perks of being a doctor was the free food. Every day there was some sort of conference being held to keep us up-to-date on our skills, and with conferences came free food. Although the night shift had to watch the recorded conference online, the day shift always saved leftover food for us in the break room.

Andy, a tall, skinny, redheaded ER doctor, was sitting at the break room table drinking coffee. "Catch last week's episode of *Game of Thrones*, Gus?"

"Nah, man, haven't had time," I said as I grabbed two pieces of pepperoni and sausage pizza and sat down next to him.

"I know the feeling." Andy nodded in agreement as he took a sip of his coffee.

I took a big bite of my pizza. "Why aren't you eating? You on some kind of liquid diet?" I teased as I motioned towards

Andy's coffee.

"I wish I could stomach pizza," Andy said with a disappointed look on his face as he eyed my food and took another sip of his coffee. "Just getting over the flu. Still not feeling all that great," he added as he put down his cup of coffee and removed a tissue from his pocket and blew his nose. "Hoping I can head out a little early if we're not too busy," he said as he leaned back to toss the tissue into the garbage can behind us.

"Yeah, yeah," I said with a smirk on my face. "My ass, you're sick! You're probably just late for a hot date!" I jokingly slapped his shoulder.

Andy and I were the two newest attending ER physicians. I had started last May, and he had started towards the end of July after completing his last year of residency at Ohio State. We were both single, and all the nurses loved when the new, young, single doctors came along. It seemed like adding an MD to the end of your name instantly attracted most girls—or guys, depending on your preference. Sometimes I felt like walking into schools and telling all the nerdy, book-smart boys not to worry, that their lives would get better after high school—that once you had an MD or a PhD behind your name, all the girls would come running.

I glanced over at Andy with his red hair and glasses. I knew that he, like many of my colleagues, had been one of those not-so-popular high schoolers. As for me, I had plenty of friends in high school, but thanks to my father, I never had the freedom or luxury of spending time with them—especially with girls. The mere thought of my father was making my blood pressure rise. But before I allowed myself to get all worked up over him, Andy laughed, bringing my thoughts back to our current conversation.

"You know me—different girl every night," he said with a wink. I laughed at his joke. We practically lived and breathed work. We had one goal, and one goal only—to survive our first year as attending physicians. Being a new doctor required that you earn your colleagues' trust and, most importantly, their respect. It didn't matter if you had a couple of years of experience under your belt or if you were brand new; if you were new to a hospital, it was important to maintain a good reputation if you wanted to succeed and have any chance of making chief one day.

Unlike Andy, I wasn't new to the hospital. About six years ago, I had completed my residency here. At the time I had worked all shifts. Now, though, there were only a few staff members working night shift with me that I even recognized—a janitor, an ultrasound technician, and a nurse named Nick. Either way, things were different for me now that I was a trauma specialist. I still needed to learn the ropes of the night shift—who I could trust, who I could depend on, who I could ask if I need a favor—and most importantly, who to never cross or tick off. Up until now, no matter where I worked, learning these few things had helped me to survive and succeed.

Beep-beep-beep-beep. Our conversation was cut short by our pagers going off. We both looked down to see the words "Code Gray" followed by this message on the PA: "May I have your attention, please. MVT—ETA, five minutes. Again, MVT—ETA five minutes."

"Ah, man!" Andy mumbled. "I don't think I have enough energy for another trauma. I'm exhausted," he said as he rubbed his hand across his forehead.

"It's okay, bro. I got this one," I said as I sprang out of my chair, threw the rest of my pizza away, and raced out the break room door.

"Thanks, I owe you one," I heard him call after me while the break room door was closing behind me.

This was the part I loved most about being a trauma specialist—the sudden adrenaline rush you got when you knew that someone else's life depended on you—your knowledge, your talent, your skills—and most importantly, your determination. You had to be on your toes at all times, especially when working in the trauma bay. One mistake could easily cost a life.

I was the first doctor to arrive in the trauma bay, where a handful of nurses were already busily making sure the room was fully stocked with all the medicine and supplies we'd need.

"Fill me in," I called out in the room as I washed my hands and tried to catch my breath from my jog to the trauma bay.

"Jane Doe. Between the ages of twenty-five and thirty. Hit while on foot by a drunk driver," Natalie announced.

"You know what that means," I replied in a solemn tone.

"Unfortunately," she moaned. This time her voice indicated concentration, not flirtation.

We all knew that if the paramedics hadn't phoned in more information about the patient by now, it was because they were too busy trying to keep her alive. They hadn't had time for anything else.

People are idiots, I thought to myself. *Why drink and drive, especially in the rain?* I thought as I dried my hands and then put on a gown and gloves.

"Okay, team, we need to bring our A game! Let's save this girl's life!" I said in my best coaching voice imitation to try and ease the tension that had already begun to fill the room.

Moments later, two paramedics were running the patient in through the doors on a stretcher. They were soaking wet with a mixture of the patient's blood and the rain. The younger of the two paramedics was bagging the patient, helping her to breathe, while the taller and older one pushed the stretcher.

I quickly examined the patient as she lay mostly exposed in her bra and underwear, with torn portions of what appeared to be a dress covering parts of her arms, stomach, and thighs. Every exposed inch of her body was covered in blood and shards of glass. Chest tubes were coming out from both sides of her chest and draining into bags hanging on the stretcher. The bags were already more than half-full of thick, red fluid. An IV bag hung on her left, and fluids were dripping at an extremely rapid rate into her left arm. She was a medical mess.

"Good job, boys!" I called as they approached. I knew the only reason the patient had a pulse was because of them.

"Rundown?" I asked.

"We believe she was crossing the street," the older paramedic with salt-and-pepper hair said. "The driver hit her then crashed into a street pole. He wasn't wearing his seat belt and was pronounced dead on arrival," he continued. "The female victim appears to have multiple facial and body fractures. When we arrived, both of her lungs were collapsed, and she wasn't breathing. After we placed the chest tubes and bagged her, she began to breathe again but has remained unconscious the entire time," he reported without taking his eyes off the woman.

"Someone call X-ray and CT!" I called out as I moved to the table and waited for the paramedics to bring the stretcher up next to it. I already knew that if her lungs were collapsed, the chest x-ray would show multiple rib fractures, but we still had to follow protocol, and imaging was crucial for trauma patients.

"Already did, Dr. Owens. They should be here any minute," Michelle, the charge nurse, answered.

The next thing I knew, the younger paramedic called out in a panic, "Her pulse is dropping, and she's losing blood—fast."

"On three, people," I commanded. "One, two, three." After I said three, the nurses, paramedics, and I all worked together to transfer the patient from the stretcher and onto the examination table.

"We'll take it from here, boys." I gave them a nod of appreciation as they turned to leave the room.

"Good luck!" the older one offered as they left the trauma bay.

I turned my attention to the woman lying before me. As I placed my stethoscope on her chest to listen, I visually examined her. Her nose was definitely broken. Her eyes were puffy and swollen shut, her lip was busted open, and the left side of her face looked as if it had suffered several facial fractures. Judging by the gash on her forehead, she could possibly have brain swelling, bleeding, or both. Her dark hair and blood-stained face made her skin appear ghostly white. Whoever this woman was, her family was going to have a hard time identifying her. She was minutes away from becoming a corpse.

"We need to move faster; I don't think we have much time!" I called out to everyone in the room as I lifted my stethoscope from her body and draped it around my neck. "Someone get this girl another bag of O negative before she bleeds out!" I ordered.

"Already on it," Michelle assured me as she hooked up the blood to the patient's IV.

As the rest of the staff worked busily beside me, I continued to examine the patient. I lifted her eyelid, shone my light into her eye, and checked to confirm that her pupils were responsive while Natalie pushed antibiotics into her IV bag. When examining her eyes, I couldn't help but notice how dark they were. I'd only seen one set of eyes that dark—almost black—but in that moment I didn't have time to think about the woman I'd once loved. In that moment I needed to concentrate on the patient who appeared to be dying in front of me. I moved on to the next task. I have been working in ER long enough to know that if there was blood in her chest, there was most likely blood in her belly as well. I placed both hands on the left, then right, side of her abdomen to feel her spleen and her liver for any obvious signs of enlargement or rupture. Before I could finish her abdominal exam, she began to code.

All at once, everyone went into survival mode. As Natalie completely removed the remaining tattered portion of her dress, Michelle cut off her bra as another nurse simultaneously placed the sticky AED pads on her chest.

"Get me a round of epi!" I ordered as I reached for the paddles of life that sat on the crash cart behind me.

One of the nurses had anticipated what I would need and was pushing it through her IV before I could even finish my sentence.

"Everyone, clear!" I shouted as I placed the paddles of life onto the woman's chest. The initial shocks jolted her body and flung her forward like a rag doll. I hadn't noticed how small she was until that moment when I saw her petite body momentarily suspended in mid-air just above the stretcher.

We all stopped and waited in silence to hear that sweet, reassuring sound of a heartbeat, but all we heard was the dreadful sound of an EKG flat line.

"Increase the voltage!" I commanded.

Natalie quickly worked to follow my command.

"Clear!" I yelled with determination as the paddles sent a furious shock through the woman's body for a second time.

Again, everyone froze as we listened for the sound of a faint heartbeat. But again, we were taunted by the buzzing of a flat line.

"Another round of epi!" I shouted. While Michelle pushed epinephrine into the IV, I reexamined the woman for anything I might have missed.

There wasn't much to her—only a little more than five feet tall and a hundred pounds. If she lived, she would require several abdominal and plastic surgeries and a long road of recovery. The left side of her face—horribly distorted—was turned towards me. I reached down to feel for even the faintest pulse on the left side of her neck when I noticed a jagged scar about three inches long that started behind her ear lobe and went down the back of her neck. My body froze for what seemed like minutes (but was really only a few seconds) while I processed what I was seeing.

"No!" I shook my head. "It can't be," I quietly said to myself in painful disbelief as my mind began to race.

The scar I used to love to trace. Those eyes darker than the night sky. Her petite figure. Suddenly snapshots of a life I used to know flashed through my mind. Memories from what seemed like a lifetime ago resurfaced. Memories I had buried deep inside and willed myself to forget flooded my mind, and a flurry of emotions overwhelmed me.

"Clear!" I called out, except this time with desperation and confusion in my voice. "This can't be her! This can't be happening to her!" I angrily mumbled to myself as I glared at the monitor and willed it to show me her heartbeat.

Again, the monitor displayed a flat line, and suddenly I was furious. Without hesitation I lowered the table and began to do chest compressions, trying to buy her some time.

"Aren't you going to call it, Dr. Owens?" Natalie asked in exasperation.

My mind was racing, searching for an answer as I pumped her chest and tried to massage her heart back to life. At this point—after several rounds of epi and shocks to the heart—most doctors would realize that they'd done all they could do, accept that the patient was gone, and make that dreadful final call—the time of death. Most doctors, however, didn't have a complex, emotional history with the patient. To everyone else in the room, this woman was just an unlucky Jane Doe lying lifelessly on the bed. But not to me. In an earlier chapter of my life—during a time when I was happy and actually liked myself—this Jane Doe had been my other half, the only girl I'd ever loved, my everything.

"Hang more blood now!" I shouted as I finished my chest compressions.

No one in the trauma bay knew this woman as I once had. No one knew that her heart was pure and kind in spite of having experienced way too much sadness in her life. Her life could not end this soon and this tragically. She didn't deserve to be a lifeless Jane Doe dying before my eyes. No! She deserved a long, happy life that was as beautiful as she was.

Dammit, Gus, think! I commanded myself as I stopped compressions, tilted her head backwards, and gave her two breaths. As my mouth touched her lips for the first time in years, instead of sending chills down my spine as it once had, I wanted to cry as I anxiously blew air into her mouth, willing her to tell me what she needed me to do to keep her alive.

"She's diabetic." Those words subconsciously slipped out of my mouth as I removed my lips from hers. "We need glucose now," I ordered in an angry panic as I began to give chest compressions again.

All the nurses looked at me, confused, before one of them moved to grab the dose.

"Blood, glucose, and epi! Faster, people, faster!" I commanded with desperation in my voice.

The way I describe the trauma bay was organized chaos. When you had the right people working together, life-changing events could occur. Unsalvageable limbs could be saved from being amputated, and bringing someone back to life after they've flatlined for what seemed like entirely too long could even be possible. That is, if—and only if—you had all the right people working together and all the stars aligned.

I had never claimed to be a religious man; however, in the emergency room there was a "force" I was constantly battling. It was present with me at all times in the trauma bay. When things went south faster than I anticipated, or when I some-how found a way to save a person whose body appeared to be nothing but an empty shell, that was when the force was its strongest. I have concluded that this force was the deciding factor between life or death. As humans, we can only do so much before something else takes control and decides our fate for us.

In this moment I knew this was it for her. Either her life would continue, or she would be joining her parents, but I had done all I could do; her fate depended solely on the force. I knew that whatever happened next, this night would haunt me for the rest of my long days and lonely nights.

Natalie pushed glucose into the IV while I frantically continued chest compressions. As soon as the glucose was in, I stopped compressions, grabbed the paddles, and desperately yelled "Clear!" as I choked back tears.

Please God—or whoever you are—she doesn't deserve this, I silently pleaded as the paddles touched her chest one last time.

SEVEN YEARS AGO

(The Girl, the Guy, & Gravity's Pull)

Chapter 3

THE GIRL, ELSIE MCCORMICK

"Come on already," Marie, who was clearly agitated, pleaded as she pounded on my bedroom door. "By the time we get to the party, all the hot fratties will be too drunk to hit on! Don't blow this for me, Smalls!" she called into my room.

"You're lucky I agreed to go to this stupid party," I snapped while examining myself in the full-length mirror that hung behind my door. "I could just skip the party and go to Battle of the Bands, ya know!" I screamed a little louder to ensure Marie heard me. "And don't forget about our deal either—" I reminded her. "Two hours at the party then we go to the concert!" I added to make sure she hadn't forgotten.

Marie and I had been roommates for two years and best friends since kindergarten. We had grown up together in the small town of Deer Park, Ohio, about thirty minutes north of the University of Cincinnati. Our friendship had begun when she was five and I was six. It was my second attempt at kindergarten. My first attempt had ended abruptly one day before Christmas break when Grandma Olive picked me up from school instead of my mom. When I asked Olive where my mom was, she said that Mom wasn't feeling well and Dad had taken her to the hospital to help her get better.

Days passed, and eventually my parents sat me down and explained that Mom had something called cancer that was making her very tired and weak. From that point on, Grandma Olive would be staying with us to help take care of Mom and me. I was too young to understand that Mom was dying.

Her cancer had spread from her breasts into her bones and then, sadly, to her brain. She was past the point of treatment. Doctors said they could try an experimental drug, but there were no guarantees. She'd have to live in the hospital where I wouldn't be able to visit because she'd be in isolation. My mom was given the choice between fighting for more time but not being able to see me, or living what would likely be a shorter lifespan but getting to stay home with me; she chose me.

By spring, everyone gathered around a grave that had my mother's name, Elizabeth McCormick, written on it. All I remember was everyone crying, hugging me, and telling me how much my mom loved me. I didn't understand where my mom had gone; all I knew was I missed her. The following fall, on my first day back to school, I ran into the bathroom stall and started to cry. (I was afraid of school. After all, school was the last place my mom had dropped me off before she got sick.) The next thing I knew, there was a knock on the stall door. I instantly froze in place, too embarrassed to move.

"Hey!" *Knock-knock-knock.* "You in there? Stop crying and come play with me," a stubborn girl's voice commanded from the other side of the stall door.

I hadn't known anyone else was in the bathroom. Embarrassed, I wiped my eyes and held my hand over my mouth to muffle my cries. I tried to be as quiet as I could, hoping the girl would go away.

"I know you're in *thereeeee*," she sang as she peeked her

head under the bathroom stall door and her blonde pigtails hung to the floor. "I'm not leaving until you come out," she added.

I didn't know what else to do, so I opened the door. Standing in front of me with her hands on her hips was a girl with blonde pigtails and a missing front tooth.

"I'm Marie," she said with a smile as she extended her hand for what I thought was going to be a handshake.

"Elsie." I sniffed and rubbed my nose before extending my hand to gently shake hers, but instead of shaking my hand, Marie grabbed my arm and dragged me out of the bathroom and to the playground, insisting that I play with her. Ever since then, Marie has been leading me around, and I have faithfully followed.

I shook my head trying to erase all the sad memories from my childhood. Tonight was to be a fun night; I needed to keep my past at bay and try just to enjoy being a college student.

I inspected my makeup. I never wore much makeup. Not only was I awful at applying it but, fortunately for me, I was blessed with flawless, pale skin and long, dark eyelashes. My eyes needed only a touch of eyeliner and a stroke of eye shadow. I had no need for mascara, as it only made my eyelashes look fake. But one thing I simply couldn't go without was blush. Without blush, my pale skin and dark eyes made me look as if I'd never seen the light of day.

"Guess this is as good as it gets," I mumbled to myself. I tucked my long bangs behind my right ear and let the rest of my natural wavy brown hair fall into place, resting on my small chest.

Next, I focused on my outfit. I have always hated clothing— correction: I have always hated clothing designed for people my size—mostly because of my underdeveloped body. I was twenty-one years old, a towering five feet tall, and I weighed one hundred pounds. Clothes designed for women my age fell off my body, and clothes designed for my body size still had Disney characters and glitter on them. Not to mention, all the stores that carried petite sizes were ridiculously overpriced and they looked like grandma clothes. No offense to grandmas, but I'm twenty-one, not seventy-one; I just wanted to look my age!

I felt like all of these things contributed to my sense of style—or what Marie would argue was my lack of style. Most girls loved going shopping with their mom and girlfriends. Unfortunately for me, I never had those moments with my mom, and clothes shopping with my only girlfriend was frustrating. Everything Marie tried on looked like it was tailor-made for her, whereas I looked like the kid sister wearing her big sister's hand-me-downs. Since my clothing options were rather limited, I stuck with the only thing I was comfortable in—a t-shirt and jeggings.

Tonight, I was sporting black jeggings, red Toms, and a longer, fitted t-shirt that covered my butt. My attempt at dressing up was putting on a necklace. For this outfit I chose a necklace with a cluster of charms dangling below. "Blame it on my ADD" was printed across my chest. I had scored my AWOLNATION t-shirt when they came and played at our local riverside venue, Riverbend, last summer. Marie and I had stood in line for hours to get a good view of the stage. Once they started to play, she looked at me, shook her head in disgust, and screamed over the band, "The things I do for you, Els."

Marie and I had different tastes in music, fashion, guys, and—come to think of it, we didn't agree on much of anything. It's amazing that we'd been friends for fifteen years and got along as well as we did.

Suddenly my door was flung open and smacked into my arm with a *thud.*

"Come on already!" Marie said as she pulled me out of my room by the back of my shirt.

There was no use trying to fight her off. She had six inches on me and more than twice the muscle. For as long as I could remember, she had been an athlete. In the fall, if she wasn't playing tennis, she was playing soccer. In the spring, if she wasn't playing softball, she was running track. She could beat me one-handed in any sport if she wanted to and sometimes liked to remind me of this—as in this instance while she dragged me out of my room, down the stairs, and towards the front door of our apartment.

"What? Time to go, *Mom*?" I asked in a sarcastic tone as I gently rubbed my arm where the door had just hit me. "Without any breakfast?" I laughed as she looked at me and rolled her eyes.

She gave me a playful shove and said, "You better watch it, Smalls," as we grabbed our purses and laughed our way out the door.

It was a typical Saturday night on campus. The streets were loud and full of drunken college students. Most were talking and laughing, but some were arguing as they stumbled off in different directions—off to parties, bars, or wherever the night would take them. Marie and I lived just a couple of blocks away from campus in a small, two-bedroom, one-bath apartment. We didn't care how small it was as long as we had our own bathroom. Our freshman year, we had lived in the dorms and had to share a small, smelly, disgusting, five-stall, three-shower bathroom with the entire floor. I'll never forget the first weekend in our dorm. I woke up on a Sunday morning to find a redhead passed out in her own puke in the middle of the bathroom floor. Tired of sharing a bathroom and listening to arguing, crying, blaring music, and fighting all night long, our decision to leave the dorm and move out our sophomore year was what I called a no-brainer.

It took us the entire summer to find an affordable apartment not too far from campus, but we finally found one a couple of weeks before the start of the school year. We'd been there ever since and were nothing but happy with our choice. Our apartment wasn't big, but it was perfect for us. It was a split-level with the kitchen, living room, and half bath on the bottom level and our two bedrooms and bathroom on the upper level. This was the standard design for most of the apartments around campus.

Although it was only the beginning of our junior year, I already felt like we were in our apartment only to shower, sleep, and eat. Between attending class, studying, going out, and taking care of Grandma Olive, I was hardly ever home; same for Marie. Both of us were looking forward to spending time together over the long holiday weekend.

"So . . . where to first—Brandon's or the Beta Bash?" Marie asked with excitement in her voice.

Marie was a social butterfly who lived for weekends. The only thing she loved more than a good party was a ton of good-looking guys at a good party. Her newest love interest—or crush-of-the-month, as I liked to call her gentleman suitors—was Brandon. She had a tendency to (a) fall for good-looking but not-so-smart guys, and (b) lose interest within a couple of months. Brandon was a year older than us. They'd met in chemistry lab, where they were put in the same lab group. Ever since then, she hadn't stopped talking about him and had taken an extra interest in chemistry. Before she mentioned going to Brandon's, I already knew she was interested in seeing if they had chemistry outside of lab.

"Do I even have a choice?" I laughed, already knowing the answer as we walked side by side down the street. Typically, I didn't like parties, but I had to admit there was something contagious in the air that night. I don't know if it was the excitement of us starting our second-to-last year in college, or it being the long Labor Day weekend, but it was hard not to feed off the night's energy and Marie's excitement.

"To Brandon's house we go!" she declared, and she took my hand as we crossed the road and headed towards Calhoun Street.

Marie was having a blast playing beer pong and flirting with Brandon. They were on the same team, laughing, smiling, flirting, and periodically finding ways to touch each other. Every time Brandon would say something funny, she would gently touch his shoulder and fling her head back while she laughed. When it was her turn to throw the ping-pong ball, she'd go up onto her toes and lean forward in order to show off her long legs dangling underneath her short denim skirt. Whenever one of them would make the ball land in their opponent's cup, they'd high-five and let their hands hang in the air a little longer than usual as they'd smile at each other. Throughout the years, she had mastered the art of flirting, whereas I could hardly say three words to an attractive guy without choking on my own spit.

Once I knew Marie was in full-on flirt mode, I grabbed a PBR, the staple college party beer, and worked my way through the overcrowded house to the back doors. The backyard was less crowded with a few groups scattered here and there. Some couples were making out while some were arguing and others laughing. In the corner a small group of boys was huddled in a circle smoking God only knew what. In the middle of the yard a decent-sized group was gathered around a keg holding up a girl and screaming, "Chug! Chug! Chug!" as beer flew every which way out of her mouth.

Oh, keg stands. I sighed as I thought to myself. *So, this is what people pay a ridiculous amount of money for? To party all weekend to get the true college experience?* I laughed as I looked around the porch to find something to sit on. With one glance at the bare porch, I was quickly reminded that I was at an all-boys house. I knew I wouldn't find any outside furniture, so the ground or steps would have to do. I looked at the step and examined it for any suspicious-looking fluids. It appeared to be dry, so I took a seat, cracked open my beer, and began one of my favorite party activities— people-watching.

Why had this become my favorite thing to do at parties? Well, put a group of stressed-out, horny, and confused young adults together, supply them with alcohol and drugs, and absolutely no good can come of it. People-watching at a college party is like watching a real-life *Jerry Springer Show* unfold. I could already predict how this evening would end for many people there. Some would drink until they puked or passed out, some would fight over a boy or a girl, and others would go home with someone only to regret it in the morning. Regardless, tomorrow morning the campus streets would be filled with hungover people doing the walk of shame.

I had spent many nights catering to Marie after she partied and drank too much. I had held her hair back out of her face while she puked her guts out. Despite how disgusting that sounds, it was small payback for all she'd helped me through over the years. Having watched her puke as I tried not to puke myself, I resolved to stick to my one—maybe two beers if I was feeling festive—and keep all my contents down, my memory intact, and remain in control of my actions for the evening.

Although I might not participate in typical college activities, I would be eternally grateful for my fellow classmates' desire for drunken stupidity. Not only had it provided me with a tremendous amount of entertainment, but it had also inspired some decent songwriting material. As I sat there on the cold concrete step sipping my beer, I wondered what drama I would witness that evening, and placed mental bets on who would fall while doing the keg stand. I had no idea that on this night the universe had a bigger plan for me. Tonight, instead of sitting around and watching others live their lives, something inside of me would be awakened, and I would be thrust into a chapter of my life that I had never anticipated living.

THE GUY, AUGUSTUS OWENS

"Ugh. They're at it again," I mumbled to myself as I pulled into a shared driveway full of random people standing around drinking out of red Solo cups. Instead of being the grumpy old neighbor and honking my horn to get them to move out of my way, I decided to flash my lights and wait for the crowd to disperse. It took several minutes, but finally everyone moved enough for me to ease my Audi up the driveway and into my garage.

It was nearing ten o'clock, and I wasn't in the mood to be up all night listening to my neighbor's party. After the night I had just had, I was done dealing with drunken people. My twelve-hour shift had quickly turned into fourteen when I got held up trying to give an intoxicated dude ten stitches across his forehead. He couldn't remember what he had done to end up in the hospital, but his buddy said he had taken a "gnarly" fall down the stairs at one of the local dance clubs.

Between his buzz and the medicine I gave him, I was surprised he was still able to move and wasn't passed out. The guy wouldn't stop laughing! And his laughing was making my stitches look like crap and left my attending, Dr. Kirk, less than pleased with my work. After staying late to wait on the results of a head CT to rule out any chance of acute head trauma, I was finally able to discharge the patient. Just as I was finishing up his discharge instructions, I had the pleasure of Dr. Kirk tracking me down to lecture me on the proper way to place stitches. As he went off, I mentally tuned him out and let the voice inside my head tell him to shut up and challenge him to give better stitches on a drunken twenty-two-year-old who was moving around and acting like a three-year-old. I had half a mind to inform him that my father taught me how to do stitches when I was eleven years old, and I could do them faster and better than anyone in my graduating class; however, I knew better than to talk back to an attending. So instead, I stood there in silence as he chewed me a new one, nodded my head in "agreement," and once he was finished lecturing me, simply replied, "I'll do better next time, sir." And then I mentally added, *Jackass*, as I turned around and walked out the door.

I was two hours late leaving work and exhausted. I needed to try and get some shut-eye before my shift tomorrow. As I hopped out of my car and walked out of my detached garage, I took another look at my neighbors' party. For all the college kids next door it was a three-day holiday weekend, which meant letting loose and forgetting about all their responsibilities until Tuesday. For me, however, Labor Day was my holiday to work. So instead of seeing a good time going on next door, I saw multiple disasters waiting to happen. I anticipated several people drinking too much and accidentally hurting themselves like the guy I'd just stitched up—or worse, someone drinking far too much and needing their stomach pumped. Either way, I predicted that at least one person from each party going on around campus would end up in the ER. I easily passed fifty parties on my way home from work. I shrugged my shoulders and thought, *Job security, I guess.*

Despite all my complaining, all these potential injuries were preparing me to become an attending physician in just two years. This was the start of the third year of my four-year residency at the University of Cincinnati Medical Center. Despite having to stay late and occasionally get lectured, I was loving every minute of it.

Well, I take that back. At the moment I wasn't loving my apartment choice. When I moved in, I didn't realize I was moving next door to party animals. It didn't matter what day of the week it was; these guys were always at it. However, the hospital sat adjacent to the UC campus, so no matter what apartment I chose, I would likely have ended up with party animals as neighbors. Sure, I could have moved away from the college scene and still been within driving distance of the hospital, but I wanted to be as close to the hospital as I could. Residents made close to nothing, and the apartments close to campus were cheaper than in any other neighborhood, so my decision was saving me money on rent and gas but forcing me to be the antisocial grumpy dude next door who hardly ever showed his face. But what did I care? After I finished my residency, I'd be moving on to someplace bigger and better. I wasn't here to make friends; I was here to better myself and move on.

At least that's what I thought until tonight. As I was leaving my garage and walking through the shared driveway to get to my back door, I looked over my shoulder and saw her. She was sitting on my neighbors' porch by herself watching the party in the backyard with what appeared to be a smirk on her face. What caught my attention was the fact that she was sitting alone, away from everyone else, but seemed to be enjoying herself. I slowed my pace and then stopped for a moment to continue watching. She laughed to herself as she sipped her beer. As I stood there and observed her, I noticed several people go in and out of the back door and walk right past her, not stopping to say hi. In fact, no one seemed to notice she was there. She didn't get up and partake in the keg stand, she wasn't smoking like almost everyone else in the backyard, and she didn't seem to care that no one stopped to talk to her as they walked by. She was content with just sitting and watching—almost as if she knew a secret that no one else knew.

The more I watched her, the more fascinating I found her to be. Suddenly, she glanced in my direction. I quickly turned and made my way to my back porch before she could tell I had been watching her. Normally, I didn't care if a woman caught me checking her out, but there was something about this girl.

She probably has a boyfriend, I thought to myself as I unlocked my back door.

GRAVITY'S PULL

He headed to his room with the intent to change out of his dirty scrubs, put on his boxer shorts, and jump into bed. However, once he reached his room, he was automatically drawn to his bedroom window—one that provided the perfect view of his neighbors' backyard. The girl was still sitting alone on the back porch. After watching her for several more minutes, he couldn't ignore what he was feeling. Instead of putting on boxers and getting ready for bed, Augustus found himself subconsciously changing into a pair of jeans and a faded blue t-shirt. He slipped on a pair of brown Reef flip-flops and headed downstairs.

In the kitchen he grabbed a glass of water. As he drank his water, he wondered why the girl hadn't yet talked to anyone. He peeked out his kitchen window to his neighbors' porch again. The view wasn't as clear here as it had been from his bedroom, but still he could see her. She hadn't gotten up, and as far as he could tell, she wasn't on her phone texting or taking videos and pictures of the party around her like practically everyone else in the backyard was doing. Most college students lived for weekend parties, but it was clear that she was different. She seemed to like being by herself. It was as if no one noticed her except him, and he was fixated. Feeling compelled to get a closer look, he walked out to his back porch and leaned over the side railing.

Although it was dark out, between the tea lights that lined the fence, the fire pit in the backyard, and the back porch lights, he was able to see her. Even in the dark, he could tell she wasn't dressed like the other girls at the party. Most wore tight or low-cut shirts to show off their cleavage, but she appeared to be wearing a t-shirt and jeggings. He was intrigued.

During his undergraduate years, he hadn't attended many college parties. He needed to stay focused on his studies in order to make the grades he needed to get accepted into medical school. He couldn't afford to waste time on girls or parties. However, every now and then, he allowed himself to kick back, forget about the stress of becoming a doctor, and take a night off to unwind, have a few drinks, and do exactly what that girl seemed to be doing— people-watch.

It had been a couple of weeks since the last time he relaxed on his back porch, cracked open a beer, and did some people-watching of his own. The difference between him and her was that he did his people-watching from afar so his neighbors were oblivious to his pastime. She didn't seem to care or to hide the fact that she was watching everyone in the backyard. Although his conscience was telling him to go back inside and get some sleep before another long day of work tomorrow, something inside him was stronger—and too drawn to the girl to listen. He wasn't going to be able to rest until he talked to her.

Maybe I have time for just one, he thought to himself as he set his water down on the patio table and headed next door. He could have just walked in the front door, grabbed a beer, and left; however, it wasn't about the beer. He was on a mission—driven by an unknown force—to walk past this girl just so he could be close to her.

As he approached the back porch, he found himself getting nervous, which was out of character for him. He had never had an issue with approaching women, but for some reason, tonight he couldn't keep his nervous thoughts at bay. What would he say to this mysterious girl? Why did he feel so drawn to her in the first place? What was it that set her apart from everyone else?

"Excuse me," he said to the girl as he tried not to step on her while he made his way up the porch steps. As he walked past her, he couldn't take his eyes off of her. She stared into the backyard, hardly realizing he was talking to her—that is, until he misstepped and began to stumble. He grabbed onto the side rail to steady himself to keep from falling on top of her. He was able to successfully brace his fall but not before his knee accidentally knocked into her shoulder just as she was taking a sip of her beer. She gasped as cold beer splashed onto her face and down onto her arm and chest.

"Geez!" she said as she tossed her now almost-empty beer can down and jumped up.

"I—I didn't mean to," he stammered as he frantically looked around for something to use to dry her off with.

"Watch where you're going!" The girl scowled as she shook her hand, trying to dry off the spilled beer. She looked down at her shirt and saw that it was wet in all the wrong places, clinging to her small chest.

"I know. I'm sorry," he said sympathetically as he ran towards a towel hanging over the porch railing, then back to the girl who was now standing at the bottom of the steps. He was back in work mode, moving quickly and efficiently to fix the problem at hand. Without thinking, he instinctively began to wipe off the girl's arm, starting at her elbow and moving up towards her chest.

"Excuse you!" she said as she quickly removed her arm from his grip before he reached her chest. "Do you always go around touching girls you don't know?" she asked in an annoyed voice as she grabbed the towel from his hand. "There's something called personal space, ya know!" and she turned around so he couldn't watch her pat her chest dry.

This caused him to snap out of the nervous "work trance" that had overtaken him. Since he'd knocked into her, he had been so focused on fixing the problem he'd created that he hadn't focused on her—until now. Now he had the opportunity to do what he had wanted to do ever since he laid eyes on her—that is, to get a closer look.

"I'm sorry," he said again as he looked the girl over. The first thing he noticed about her was how small she was. Her head barely reached his chest. She couldn't have been more than five feet tall. Not only was she short, but she was small all around. He smiled when he realized how petite she was.

He continued with his apology as she turned back around and wiped off the rest of her arm. "You're right; I should have been more careful. I didn't mean to knock into you or for your beer to spill all over your—" He was about to say breasts but reminded himself that he wasn't at work, so instead said, "yourself," as she continued to wipe off her arm.

The next thing he noticed was her outfit. He was right; she wasn't dressed like all the other girls at the party. Instead of dressing to impress—meaning showing off her body—she was wearing a t-shirt and jeggings. He smiled as he read the writing on her shirt and realized they had similar tastes in music. So far, all the girl had done was yell at him, but now that he was only inches away from her, he could feel the tension lingering in the air. He was determined to turn his mistake around and strike up a real conversation with her.

"I was on my way in to grab a beer when I stupidly tripped into you. Do you want me to grab you a new one?" he offered, thinking they could talk over a beer.

She let out a little laugh. "Didn't your parents ever teach you not to accept drinks from strangers—you know, in case they slip something into it?" She laughed as she threw the towel down next to her empty beer can. She was annoyed that her peaceful night of people-watching had been interrupted by a guy she presumed was stumbling drunk up the stairs. From her experience, when a random guy offered you a drink, it meant one thing: he was trying to get you drunk enough to hook up. She put her hands on her hips and, for the first time since he'd walked past her, looked him directly in his eyes.

Their eyes met. For a brief moment in time, eyes darker than the winter's night sky met eyes as clear blue as the ocean, leaving them both speechless.

He had never seen eyes so intense. It was almost as if she could see through his eyes and into his mind, able to hear his thoughts and feel his feelings. Not only was he taken aback by the way she looked beyond his stare, but he was also intrigued by her accusatory comment. It took guts to say something so sassy to someone she didn't know—especially to a guy twice her size. She was being cautious, and he understood why. Working in the ER, he had seen too many girls come in needing their stomach pumped who had similar stories that went a little something like this: "I was at a party and some guy kept handing me drinks. The next thing I knew, I started to get dizzy and felt really out of it."

He opened his mouth to say something—anything—but he couldn't find the words. He needed to rethink his game plan. He motioned to the door as if to say something, anything really, but instead he found himself breaking her stare in order to think straight. *I'm sorry* was all he could think to say as he turned to walk away. At that moment he felt defeated, but his heart was pumping so hard in his chest as if it was telling him not to give up. As he reached the door and began to open it, he was surprised to hear the girl call out behind him.

"Grab me one, would you?" she called to him. "But don't open it," she teased.

He glanced back at her, confused but relieved that she was giving him a second chance. The nervousness that had taken over him as he approached her was replaced with hope. Several minutes later, he returned with two unopened cans of PBR, his confidence restored.

"One can of unopened PBR for the lady, just as you ordered." He smiled, and even in the dimly lit backyard, she could tell his teeth were perfectly straight and most likely very white.

"Thank you, but I don't accept beers from strangers." She smiled. "You are . . . ?" She paused, waiting for him to introduce himself.

"Augustus Owens," he said as he balanced one can of beer in his left armpit, held the other in his left hand, and extended his right hand for a handshake.

"Augustus," she repeated. "No, that's not going to work for me. Seems too old-fashioned and formal for someone our age," she teased, letting his hand hang there in mid-air between them.

He smiled at her quirkiness. "Well, my friends call me Gus," he said, his hand still extended and waiting for her to introduce herself. He nudged his hand a little higher.

"Oh, sorry," she said as she realized she hadn't yet told him her name. She wasn't used to talking to attractive men. Normally, when she went out with Marie, Marie was the one to get hit on.

"Elsie," she said, extending her right hand to shake his. "Elsie McCormick." When their hands touched, her fingers tingled.

"Elsie," he repeated. "Nice to finally meet you," he added, exaggerating the *finally*. As he shook her hand, he noticed how small hers felt in his, and instantly a cool chill ran up his arm and down his spine.

"Most of my friends call me Els," she said, interrupting his thoughts as she let go of his hand.

"Does that mean we're friends?" He smiled, flashing his straight, bright, white teeth as he handed her the unopened can of beer.

"Ask me again at the end of the night." She shyly smiled back as she took the beer from his hand and popped open the tab. She reminded herself to stay calm and just be herself— something Marie was constantly telling her to do.

"I'll be sure to!" He gave her a mischievous look. His nervousness subsided, and now he was feeling a feeling he wasn't familiar with. The more she smiled and talked to him, the more he wanted to talk to her—not to try to get something out of her like he had done with other girls during his college days, but to really talk to her and figure out what it was that had drawn him to her.

Her heart quickened as she realized Gus was not only a good-looking guy, but he was a witty, good-looking guy who was flirting with her! With her track record, she wasn't sure she'd be able to flirt back. Guys were Marie's area of expertise, not hers.

"You, um, go to school here?" she asked, trying to keep the conversation flowing and remain cool.

"Yes. I mean, I used to," he answered as he glanced around the backyard, observing the party and trying to think of a way to avoid telling her he was a doctor.

"Used to?" she asked. "Does that make you one of those creepy old guys? You know, the ones who graduated but can't seem to move on from the college life so they stick around to crash college parties and reminisce on the good old days?" and she gestured towards the party in the backyard.

"Yep, you caught me! I'm a total creeper," he said as he threw his hands up in defense, careful not to spill his beer. "I just can't get enough of these parties! Party on!" he yelled a little as he glanced around the yard smiling, marveling at her sense of humor.

When he turned away, she had the chance to get a good look at his face without him knowing she was staring at him. He was tall—but everyone was taller than her—five feet eleven maybe? He had bright blue eyes, which she had noticed before, and light brown hair. When he smiled, big dimples on both sides of his cheeks appeared. He was good-looking, and she liked the fact that so far, he could handle her sense of humor. The more they talked, the more at ease she felt, which was unusual for her.

She liked that he wasn't wearing a polo or collared shirt like the rest of the fratties wore. So far, he seemed decent enough, but she didn't want to get too excited just yet. She had never had a real boyfriend and planned on keeping it that way until she finished college and had a career of her own. Then and only then would she have the time and energy to focus on a relationship.

"No, I already graduated. I'm just finishing my training," he said as he turned his head back to her. He didn't want to tell her what type of training he was doing. It seemed every time a girl found out he was a doctor, she saw one thing and one thing only—a giant money symbol all over his face. He knew he needed to ask her a question before she could ask him about his training. "How about you?" he asked.

"I'm a junior," she said and then sipped her beer.

He nodded. He realized he was several years older than her, but that didn't bother him. From what he could make of her so far, she seemed pretty mature for her age.

"What's your major?" he asked. And at that moment their conversation was interrupted by another girl.

"Hey, hottie." A girl stumbled up beside Augustus and leaned into him, placing her hand on his shoulder.

"Wanna do da keg stand?" she slurred as she drunkenly began to pull him towards the keg in the yard.

He immediately noticed that she was nothing like Elsie. She was wearing a tight-fitting black dress and way too much makeup. He gently removed the girl's hand from his shoulder and took one step away from the girl and another step closer towards Elsie.

"No, thanks," he replied, hoping the girl would get a clue and walk away.

"You sure?" she asked in a whiny voice as she made a pouty face.

"Yes," he said firmly. "Actually, we were just leaving," he said as he gently nudged Elsie towards the driveway.

"We were?" She looked at him, somewhat annoyed. Yes, she was flattered that his attention was on her and not the drunken girl with her huge boobs hanging out, but if he thought she was going to go home with him that easily, he was mistaken, and she had misjudged his character.

"Yes, so we can find a quieter place to talk." He smiled down at her as he gave her another gentle nudge towards the driveway. Elsie, however, was hesitant to follow, and he could feel resistance as he took a few steps in front of her.

"Relax," he reassured her. "I know the guy next door. We can sit on his back porch and talk where it's a little quieter and there's not as many interruptions," he said as he glanced towards the girl who was now stumbling off towards the keg stand.

She looked at how many people were in the backyard. Although they were drinking, she knew that if he ended up being a creep, all she had to do was yell for help and someone would surely come. As far as she could tell, he seemed like a nice guy, and her gut was telling her to listen to him. She took a breath in and slowly breathed out, helping her to relax. She followed his lead to the neighbor's back porch. After walking up the porch steps, she was surprised to see the porch actually had a table and chairs, unlike the fraternity house next door.

"So, do you always leave parties with complete strangers?" he teased as he pulled out a chair for her.

"Oh yeah, all the time." She was trying to hold back a smile as she took a sip of her beer and sat down. She was glad to be sitting in a real chair instead of on a cold, hard, concrete step. She looked over to Brandon's backyard, where the party was still in full swing. Augustus had been right: it was much quieter over here. She hadn't realized how loud the music was playing in the backyard until she sat down on the neighbor's porch.

Music! Ugh, she groaned to herself as she realized it was entirely too late. She had missed Battle of the Bands. At the beginning of the night, Elsie knew Marie would get too wrapped up in the party to remember her promise, but she didn't think she'd be the one to forget.

Surprisingly, however, sitting next to Augustus, she wasn't too upset with Marie or with herself for letting time slip away. Had she left the party to go to the concert, she wouldn't have met Augustus. She blushed. There was some-thing about him.

"What's wrong?" he asked as he sat down in the chair next to her. He could tell by the look on her face that she was thinking about something else.

"It's nothing." She smiled. "Don't worry about it."

"Come on." He flashed his perfect smile. "You can tell me; I can keep a secret," he said as he winked at her. His confi-dence had fully returned. He was drawn to Elsie in a way he'd never known. She was different from any girl he had hit on before. She was cute in a way he'd never considered attractive—small, feisty. She had no problem joking around with him or standing her ground, but at the same time she seemed to have a good head on her shoulders.

Not only was he good-looking and nice, but he could make her laugh. "I wanted to go to Battle of the Bands tonight, but there's no use now; it's too late," she said as she took another sip of her beer and looked over at the party, hoping Marie was still playing beer pong and not getting into too much trouble.

"Ah man, that was tonight?" he asked. "I heard that local band, um, Minus One, was going to be playing," he said.

"Yes!" she said, surprised that he knew who Minus One was. "Tonight's their big debut—post-record that is. They all went to school together here in town," she said, thinking back on the day the band had asked her to be their lead singer. As flattered as she was that they would consider her, she had politely declined. She wasn't ready for the commitment and didn't want to be the only female band member.

That's when the drummer, Rory, said, "Ah man, now we're out a singer and a band member. Man Down—hey, that should be our name!" Then she chimed in with, "What about Minus One? That has a cool ring to it, don't you think?"

"I like it when a small-town band lands a record deal," he said, interrupting her thoughts.

"So do I," she agreed, grateful they seemed to have similar taste in music.

"I've heard a few of their songs; they sound good." He smiled and then added, "Sounds like we might have a few things in common."

"Sounds like it!" She smiled.

"Some nights I sit out here, listen to music, and watch all the stupid things people do next door. I even make my own drinking game out of it," he said. "One sip for every argument, two for some random couple making out." He looked over at her and took a sip of his beer.

"Ha! Sounds like a game I'd like to play." She laughed. Then she thought about what he had just said. "Wait, what? You sit out here? As in, this is your porch?!" she asked as she looked him in the eye, eager for him to answer. Even in the dark, his eyes looked bright blue. She longed to see them in the daylight.

"I told you I knew the guy next door!" he said, slyly grinning from ear to ear.

She had to look away from his dimples to keep from blushing. She shook her head as she secretly admired his sense of humor. "Oh, you think you're clever, don't you?" she taunted in a flirty but somewhat annoyed voice as she took another sip of her beer and glanced back at him just in time to catch him winking at her.

Her heart raced. He was flirting with her! She marveled at how it all had happened. One minute she was sitting on the porch steps minding her own business when out of nowhere this charming, good-looking, funny guy comes along. Now she was sitting on his back porch on a candlelit evening, sipping a beer and trying to keep her cool while every time he looked at her all she could do was smile and blush. Stuff like this never happened to her. She could feel her palms starting to sweat and realized she was out of her comfort zone. She was a rookie when it came to flirting and wasn't sure she knew what to do next. She was starting to feel uncomfortable, worried that she might say the wrong thing and ruin it all. *Just keep the conversation going,* she told herself. *Don't blow it!*

"So, um," she began to stutter, "how long have you lived here?" She cursed herself as soon as she asked. *Come on, you can think of something better than that!* She mentally scolded herself, then gave herself a mental pep talk: *Don't be boring and dull! You are NOT boring and dull!*

"I've been in this apartment for two years; in Cincinnati

for ten," he answered. And he noticed the sudden nervousness in her voice. "How 'bout you?" he asked as he turned his head in her direction.

"Born and raised in Cincinnati." She managed to look him in the face again but only for a second. She continued, "I know. I'm pretty boring, right? Never really ventured out." Again, she regretted her choice of words. *Now you're telling him you're boring?!* she scolded herself as she took a big sip of her beer.

"Nothing wrong with that," he replied. "Why move if you know what you like? You said you're a junior?" he asked her. He didn't seem to have trouble keeping the conversation going.

"Yup." This time she kept her answer short and simple. She wondered if first conversations with a good-looking guy were supposed to be this awkward, or if she just sucked at everything that came naturally to most girls.

"Can I guess your major?" he asked as he leaned back in his chair and held his beer between his legs.

"Um, sure." She was caught off guard by his question.

"Communication." He chuckled as he grinned and took a sip of his beer.

She glanced up at him to see a huge grin on his face. She was relieved that he had the ability to make her laugh. Although she was completely embarrassed, Marie had always told her she couldn't hide a single emotion from anyone. She was grateful that it was too dark for him to see how red her pale cheeks had just turned. She took a deep breath in and asked, "Is it that obvious that I suck at talking to guys?"

"No, no. I'm just teasing you." He smiled as he set his now empty beer down on the table. "You didn't seem to mind telling me what to do when we were at the party, half-pint!" he teased her some more.

That was before I realized you were hot, funny, and flirting with me, she thought to herself but instead said, "Oh, so you're calling me names now!" she teased back at him. "What are we, fifth graders flirting with each other at recess? What's next, hair pulling?" She smiled to herself, pleased with her comeback. With more confidence, she was able to look him dead in the eyes.

Suddenly, his face got very serious as he stared back at her and said, "Who said I'm flirting with you?" as he maintained his best poker face.

Her confidence began to quickly fade until the corner of his mouth began to curl up, and he started to laugh. Once she heard him laugh, her body instantly relaxed. She then laughed along with him as she reached over and playfully punched his arm and teased, "Why am I hanging out with such a jerk?"

There was something about him that allowed her to be herself—something that until tonight she hadn't been able to do with anyone but Marie.

An hour passed, and as the party next door continued, Elsie and Augustus sat on his back porch talking, laughing, and enjoying each other's company. Thanks to her AWOLNATION t-shirt, their conversation had focused mainly on music. Elsie's favorite hobby was writing and composing songs. For her, music was the only connection she still had to her parents. She wasn't ready to tell him about her hobbies just yet, but she was enjoying talking to him about her favorite bands and concerts. When she learned that they both wanted to see The Killers, she secretly wished they'd one day go together.

After talking about music, they made up their own people-watching game. They'd pick a couple in the backyard and try to figure out what they were saying to each other.

"Yo, my name's Ken. What's your name, sexy?" he said in

his best surfer dude voice. He was imitating a tall, thin guy standing in the backyard talking to a girl leaning with her back against a tree.

"Barbie, duh! With blonde hair as fabulous as mine?" she said as she tossed her hair over her shoulder with her right hand. She was imitating the big-busted, blonde girl talking to the guy.

" 'Sup, Barbie? This party is like, um, totally rad," he said, still in his surfer-Ken voice.

"Yeah, like totally," she reacted in her Barbie voice and pretended to chew on gum.

"So, Barbie babe, what ya say about giving me your digits so we can hit up the beach sometime?" he replied again as surfer-Ken.

"Yeah, for sure!" she said, still in her Barbie voice, and started to giggle.

He opened his mouth to say something just as "Ken" and "Barbie" started to make out. Both Elsie and Augustus got quiet for a moment, not sure what to say in the awkward moment of watching the random couple next door go at it.

He cleared his throat and turned his attention back to Elsie, trying to ease the awkward tension that now lingered between them.

"So, anyway," he said in his normal voice, "I was having a real good time until that awkwardness just happened." He laughed. She nodded her head and laughed along with him.

"How do you feel about giving me your number so we can do this again sometime? You know, minus watching strangers make out," he said in a playful, flirty way.

She was again thankful that it was dark so he wouldn't notice her red-hot cheeks. She was practically exploding at the thought of getting to spend more time with him. She opened her mouth anxious to answer until she realized she didn't have a cell phone number to give him.

"Um, actually, I can't," she replied.

"Really?" He was surprised by her response, "I thought we were having a good time," he continued, sounding a little confused and thrown off his game. Although he didn't go out often, in the past whenever he had asked a woman out on a date, she'd always said yes. Until tonight, he had never been turned down.

"Yes, I'm having a good time, but . . ." She tried to explain her dilemma, "I don't have a number to give you." She had a sinking feeling that she was throwing away her only chance to go on a real date with Augustus and tried reassuring him that she wasn't just blowing him off.

"What I mean is, I don't own a cell phone, so I don't have a number to give you," she said, clarifying what she had just previously stammered.

He was relieved when he realized she wasn't turning him down. Then he started to laugh. "Of course, you don't. Because that would be too easy. I have a feeling you're a bit of a . . ." He momentarily paused before adding, "challenge."

She couldn't help but notice how his blue eyes seemed to dance as the porch light reflected off of them. Again, she longed to get a good look at those bright blue eyes in the daylight and see just how blue they really were.

"Me? A challenge? Never!" She playfully chuckled and then added, "But really, I don't have a cell phone."

"Who doesn't have a cell phone?" He continued to poke fun at her, but truthfully, from the moment he saw her, he knew she was different. The more he learned about her, the more interesting she became. He wanted to get to know her better. He wanted to discover more things he liked about her.

"I don't know." She shrugged and simply said, "I just don't feel the need for one." Although she'd only met him a couple of hours ago, she believed he had the potential to become someone she could trust and confide in. No, she wasn't ready to reveal that she was an orphan with only one living relative or that her only close friend was Marie, but in this short time she was feeling more comfortable talking with him than she had felt with some people she'd known for years. In reality, she knew plenty of people—people from class, people from church, and all of Marie's social circle—but she didn't feel the need to hang out with those people. Marie and Grandma Olive were the only two people she wanted to talk to on a daily basis. She lived with Marie and drove home at least two, sometimes three, times a week to visit with Olive. That's the reason she didn't feel the need for a cell phone.

"If only we could all live as simply as you do, Miss Elsie," he said. He was fascinated with the way she lived. She seemed so carefree. He thought about the new iPhone he had recently purchased. He couldn't go a night without having his phone on or near him, especially when he was on call. Most of the time he felt as if the phone owned him and not the other way around. He was constantly connected to it, religiously checking his work email for updates for fear he'd miss an important message or opportunity and fall one step behind all the other residents. Even now as he sat here off duty talking with her, his phone was in his back pocket on vibrate. Then he realized he hadn't checked it since they started talking. That thought intrigued him. No one had had that effect on him before. He wondered what it was about her, a girl he hardly knew, that made him forget about work.

"Well then," he said, "how can I get ahold of you? When can I see you again?" He was being more direct than he had been before. He realized that without her having a cell phone, he wasn't going to be able to send her a quick text or call her whenever he had a spare moment, and when you're a doctor-in-training, spare moments are few and far between.

She thought about it and remembered her apartment landline. The only reason she had it was for emergencies or if she needed to talk to Olive. Half the time she forgot they even had a phone in her apartment, and needless to say, she'd never given the number to a boy before. Just when she was about to give him her apartment phone number, a loud, thunderous roar rolled across the dark September sky. Immediately following the roar, a cool and humid Cincinnati rain began to fall hard and fast.

"Ah!" she shrieked as the cold raindrops began to fall on them, and she jumped up out of her chair.

He was already on his feet, reaching for her arm to pull her close to his back door where they could seek refuge from the rain.

"Quick! Come inside," he spoke loudly so he could be heard over the thunder and lightning.

They could hear other people shrieking from the party next door. The storm had taken everyone by surprise.

She pulled back at his arm towards Brandon's house. "I—I can't. I have to find Marie," she gestured towards the party. "I can't just leave her!" she shouted over the rain as she broke loose from his grip and headed towards Brandon's house.

He balked at the thought of letting her go. He had no way of contacting her and was just starting to get to know her. So, he did what any guy in this situation would do: he followed his heart and chased after the girl through the storm and into the house next door.

The house was packed wall to wall with people. Everyone was talking loudly to be heard over the music playing. The tile kitchen floor was a muddy, slippery mess from everyone racing in from the storm. They had just entered a full-blown, chaotic college party.

He was standing directly behind her in the crowded kitchen. He leaned down to talk into her ear so he wouldn't have to scream over everyone else. "Once we find Marie," he began, "I can take you guys home."

She nodded, giving him the okay. As he straightened his body back to an upright position, his nose gently brushed against her hair, and a hint of lavender hit his nostrils. *Her hair smells so good*, he thought to himself.

As they shuffled through the crowd, he found himself comparing Elsie's height to everyone around them. He knew she was small but hadn't realized just how small until now as he was watching her push her way through the crowd to the basement. He laughed, she looked like a middle schooler crashing a college party.

Although she was small, she was fast. For every step she took he had to take two; otherwise, he'd lose sight of her. Once he caught up to her, he subconsciously rested his hands on both sides of her tiny waist to keep them close together. His hands stayed that way for several moments until he realized how intimately he was touching her without her permission. With this realization, he quickly removed his hands to prevent giving her the wrong impression. When he let go, his hands tingled and his heart quickened. He was standing very close to her, with his front side pushed up against her back. Amid the chaos of the party, he hadn't realized how much he'd been touching her until now. Thankfully she didn't seem to notice— or if she did, she didn't mind; because if she did mind, he knew she'd tell him!

As they attempted to push their way through the tangled mass of partygoers, they came to a standstill. Augustus took this opportunity to see where Elsie stood compared to him. The top of her head barely reached the bottom of his chest. They were both soaking wet from the rain, and her t-shirt was clinging tight to her body. He could almost make out her ribcage. When his hands had rested on her hips, he realized how tiny her waist was. She was probably the smallest woman he'd ever met. Everything he knew so far about this girl was out of the ordinary, and he found that extremely attractive.

The large crowd began to disperse. His thoughts were interrupted as they worked their way downstairs to the beer pong table. Here, Elsie found Marie in the same spot she'd left her hours ago. Clearly, Marie hadn't stopped drinking. Even with her heels off, she was wobbling around and had that hazy, drunken gloss in her eyes.

"Els!" Marie screamed when she saw her friend standing directly in front of her. "You are all wet!" she said as she patted Elsie's head.

Marie knew she hated when people, especially random people, patted her on the head like she was a cute little child. The fact that Marie thought it was okay to pat her on the head verified that she was beyond drunk and that it was time to call it a night.

"You're drunk. It's time to go!" Elsie said as she searched the nearby floor looking for Marie's high heels and purse. Considering Marie hadn't moved from the same spot she left her a couple of hours ago, she knew Marie's belongings shouldn't be far. She walked over to the closest corner, about twenty steps from where Marie was standing, and found her purse and shoes.

When she picked up Marie's purse, she noticed it was wet. A look of disgust blanketed her face as she brought the small purse close to her nose to give it a quick sniff test. She let out a sigh of relief when it smelled like beer instead of vomit. Marie was notorious for leaving her shoes and purse on the floor at parties. Sometimes if they were covered in a suspicious fluid, Elsie would just leave them behind. They had a rule: Marie was allowed to bring only her makeup in her purse. If they were going somewhere where she'd need an ID, Elsie kept it safe. And Marie's cell phone normally ended up in Elsie's back pocket, except for tonight. Tonight, she had been so busy talking with Augustus that she hadn't thought of keeping track of Marie or her belongings.

Elsie walked back over to her friend, carrying her shoes and purse. "Let's go home," she said as she pulled her arm, leading her towards the basement stairs.

"Nooo!" Marie whined in drunken protest.

Until this point in time, Augustus had stood quietly to the side, arms folded across his chest, observing. However, once he realized that Marie wasn't willing to leave the party, he quickly stepped in. Marie might be tall compared to her small friend, but compared to him, Marie was nothing he couldn't handle.

He walked over to her, put his arm around her, and said, "Hey, Marie, I'm Elsie's friend Gus, and I'm going to take you guys home now," and he began to lead her from the basement corner to the stairs.

"Well, helllloooo, hottie!" She laughed as she stumbled aside Augustus, putting one arm around his shoulder. "Els, where'd you find him? I want one!" she slurred as he helped her up the steps, and Elsie followed behind them.

Getting Marie up the stairs, through the crowd, and out the back door wasn't an easy task, but he managed to do it in about five minutes. If Elsie had been trying to do it alone, it would have easily taken her close to an hour. She smiled. Tonight, she was grateful for Augustus's help.

As they headed out the door to his driveway, both Elsie and Augustus were happy to discover the rain had slowed from a downpour to a light drizzle. When they made it to his garage, he reached into his pocket and pressed the button on his keychain to open the garage door. Elsie kept Marie off to the side as he backed his black Audi out of the garage. Marie put up a struggle as Elsie and Augustus worked together to get her into the back seat of his car. After a few minutes, she practically fell into the back seat, sprawling out and making herself more than comfortable. Elsie didn't bother trying to buckle Marie in. Instead, she shut the back door, jogged around to the passenger side, and jumped into the front seat. Once Elsie sat down on his leather seats, her butt was instantly warmed by the seat warmer. She smiled as she realized how considerate Augustus was. He knew she was soaking wet and most likely cold, so he took it upon himself to turn her seat warmer on before she got into the car.

As Elsie gave Augustus directions to their apartment, Marie slurred a drunken version of "If All the Raindrops Were Lemon Shots" from the back seat. Occasionally, she would stop singing and insist that Gus take her to get food. Augustus and Elsie just laughed at Marie until she passed out in the back seat.

"I'm truly sorry," Elsie apologized for Marie's behavior. "She isn't like this every weekend, I swear," she continued to explain. "She gets a little extra festive around holidays."

"Trust me." He let out a little chuckle and then added, "she's not the only one," as he thought of all the "festive" patients he'd treated during his shift earlier that night.

He looked over at Elsie and noticed the confused look on her face. Now was not the right time to divulge his job to her. Instead he said, "Remember who my neighbors are? Every holiday they throw parties, and it's always a disaster waiting to happen."

He smiled at her, and she nodded her head in agreement. Brandon's house was definitely a party house, and that party had been one of the biggest parties she'd been to so far.

"Turn left at the next street," she instructed as they drew nearer to her apartment.

He turned left and then began to slow his car down, not wanting their time to end. He was practically inching towards her driveway.

"It's, uh, the third apartment on the right," she said, taking note of the change in his speed and assuming it was because he was waiting on her to tell him where to go.

He pulled into their driveway, parked his car, and looked over at Elsie as he took off his seatbelt. He wasn't sure what to say or do next. Not wanting the night to end, he sat frozen in place. He looked at Elsie, sitting still and looking out the window at her front porch. She seemed to be feeling the same way.

Marie was snoring loudly in the back seat. He said to Elsie, "I should probably help her get inside."

She nodded in agreement and unbuckled her seatbelt. Augustus opened his door.

"Marie, you're home," he said as he gently nudged her, trying to wake her up. She rubbed her eyes and let out an audible moan.

"Ugh, go away. Let me sleep," she pleaded.

By now Elsie was standing next to Augustus. She let out a sigh. "Come on, Marie. Time to get into bed," she said as she pulled at her arm.

Suddenly, Marie's eyes popped open and she sat up. Elsie had seen that look on Marie's face many times before.

"No!" she raised her voice at Marie. "Do not throw up in the car!" she ordered. On that note, Gus leaned forward, grabbed Marie, and in one swift motion lifted her up and out of his car. She was holding her hands over her mouth and making a gagging noise. As he helped her up the porch steps, Elsie ran ahead and unlocked the front door. As soon as the door was unlocked, Marie jumped out of his arms and took off towards the bathroom, leaving Gus and Elsie alone in the doorway.

They were both still damp and cold from the rain, and neither of them seemed to notice the steady rain falling down around them. Elsie glanced at the t-shirt clinging to his chest and arms, showing off his thick muscles. Until now she hadn't realized how built his upper body was. Although he was tall and thin, his arms were thick and muscular. She felt physically inferior to him and exposed as her clothes clung to her thin, fragile body, outlining her small chest and butt. She crossed her arms across her chest to hide her nonexistent figure and smiled to herself. He was very attractive. She couldn't believe she had spent the evening with this chivalrous, funny, good-looking guy.

Augustus looked down at Elsie, who had a shy smile on her face. She was the first to break the silence. "Thank you," she began, "for everything. I don't know how I would have gotten Marie home without you," and she uncrossed her arms and motioned towards Marie somewhere inside of the apartment. She could hardly handle the nervousness that was intensifying inside her.

He was a smart guy. It was obvious that she was nervous wondering how tonight would end, but what surprised him the most was that deep down inside, he was too. Normally, he didn't get nervous. He lived for excitement and was quick to respond in chaotic situations. That was the main reason he'd decided to be a trauma specialist. When it came to women, he had always instinctively known the right thing to say and do. That is—until tonight when he approached Elsie. There was something different about her. She threw him off his game. She challenged him, and he liked that about her. Not to mention that ever since he saw her sitting on the back porch, something was drawing him towards her. Like gravity, she was impossible to escape. He'd been forced in her direction from the moment he set eyes on her. He had never felt this way before. Although he was looking directly at her, he longed to see her again.

"No problem," he said, "I had a great time tonight too." He paused before adding, "Els." He smiled at her, recalling their conversation from earlier in the night, when she had told him that only her friends called her "Els" and that he should ask her at the end of the night if they were friends.

She looked up at him and smiled, pleased that he remembered their conversation. She replied, "Ditto . . ." then added, "Auggie."

"Auggie?" he said, a little befuddled. He stared back at her, willing her to make full eye contact with him. Then, right on cue, as if she knew he was willing her to look him in his eyes, their eyes met. Chills went down Elsie's back, and Augustus too felt a tingling sensation all over his body.

"If we're going to be friends," she said in a breathy voice, finding it hard to concentrate as he stared so intently at her, "you need a nickname too." She smiled. "And I like Auggie." She took in a deep breath and tried to calm the flurry of emotions swirling inside her.

"So, we're going to be friends, huh?" he said playfully as he took one step closer to her, closing the distance between them. The closer he got to her, the stronger the tingling sensation became. He crossed his arms against his chest and leaned up against the side porch wall and tried to play it cool.

Unable to handle his intense gaze and intimately close proximity, she broke eye contact and looked down at the concrete steps to try to keep from blushing, but it was too late. She could feel the cool raindrops trickle down her hot cheeks, cooling them from her embarrassment. Every time he had looked her directly in the eyes tonight, her heart had started to beat faster and her hands had felt sweaty and shaky. Continuing to look down at the ground, she shrugged her shoulders and nonchalantly replied, "Maybe—if you're lucky." She looked back up at him, careful not to make direct eye contact, and gave him a mischievous smile.

"Auggie," he repeated with more certainty in his voice this time. "I think I could get used to that," he said as he looked into her eyes and smiled. "Go out with me," he petitioned in a serious voice.

Although they had just met, he needed to know her better.

He wasn't ready for the night to end. He inched himself closer to Elsie, feeling the need to be as close to her as he possibly could be. As he gently lifted her chin up towards his face, the porch light began to shine through her hair and onto her face, making her eyes sparkle like little diamonds.

He could tell she was intimidated by his actions. It was clear to him that she wasn't used to being touched so intimately. He gently put his other hand under her chin and tilted her face towards his. He leaned forward, lowering his face close to hers. Their eyes met for a moment, then she closed her eyes, afraid to watch as his mouth moved towards her lips.

As his lips gently brushed up against hers, he could feel her lips quiver. He paused, making sure she was okay with him touching her. She didn't pull away, so he took that as an invitation to continue. Her warm breath instantly warmed his cool, wet lips, and she gently pressed her lips against his. As their lips gently massaged each other's, he felt like he couldn't get enough; he needed more. As they continued to gently kiss, her mouth opened, and he could feel her warm, wet tongue touch his. He could feel his heartbeat quicken, and he gently pulled her small body up close against his. Their wet shirts provided only a thin barrier between their bodies. With their warm bodies pressed against each other, the urge for more began to grow stronger. Instinctively their kissing went from gentle and not too intense to passionate and wet.

Suddenly a bolt of lightning lit up the sky, and a loud crack of thunder broke the spell they had fallen under. Elsie was the first to open her eyes and then quickly looked away, somewhat embarrassed at the way she had just behaved. She had never kissed anyone that passionately before—and certainly not someone she'd only just met. She was taken aback by the degree of intensity still coursing through her body even after they'd stopped kissing.

She hadn't realized that she'd been up on her tippy-toes

the whole time in order to reach his face, and now her calves were tight from the tension. As she slowly lowered herself back down, she felt unsteady on her feet. She wobbled backwards, creating a gap between them. Once she had steadied herself, she peeked up at Auggie's face as she gently touched her fingers to her lips, which were still tingling, and smiled. He was looking back at her and smiling ear to ear. From the look on his face, he was just as pleased as she was with their kiss. Her heart was beating so hard and fast, she felt like she could hear it pounding in her chest.

He didn't say anything but reached for her hand and gently rubbed her palm with his thumb. Although he was only inches from her, it felt as if he were miles away, and she couldn't stand the distance between them. The urge to be as close as possible to him was consuming her. She longed to again feel the warmth of his body pressed up against her and the softness of his lips upon hers. Before she knew what she was doing, she took two steps closer. At exactly the same time, he gently wrapped his arms around the small of her back and pulled her in close.

There were moments in life when a touch could say so much more than words ever could. Though Auggie and Elsie spoke not a word, they knew that whatever was happening between the two of them, it was the very first time for both. Never had they known an attraction so undeniable, a connection so intense, as the one they felt in that moment. Speechless as they stood there in the rain, they got lost in each other's embrace and just let their bodies do the talking.

Despite the cold rain, she could have stood on her front porch kissing Auggie all night long—that is, if Marie hadn't kept interrupting them by yelling for help.

She was now sitting on the bathroom floor with her back up against the wall while Marie lay passed out beside her. Marie had already thrown up three times since she joined her, and each time she faithfully held Marie's hair back and wiped her face with a cool, wet cloth.

She was near certain that Marie would get sick at least once more before she could leave her alone and make her way to her soft, warm bed. For the moment, however, Marie was snoring, so she knew she would have time to let herself get lost in her thoughts before she was called up for hair-holding and mouth-wiping duty again.

Elsie closed her eyes and reminisced on how the night had unfolded. She blushed at the memory of Auggie's warm lips pressed up against hers. She'd never kissed anyone she had only known for a few hours; in her book that was a definite no-no. She shook her head and laughed. There was something about him that made kissing him seem so right. From the moment their eyes locked, she had felt an instant attraction but never imagined her night would end with a hot, steamy make-out session. She felt as if she had had no control over the night's events; they were just destined to happen.

In the past, she had dated a few guys—a casual date every now and then—but no guy had ever stuck around for more than a few months. She didn't know if it was because she sucked at dating, or because of her obvious lack of interest in the guy, or a combination of both; but whatever the case may be, she had never felt the need to seriously date anyone. After a few dates, history would repeat itself with the guy giving her the ol' *You're a really nice girl, but* and *It's not you, it's me* speeches. Secretly, she never minded when relationships ended. Instead of crying like most girls did, she would let out a sigh of relief.

She didn't mind being chronically single. Dating boys had never been a priority in her life. She always had other, bigger issues to deal with than something as trivial as boys. Tonight, with Auggie, she had experienced something she'd never experienced before—an irresistible connection with a very attractive, smart, and funny guy. She smiled and blushed again as her thoughts led her back to the way her body tingled as he pulled her close and kissed her. She had never felt tingling as she kissed a boy. Until tonight, kissing had seemed sloppy, wet, and awkward. With Auggie—well, kissing him was like losing herself in one of her favorite songs—exciting, blissful, and never long enough. She was surprised by the desire his kiss had left her with. Even now, hours later, she still longed to feel his warm lips pressed against hers.

She glanced at Marie and silently thanked her for dragging her to Brandon's party and for drinking too much, causing her to miss Battle of the Bands. For months, Elsie had been looking forward to that concert and seeing her old friends on stage, but now having missed it, it didn't seem like such a bad thing at all.

Auggie . . . just thinking of him made her smile. The evening they'd shared together had been worth missing every minute of the concert—and that was saying a lot for her, a music major and aspiring singer-songwriter. Whenever she tried memorizing a song, she'd listen to it over and over again until she knew every single lyric. In the same way, she re-played her time with Auggie over and over until she was certain she'd remembered every detail.

"Ugh . . ." Marie groaned, interrupting Elsie's train of thought, "I feel like . . ." She stopped mid-sentence as she sat up quickly. She let out a little burp and then mumbled, "False alarm," as she turned herself around and placed her head back down into Elsie's lap.

"Oh, Marie," Elsie began as she gently moved a piece of her hair that had fallen out of the sloppy ponytail she had given her. "Why do you do this to yourself?" she asked, knowing she was too drunk to give her a serious answer.

"I dunno," Marie mumbled. "Els?"

"Yes," she answered.

"Sing to me."

"Ugh." Elsie was the one moaning now.

Her throat was dry and scratchy from being up too late. Luckily for Marie, Elsie was in a particularly good mood and although she was tired, she had regained some energy from mentally reliving her night with Auggie. "Fine, but don't say I never did anything for you." She gently ran her fingers through Marie's blonde hair as she quietly sang to her. As Marie drifted off to sleep, Elsie thought back to the first time she'd ever felt this alive. It was their junior year of high school.

Chapter 4

In high school, Elsie believed she was thought of by her class-mates as the pitiful girl who had lost both her parents. She'd catch others staring at her as she passed them in the hall, at lunch, or in class, as if she were a different breed—never knowing what to say or how to act around her. She marched to her own beat, and that made her even more unusual. She didn't care who was taking whom to the homecoming dance, and she wasn't up on the latest fashion trends. She wasn't one to play sports, and she didn't gossip or hang out at the park or the mall. In her spare time, she'd rather read, compose music, or play her guitar.

Many people found it odd that the captain of the cheer squad and all-around athlete, Marie, gave "Oddball Elsie" the time of day. The truth be told, Marie's perfect life was only perfect from the outside looking in. Marie kept her personal life a secret from everyone but Elsie. Although she was the most popular girl in their grade, she would never host a slumber party or have friends over.

Marie's father had cheated on and then left her mother, Carol, to start a new family with his mistress. By the time she was ten and her brother Marc was eight, they were old enough to realize that their dad was never coming back. Marie and Marc were both very athletic, and they had a need for track and field shoes, soccer, softball, baseball, and football equipment, and—well, all of those things added up faster than Carol could keep up. She didn't want them to go without, especially since they were counting on sports scholarships to get them into college, so she picked up a second job. With her mom constantly working to provide for the family and her dad nowhere in sight, she could relate to Elsie; she too felt abandoned. Neither of her parents was around to watch her in all that she participated in. What her father had done tore her apart inside. She had no idea where he was or if he'd ever try to be a part of her life. Although their reasons were different for not having a father in their lives, Elsie and Marie could relate to each other, and that made the bond between them stronger.

Although they didn't have class together, they'd arrive at school together, eat lunch together, and leave together. Every day during lunch, Marie would make her way through the cafeteria, stopping at different tables to chitchat and catch up on all the latest gossip and to see who was throwing a party that weekend, while Elsie would sit quietly at her own table working on assignments and eating until Marie joined her.

"What's new in the gossip world?" she asked Marie as she shut her copy of *Macbeth*.

"Ha, like you care, Smalls!" Marie said as she placed her lunch down, then sat next to Elsie.

"Not really," she agreed, and ate her chips.

"So, we've been friends basically our whole lives, right?" Marie was giving her a mischievous smile.

"Right." She knew that look all too well; she wanted something from her, and she could tell it was something big. Elsie braced herself.

"So that makes us more like sisters than friends," she

continued as she batted her eyes at Elsie.

"Okay, first off, batting your eyes only works on the boys," Elsie said as Marie gave her a fake frowny face. Her pouting didn't faze Elsie, so she continued, "Secondly, I know you want something, so just spit it out already," and she took a sip of her drink.

"Man, am I that predictable?" Marie's frown was replaced by a smirk as she laughed.

Elsie laughed with her. "Why, yes! Yes, you are that predictable. And none of your tricks you use with the boys work on me!"

"Bummer," Marie lamented as she took a sip of her Cherry Coke and a bite of her turkey sandwich, then casually added, "So . . . Parker's auditions are next month."

"Ugh!" Elsie moaned and stopped eating. Just the thought of Parker's made her instantly feel sick to her stomach with nervous energy.

Parker's was their high school variety show held every year in the spring. Auditions started before winter break, and students could enter just about any act from dancing and singing to a boys' kick line or comedy sketches. The show was performed five times in one weekend, and proceeds went to help fund school events such as pep rallies and dances.

"Come on, Els," Marie pleaded. "It's our junior year. Besides, you need to put another extracurricular activity besides the writing team on your college resume." By now Marie was practically begging.

Elsie sat in silence with her elbows on the table and her head resting in her hands as she considered what Marie was asking her to do. She didn't want to disappoint Marie, but just the thought of being on stage performing in front of everyone at school—*no, thank you.* That sounded like a nightmare, not a good time!

"Please," Marie begged as she grabbed Elsie's hand so that

her head wasn't supported anymore, and she was forced to look at Marie. Marie was giving Elsie her best pouty lip.

Elsie laughed. Marie did have a good point. Currently all Elsie had to write under extracurriculars on her college application was writing team and volunteer work.

"You wouldn't have to sing," Marie promised, "although your voice is much—and I mean much—better than mine!" She made sure to emphasize the much to earn some brownie points with her friend and continued, "You could just sit in the back—way, way, far back, in the corner of the stage, in the dark, where no one would recognize you—and play your guitar." Marie gave Elsie a sly smile.

"Why do you even want me on stage?" Elsie inquired. "Why don't you just sing along to a recording—you know, karaoke-style?" Elsie made her only valid argument.

"Because, Els, you need to get on stage and get over your stupid stage fright. And besides," she reasoned, "singing to a recording is lame, and it's been done before. An original duet, on the other hand, has never been done before! And no one in this school, except for you, of course, has the talent to compose and play an original."

Marie was like a child, knowing just how to sweet-talk her parent into giving her what she wanted. Elsie put her head back in her hands and gently massaged her temples, let out an audible sigh, then peered over at her friend. "How much time did you say we have before auditions?"

As soon as that question escaped her mouth, Marie jumped up out of her little black cafeteria chair, hugged her from behind, and yelled, "Thank you, thank you, thank you!"

They had one month to come up with song lyrics and the music to go along with it, but Elsie welcomed the challenge. Composing music wasn't an issue; not only did it come naturally to her, but it also brought back so many cherished memories of her childhood. Her passion for music began when she was a toddler; her father, Lee, would play guitar as her mother, Elizabeth, would make up silly lyrics and dance with her. Performing on stage, on the other hand, was what she worried about. She'd never performed for anyone other than her family. However, if she wanted to take her love for music to the next level, and pursue it in college, then she'd have to get over her reservations about performing on a stage. That was one of the main reasons she'd agree to Marie's request.

Elsie knew that this project, like many projects Marie had put her up to, would be accomplished primarily alone, with little help from Marie—especially since she was the one who knew how to play guitar and compose music. Marie only had to learn lyrics. On days that Marie didn't have practice, she would come over after school to work on their audition—that is, to see what progress Elsie had made. Grandma Olive would make them an afternoon snack, then they'd head downstairs to the basement and get to work.

The basement was Elsie's favorite part of the house. After her mother passed, Elsie's father, Lee, had used some of the insurance money to finish their basement. With Olive getting older, and Lee not wanting her to end up in a nursing home, he converted the basement into a living room, a large bedroom, and a bathroom. He didn't anticipate that Olive would be living in the house until after Elsie was grown, so until then, they would use the bedroom as a place to have jam sessions. Lee would play keyboard while Elsie played guitar, and they'd take turns singing. The two shared a dream of having a recording studio in the basement, but Lee couldn't afford the equipment. The funny thing about life is, no matter how hard you prepare for it, you can never predict it. When Elsie was thirteen, Lee was diagnosed with metastatic prostate cancer and given less than a year to live. He drew up plans for a studio and looked for a contractor. He'd wanted Elsie to have a place to escape what would be the hard reality of continuing on without a father or mother. He had hoped a recording studio would help to inspire her to keep living and to follow her dreams.

Olive promised Lee she would take care of Elsie and make sure all her dreams were fulfilled. After Lee's death, Olive put her house on the market and moved into Elsie's house. She wanted Elsie to grow up in the house her parents had raised her in. Once Olive's house sold, she put some of the money with what Lee had left and hired a contractor to finish the studio.

Every time Elsie entered that studio, her mind was flooded with happy memories. The memories began with her as a toddler, dancing around the back porch as her mother sang and her father played guitar. The older Elsie got, the more interest she showed in music, and Lee began to teach her to play guitar and piano. Soon they were playing and singing together.

"Els, have I told you lately how jealous I am of your awesome house?" Marie cooed as she entered the studio.

"The awesomeness didn't come without a price, ya know," Elsie quipped as she began to set up everything she thought they'd need.

"Don't play that pity card on me, girlie! I know you better than that," Marie teased. This was their way of dealing with grief—teasing each other. Yes, there were times when they had serious conversations about their parents and how difficult life could be, but mostly they coped by making each other laugh. Life was too important to be taken so seriously.

"Alright, Marie," Elsie began after she had a notebook and pencil in hand and her guitar sitting next to her. "Pick your poison. What do you want for this song—fast, slow, country, rock and roll?" she asked as she twirled a pencil between her fingers.

Marie idly ran her fingers across the keyboard, which sat along the back wall. "Hmm, I don't know." She shrugged nonchalantly. "I know you'll make it good."

"Yeah, right," Elsie laughed. "I know you have something in mind. And let me remind you that I will be sitting far—and I'm talking in the farthest back corner of the stage—just playing my guitar, so I don't care what you sing about!" she sassed.

"Okay, okay." Marie turned and looked at Elsie. "How about . . ." she paused before finishing. ". . . love?" Marie suggested.

Elsie bellowed, "Oh, yeah, because I've had a ton of experience in that department!" She rolled her eyes at Marie.

"Well, I think I'm in love," Marie confessed as she grinned and sat down on the chair in front of the keyboard.

"Ha! With who, Will?" Elsie laughed. Marie had never had a boyfriend for more than a month. It seemed she was constantly replacing her boy of the month with a new love interest.

"Don't laugh, Els! He's different, I swear!" Marie protested as she got up from her chair and gave Elsie a gentle smack on the arm.

"If you say so!" Elsie laughed, then instructed, "But how about we focus on song ideas now, and save boy talk for later."

"Fine." Marie rolled her eyes. "Love or summertime," she offered.

"Love or summertime," Elsie repeated, giving Marie a sour look. "Thank you for giving me *so* much to work with. Okay then, let's get started!" Elsie sighed as she began to brainstorm ideas on her notepad.

Their routine continued this way for several weeks. Most nights Marie would stay at Elsie's until close to bedtime, breaking only briefly to eat dinner with Olive as a "family." During dinner the girls would listen intently to Olive's stories from when she was growing up in the 1930s.

"When I was your age, I could buy Pepsi-Cola for just a nickel. Can you believe that? A nickel! Five cents won't buy you diddly-squat anymore," Grandma Olive lamented as she passed the meatloaf to Elsie. Marie and Elsie smiled and encouraged Olive to tell more.

"Marie, you remind me of my best girlfriend, Ruthie," Olive said in between bites of meatloaf and carrots. "That Ruthie, let me tell you, boy, she was a pistol! Always putting me up to things I didn't want to do. Kind of like getting my little Elsie up on stage," she said as she winked at Marie.

"Grandma, I'm not a little girl anymore," Elsie reminded Olive.

"Well, hon, I hate to break it to ya, but you'll always be my little girl. And no matter what happens at the audition," she continued, "you should know that I am always proud of you— the both of you!" Olive reached across the table and patted the top of Elsie's hand. "I sure am glad you girls have each other." And she flashed them a kindhearted smile.

Elsie and Marie looked at each other. Marie stuck her tongue out at Elsie, and they both laughed. They helped Olive clean up dinner before heading back downstairs. As Olive cleaned up the dinner mess, she began to sing.

"How 'bout this song, girls?" Olive asked Marie and Elsie. "This is the kind of stuff I grew up on. It's by Dean Martin. You ever hear of him?"

"No, Grandma, we haven't." Elsie and Marie shook their heads.

"I didn't think you had. You know why?"

They looked at each other and shrugged.

"Because I'm older than dirt, that's why!" Olive chuckled as she handed more dirty dishes from the table to Elsie. Elsie and Marie laughed along with her as Olive began to sing:

I'll be down to get you in a taxi, honey.
You'd better be ready about half past eight.
Ah, Baby, don't be late.

Olive continued to sing as Marie and Elsie did the dishes. When she finished, they both clapped, and Olive gave her audience a little bow.

"Thank you, thank you. I'll be taking requests all night," she smiled as she teased the girls.

Marie looked at Elsie and said, "Now I know where all your talent comes from." They both laughed.

November came and went, and before they knew it, audition day had arrived! Elsie woke up feeling more nervous than she'd ever felt before. Getting ready for school was all a blur. Once Elsie arrived at school, the day seemed to drag, minute by minute, second by second. During class, she could hardly concentrate on her schoolwork. She felt like she had to pee every ten minutes, and her stomach was churning. Then 2:40 arrived, and the end-of-day school bell rang. Elsie grabbed her stuff from her locker and nervously walked to the cafeteria for one last run-through with Marie before their three thirty audition time.

After their final practice, they headed to the auditorium. "Why did I let you talk me into this?" Elsie asked nervously as they stood outside the auditorium awaiting their turn.

"Relax! We're only performing in front of like five teachers. And honestly, who cares about them? In a year and a half, we'll never see them again," Marie reassured her. "Besides, the spotlight's going to be on me. You're just background noise." She smiled and winked at Elsie.

Elsie couldn't help but smirk. In awe of her best friend, she closed her eyes and willed herself to have a fourth of the confidence Marie had.

"Marie Scarborough and Elsie McCormick," Miss Carey, the dance team coach, announced through the microphone, "please report to the stage." She repeated their names one more time, then placed the microphone back in its stand in the middle of the auditorium stage.

"Showtime!" Marie squealed with excitement and jumped up and down as she pulled Elsie by the hand through the auditorium's entrance. She continued to drag her down the aisle, to the front of the room, and then finally up the stairs to the stage.

Elsie felt as if her body was on autopilot as she took a seat on a stool towards the back of the stage. She let Marie do all the talking.

"Hello everyone! I'm Marie Scarborough. And behind me," she motioned to the back of the stage, "is Elsie McCormick."

Elsie gave a slight wave to the judges, then wiped the sweat from her forehead. "We are juniors," Marie continued, "and we will be singing and playing an original by Elsie." She strongly emphasized *original* to get the judges' attention. "The song is titled, 'Stay.' "

"Okay, ladies. Begin when you're ready," Mrs. Hubbard, a history teacher, said as she took her seat in the front row next to the other three teachers who were serving as judges.

Marie looked back at Elsie, gave her a thumbs-up, and smiled. Elsie half-smiled back and recalled the advice Olive had given her before leaving the house that morning: "Close your eyes and picture playing with your dad in the basement. Imagine no one else is around, just the two of you having a good old-fashioned jam session."

Elsie took a deep breath, closed her eyes, and pictured her dad's face. As she pictured the two of them playing together, all her inhibitions and anxieties about being on stage seemed to fade into the far unreachable corners of her mind. Before she realized it, she was playing her guitar and Marie was singing.

> *My whole life*
> *I'm so tired*
> *People coming, always going*
> *Never staying*
> *To*
> *Take a chance*
> *On*
> *Loving me.*
> *Well,*
> *You walked in*
> *Tall, pale skin*
> *And your blue eyes*
> *Are my summer skies.*
> *Then I fell for you,*
> *Without knowing*
> *How you stole my heart*
> *Without asking.*

Not only was Elsie performing, she was enjoying herself! Now, though, was the true test. Could she open her mouth and join Marie on the chorus?

> *So, won't you please*
> *Show me*
> *How it feels*
> *To be loved*

As she sang the chorus, she couldn't help but notice Marie was slightly off-key. Something deep inside of Elsie urged her to sing louder, more powerful, and take the place as lead. So, she did.

And
Will you
Stay
For a while?
Oh, show me
How it feels
To be loved
And
Stay
For a while.
La-la-la-la-la-la-la-la

As the chorus ended, instead of allowing Marie to take back over as lead, Elsie found herself completely entranced by the music. Standing up from her stool, she continued to sing lead as she joined Marie at the front of the stage.

Marie allowed her to take over and counited to sing as the backup vocalist in the song.

As she continued to play and sing, something inside of Elsie changed. Adrenaline like she had never felt before was rushing down her arms and through her fingertips. She was feeling her guitar like she had never felt it before. As if she were in a marathon, racing for first place, giving each stride every ounce of energy she possibly could; with every string's vibration, her heart beat faster and faster. It wasn't just the music, it was in her voice too. She felt the lyrics like she had never felt them before, almost as if each word had its own emotion and it was her purpose to bring them to life through her heart and voice.

Then, just as abruptly as the changes within her had occurred, the song ended. Before she could comprehend what had just transpired, the judges were applauding and Marie was grabbing her hand, and they were taking a bow together then running off the stage.

"OMG! OMG!" Marie was screaming with excitement.

Adrenaline was still coursing through Elsie's veins and her mind was trying to process what had just transpired.

"You were AMAZING!" Marie screamed as she hugged her. "I don't know what came over you, I've never seen you sing and play like *that* before. I mean one minute you were sitting at the back of the stage singing backup, then all of a sudden, you were next to me, taking over as lead and playing like a freaking star!" Marie exclaimed. "You owned the stage!"

"I have no idea what just happened!" Elsie said confusedly. "But, I want to do it again!" she shouted, smiling ear to ear.

"That's what I'm talking about!" Marie screamed back. "My friend, the future rock star!" She laughed.

Back at home, the girls laughed and smiled as they gave Olive the play-by-play recap of their audition. Elsie couldn't explain what had overtaken her, but all she knew was she'd never felt so in tune with her music before. Before tonight, she had feared the stage, worried about others judging her voice and music, but now, she wanted nothing more than to get back up on the stage and make the music come alive through her hands, her voice. She wanted the audience to feel the music as she felt it.

"I'm so proud of you," Olive told Elsie as she hugged her goodnight. "And I know your parents are just as proud as I am, and they were with you tonight."

"Thanks, Grandma." Elsie beamed. "I know this probably sounds strange but tonight, up on stage, I felt at home. Happy. Kind of like I do when I'm in my studio and it's just me playing by myself, and the memories of Mom and Dad really come to life. All the time in my studio has been preparing me for my audition."

"Not only tonight kiddo, but for what's to come." Olive smiled and kissed her cheek. "This is the start of something big!"

"You really think so?" Elsie asked.

"Yes, but that all depends on you, and what you want," Olive said encouragingly.

The next day at school, the Parker's audition results were posted. Before heading to homeroom Elsie and Marie raced to the auditorium's front doors.

"We're the opening act!" Marie shrieked. She grabbed Elsie's hand and they began to jump up in down excitedly.

Elsie was speechless—she couldn't believe it! Opening and closing acts were reserved for the best acts. She found herself at a loss for words as she joined Marie in celebrating.

All day long, the halls were buzzing. It came as no shock to anyone that all-star Marie had landed an opening act, but Elsie McCormick? No one in school knew anything about her, let alone knew that all these years she'd been hiding a secret musical talent.

As she walked the hall that day, random classmates who had never spoken to her before would call to her, high-five her, or give her a head nod. It was as if suddenly she was no longer invisible, and all the new attention made her uncomfortable. Much to her despair, unlike when she was on stage, in the hallway she was unable to tune out everything and everyone around her.

"Get used to it, girl," Marie said as she put her arm around her best friend. "You're going to be the Parker's star. Your life is about to change."

"Awesome," she said sarcastically. "That's exactly what I was going for when I agreed to audition with you. You know, forget about sharing my love of music with others. I only care about being the *star*," she said as she rolled her eyes at Marie.

In the weeks to come, during Parker's practice, more and more classmates would gather in the auditorium to watch oddball Els and all-star Marie rehearse. With each run-through, Elsie didn't even notice the crowd until after the song had ended. When her classmates would applaud and cheer

Elsie's face would turn red in embarrassment. She'd never liked being the center of attention; however, at the same time, her heart would swell with love. She realized there was nothing more in life she'd rather do than share her love for music with others. She was an entirely different person on stage than off stage. On stage, she was full of life, passion, and energy. Offstage, she was still her private introverted self.

By the time opening night had arrived, Elsie was more than ready to share her love and passion for music with the audience. With Olive sitting front and center all Elsie could see was her family smiling back at her. That night, as she filled the auditorium with the sound of her guitar and voice echoing back at her, she was filled with more confidence than she'd ever felt before. Opening night, she realized she was a natural, born to tell a story through the strum of her guitar and her heartfelt lyrics. Unknowingly to her and everyone watching, that was the first of many performances to come for Elsie McCormick.

Chapter 5

Elsie woke with a sore neck and back. She blinked several times, then rubbed her eyes. It took a minute for her to realize she was lying on the bathroom floor. She sat up, rubbed her neck, and looked around. Marie was nowhere to be seen. The last thing she remembered before falling asleep was singing to her drunken friend. She silently cursed her for leaving her on the bathroom floor when she knew Marie could easily have picked her up and carried her to bed.

It was Sunday of Labor Day weekend, and Elsie needed to get home to spend time with Olive. Sunday night family dinner had been a tradition in their family for as long as she could remember. They'd spend the entire afternoon talking while they cooked, then after dinner they'd play cards or dominoes. She moaned as she peeled herself up off the bathroom floor and headed downstairs for some breakfast and much-needed coffee. Upon entering the living room, she was surprised to see her friend sprawled out face down on the couch. She had assumed she was in bed.

"Well, hey there, sunshine!" she said as she plopped down on the couch next to Marie.

"Ugh," Marie groaned as she turned her face towards her.

"Feeling that great, huh?" she teased. "And thanks for leaving me on the bathroom floor, punk!" she added.

"Yeah, sorry about that. I tried to pick you up, but my head was still spinning," Marie explained in a gravelly voice.

She shook her head in disapproval and said, "That's what happens when you drink too much."

"I know; I'm an awful person," Marie mumbled. Suddenly her eyes widened and she perked up, then asked, "Hey, did I have one too many tequila shots last night, or were you actually hanging out with a really hot guy?"

"Really? That's the first thing on your mind?" She had known it wouldn't take long for her nosy friend to inquire about last night's events, but she hadn't even had a cup of coffee yet!

From the happy, playful tone in Elsie's voice, Marie knew there was a good story to be told. She sat up and gently rubbed her pounding head as she smoothed her hair back into a perfect ponytail and probed, "Tell me everything, and don't you leave out a single detail!"

"I'm going to need a cup of coffee first, and you're going to need some Advil!" she prescribed as she got up from the couch and headed into the kitchen. Marie didn't argue.

She returned from the kitchen with a cup of coffee, a Gatorade, and three Advil. Marie sat up, and Elsie handed her the Gatorade and pills, then sat down on the couch facing her. Marie eagerly swallowed them and drank her drink.

"Okay," she declared with anticipation, "now I'm ready." Marie encouraged her to tell her the whole story.

Elsie filled her in on all the night's details, from meeting Augustus "Auggie" Owens, to hanging out on his back porch, to him taking them home, and then the big finale, ending the evening with a passionate make-out session. By the end of the story, her pale white face was beet red, and her cheeks were sore from smiling so hard.

"Oh, my, goodness!" Marie was smiling ear to ear. "I can't believe this is *finally* happening to you!" She let out an exasperated sigh of relief and fell backwards onto the couch pillows.

"Geez, thanks. Has my life really been that boring?" Elsie halfheartedly teased her.

"Yes! Yes, it has been!" Marie quipped as she laughed and sat back up. "So . . . when are you seeing Hottie Auggie again?" And she moved her eyebrows up and down when she said hottie.

"Yeah, about that . . ." Elsie began.

"Oh, come on, please don't tell me he asked you out, and you turned him down." Marie sounded annoyed.

"No! But, we were kind of interrupted by my puking roommate before we could make plans to see each other again." She emphasized roommate as she stared directly into Marie's eyes.

"Man, I'm such a buzzkill!" Marie groaned apologetically.

Elsie laughed at her overly dramatic friend. "I'm not too worried about it. He didn't say how he'd get hold of me, but if he wants to see me again, he'll find a way," she shrugged. She was trying to stay cool, but she wondered when she'd see him again.

"Geez, do us all a favor and join the twenty-first century! Go buy a damn cell phone already!" Marie lectured as she snatched the coffee cup right out of Elsie's hand and drank the last few sips.

"Yeah, yeah, okay, Mom!" she sassed. "And I wasn't finished with my coffee! You're going to make me another cup!"

An hour later, Elsie was showered, dressed, and ready to head home for the day. Normally on Sundays Marie would ride home with her, but not today. Today Marie was headed to watch Marc in the semifinal state soccer tournament, then to the Labor Day firework show. Elsie was invited; however, she wanted to spend some time with Olive, so she grabbed her guitar, hopped in her beat-up Jeep, and headed home.

She loved her old Jeep. It held so many fond memories of a younger version of herself riding beside her dad. After he was diagnosed and given a year to live, he was on a mission to help prepare her for what was to come. He took her to a church parking lot and let her get behind the wheel. When she protested that she was too young to drive, he reassured her that she was never too young for him to teach her life lessons. And he reassured her that the church had been abandoned for years.

Lee knew he wasn't going to live to see her through all of life's rites of passage, so one night after she turned fourteen, he made her try a sip of whiskey.

"You feel that burning?" he asked.

"Yuck!" she gagged as she ran to the kitchen sink and rinsed her mouth with cold water. "Why are you making me try this garbage?" she complained.

"I want you to remember that burning feeling. If you think this stuff hurts going down, it hurts twice as bad coming back up!" he warned her. "I want you to remember that when you're in high school or college, and you're at a party where people are drinking and doing stupid stuff they're not old enough to be doing."

"But I'm not stupid, Dad!" she protested.

"I know you're not. But you're my daughter, and I want you to be prepared."

She smiled thinking about her dad. She wondered what he would say about his little girl kissing a man she hardly knew.

She pulled her Jeep into the long, gravel driveway and saw Olive in front of the house picking flowers. Recognizing the sound of the Jeep, Olive turned and waved to her.

After dinner, the two sat at the dining room table and

played rummy and talked about their week.

"Did you have fun at that concert?" Olive asked as she lay down three queens.

"I actually didn't make it to the concert," she said as she laid down the queen she was holding in her hand to play on Olive's set of three.

"Oh really?" Olive inquired. "That's very unlike you. I'm sensing there's a story behind why you missed your friend's performance."

"It's okay, Grandma. Marie and I got caught up at a . . ." She paused and looked away from Olive's eyes and down at her cards before adding, "an event." Then she played a four, five, six, and seven of hearts and discarded.

"Please, dear," Olive remarked, "I'm no fool. You're an adult in college. You can tell me you went to a party. But," she continued, "you are my granddaughter, and I know you very, very well. You wouldn't miss that concert for just any party." She sounded concerned as she played the eight and nine of hearts on Elsie's straight and then went out.

"You caught me," she confessed. "I can't hide anything from you." She could feel her face turning pink as she mentally debated as to which details she would tell Olive while simultaneously adding up the points from the cards in her hand. Somehow sharing *I had the hottest kiss I've ever had last night from a guy I only knew for a couple hours* didn't sound like something she should tell her grandmother, no matter how close they were.

She wrote down seventy-five points under her name on the scorecard and asked Olive how many points she had.

"A hundred and twenty-five," Olive answered with a sly smile on her face. The game was close, and Olive had just taken the lead. Typically, this would bring out the competitive side of Elsie; tonight, however, her mind was elsewhere.

"You were saying?" Olive encouraged her to continue with

her story as she gathered the cards and started to shuffle them.

"Well," she began, "Marie really wanted to go to this party, so I told her I would go with her only if we left in time to catch the last half of Battle of the Bands."

"Go on," Olive said.

"At the party this guy came up to me, and we got to talking. Time just kind of . . . slipped away." She could feel that her pale face was on fire, and she deliberately avoided direct eye contact with her grandmother.

"Oh, well, that's nice, dear! What was this young man's name?" Olive asked with a smile on her face.

"Augustus. But I call him Auggie," she answered as she looked down at the pad of paper she was keeping score on. She hadn't realized that she'd been subconsciously doodling little hearts at the bottom of the page. She quickly scribbled through them with swirls and stars so Olive wouldn't notice. She felt like a silly schoolgirl pining over her first crush.

"And does he go to the university with you?" Olive inquired as she dealt the cards.

"No, he's here for training, but I'm not sure what kind." She stopped talking as she realized she didn't get much personal information on Auggie. "I still don't know that much about him," she confessed. "Like I said, I just met him, and we only talked for a while."

"Well, if he's smart, he'll make an effort to see you again," Olive simply replied. She always knew when enough was enough and didn't pry.

They finished their game while talking mostly about Olive's volunteer work through their church and Elsie's schoolwork. Once it started to get dark, Elsie gathered her stuff and gave Olive a hug goodbye. Olive wasn't much taller than Elsie. She was a frail five foot three with gray hair and bright green eyes. Elsie loved looking into her eyes because they reminded her of her dad's eyes. She gave Olive a kiss on the cheek, jumped into her Jeep, and headed back to her apartment.

As Elsie walked into the dark, quiet apartment, she let out a sigh of relief. She was glad to make it home before the fireworks started. UC's campus was only ten minutes north of downtown Cincinnati, where the fireworks were being set off. Although she wouldn't be able to see the ground show, she knew her balcony would give the perfect view without having to be a part of the crowd.

She went upstairs to her room and grabbed her favorite sweatshirt and put it on. She looked in the mirror and saw the sweatshirt hanging down to her knees. In that old, worn-out, gray Beatles sweatshirt that had been one of her dad's favorites, she looked like a small child, but she loved wearing it because she was reminded of the countless jam sessions, smiles, and laughter she had shared with her father.

She turned from the mirror and walked over to the far window in her room. Next to the window was a narrow door. She opened it and stepped out onto her tiny balcony. It was as if that balcony had been designed for people her size. And thankfully, since Marie had no interest in squeezing through that door, she ended up with the bigger room. Elsie would come out onto her balcony almost nightly, stare up at the stars, and think of her parents. Sometimes she'd bring her guitar out there and play, or her notebook and write. At home, whenever she needed to get away and clear her head, she'd escape to her backyard woods or her screened-in porch where she and her parents used to sing and play music. Here, in the city, in the middle of campus, her balcony was the closest thing she had to a private escape.

It was a dark, clear, cool September night. In the distance, she heard a faint boom and knew the fireworks were just getting started. She took a seat on the wooden balcony floor, brought her knees to her chest, and pulled her dad's sweatshirt over her knees and down to her ankles. She looked up at the sky and waited for the fireworks.

About ten minutes into the show, Elsie noticed headlights pull into her driveway. The car pulled in, parked, and turned off the headlights. She stood up, pushed herself close against the wall, and slightly leaned over the front of the balcony to try to get a better view. The balcony was small, and it was dark out, so she was sure that whoever was in the driveway wouldn't see her.

The driver made it almost all the way to the front door then turned around and headed back towards the car, only to turn back around and continue towards the front door again. It was too dark to make out any details about the person; however, the fireworks were lighting up the sky, providing just enough light to see what the driver was doing.

She thought it was strange that the person couldn't decide whether they were coming or going, so she turned her attention back to the car. Several large fireworks went off simultaneously, providing just enough light for her to see the car in the driveway. Her heart sped as she recognized the Audi from last night. It was Auggie's car! Instantly her stomach began to churn as she wiped her clammy hands on her sweatshirt.

She was hoping to hear from him again, but she didn't think she'd hear from him this soon. She watched as he finally walked to her porch, spent about a minute there, then walked back to his car and drove off.

She stood on the balcony and watched his car head down the street to the stop sign. Once she was sure he had turned the corner, she eagerly went inside and ran downstairs to the front door. She opened the door to find a small vase of assorted flowers sitting on the front porch.

She picked up the vase and noticed her hands were

shaking. The flowers were beautiful—a bouquet of white calla lilies. She brought the flowers to her nose, breathed in, and smiled. No guy had ever brought her flowers before. She turned around and took her flowers inside and sat down on the couch to get a better look at them. Poking out of the flowers was a small, white envelope. She set the vase down on the coffee table in front of her and opened the envelope.

As she pulled out the card, she couldn't keep her hand from shaking. She was grinning ear to ear, nervous about what the card would say. It read:

> *Elsie,*
> *Thank you for a night I'll never forget! Will you*
> *have dinner with me this Wednesday? How*
> *about 6? I'll pick you up.*
> *Auggie,*
> *513-213-0921*

Four sentences. Four sentences made her heart beat so hard and fast that she felt as if it was going to come right out of her chest. It wasn't her imagination. Last night's events really did happen, and Auggie wanted to see her again. Elsie fell asleep that night counting the hours until Wednesday.

Chapter 6

Labor Day had finally arrived. Auggie was in the break room making a cup of coffee that would give him the caffeine fix he needed to make it through the last two hours of his shift. He felt his phone vibrate in his lab coat pocket. He steadied his cup of coffee in his right hand and reached into his pocket and pulled out his cell. He glanced at the screen to see that he had a new voice mail. He hadn't heard or felt his phone ring. He cursed the hospital for having terrible cell service. His phone was constantly dropping calls, not recognizing numbers, not ringing, or forwarding calls to voice mail. Even worse, he received text messages ten minutes after they had been sent.

He pushed play and listened to the voice mail from the "unavailable" number: "Hi, Auggie, it's Elsie!" His eyes widened as he heard her sweet voice coming from his phone. Instantly a smile appeared on his face. Her message continued: "I wanted to thank you for the flowers. They were beautiful. And the card; it was, um, so thoughtful." There was another pause. Auggie continued to smile. The message continued: "Eh, anyways, yes, um, yes, I'm free Wednesday night so, um, I'll see you at six! K. See you then!"

After her message ended, he hit save to make sure he

didn't delete her message, placed his phone back into his lab coat, and smiled. He mentally gave himself a pat on the back for having scored a date with Elsie. She had been on his mind ever since he left her apartment Saturday night. He had second-guessed himself about having left the flowers and card on her doorstep on Sunday, thinking it might be too much too soon, but now that she had called him back and agreed to go on a date with him, he knew he had made the right decision.

He took a sip of his coffee and realized he didn't need it anymore. Hearing from Elsie had given him the burst of energy he needed to get through the rest of the night. Just then his friend from college, Bobbie, walked in.

"Yesss, coffee!" she said as she grabbed the cup out of his hand. "Thanks, loser. I needed a pick-me-up!" She smiled as she sipped the coffee.

"Take it, Bob. I don't need it anymore," he offered.

"Good! More for me, Gus-Gus!" she said cheerfully. "And stop calling me Bob! You know it drives me crazy," she said in a playful tone.

"I'll stop calling you Bob when you start acting like a lady and stop stealing all my stuff," he bargained. "And stop calling me Gus-Gus!" he added in a mocking tone.

"You never seemed to mind either before," she remarked as she picked up a cookie from the break room table and took a bite.

"Both have always driven me crazy," he admitted.

"Even when we dated?" she asked as she laughed and took another sip of coffee.

"Especially when we dated," he said as he nodded his head and smiled back at her.

"Ugh, I'm so tired and hungry, I don't think I can finish my shift," she grumbled as she grabbed another cookie.

"Come on now, Bob, two hours to go. We got this!" he said, and he clapped his hands as if he was giving her a pep talk.

"You're in an annoyingly good mood," she observed as she took another bite of her cookie. "This wouldn't have anything to do with a girl, would it?" she probed as she took another sip of coffee, then threw the rest away.

"A gentleman never kisses and tells," he declared as he winked at her then put his arm around her shoulder and led her out of the room.

"Don't flatter yourself; you're no gentleman," she laughed. "Remember, I know you *far* too well." And she stressed the word *far*.

"Yeah, don't remind me," he said as they laughed their way down the hall and back to the ER.

Tuesday was another long day for Elsie. No one, not even the professors, seemed to be back into the swing of things after the long holiday weekend. Everyone was dragging. She found it especially hard to concentrate. Her eyes would scan the lecture hall until they spotted a clock hanging on the wall and then would watch the minutes slowly tick away. When she got home from class, she changed into comfy clothes, parked herself on the couch, and flipped aimlessly through the channels. She felt like a zombie staring at the TV screen but not really paying attention to what was on. All she could think about was tomorrow. She was filled with both excitement and anxiety as she eagerly anticipated her date with Augustus "Auggie" Owens.

When she couldn't stand the mindless channel surfing any longer, she made her way to her room and lost herself in her music for the rest of the night. Marie was out with friends, so she had the apartment to herself. She turned up her Bob Dylan and lay down on her bed with her songwriting book. She filled several pages with her thoughts and then pulled out her

Gibson and began strumming. She continued composing for several hours until her bedroom door flung open and Marie came in and sat down next to her. The two talked 'til nearly midnight when they both fell asleep on her bed.

While Elsie was finding it difficult to pass the time, Auggie couldn't find enough hours in the day for everything he needed to accomplish. His Monday shift had ended at midnight, so by the time he got home, showered, and got everything lined up for his next shift, it was close to two a.m. Running on only five hours of sleep, he grabbed his second cup of coffee as he arrived for an eight o'clock conference, sat down next to Bob, and listened to a case review from the previous weekend. Before he knew it, it was nine a.m., time for his twelve-hour shift to begin.

As the day progressed, he was having a hard time keeping up with the fast pace of the ER. Running on five hours of sleep and anticipating his upcoming date with Elsie were not making it any easier.

The ER was busy, and things weren't running as smoothly as they typically did on a Tuesday. One of his attendings had ordered an abdominal CT with contrast on a patient with a concussion instead of a head CT with contrast. When he realized his mistake, he immediately blamed Auggie for ordering the incorrect imaging under his name. So instead of catching up on work, Auggie found himself in the break room on the receiving end of an irate doctor rant until the attending felt better.

Later that day, a four-year-old girl tried to bite him as he was taking her vitals. Not to mention, he was puked on several times and bled on by multiple trauma patients. Auggie had to change his scrubs three times within two hours.

Just when he thought things were turning around and that his shift was about to end, a pregnant woman was dropped off unconscious in front of the ER and left there for someone to find her. She was bleeding from her eyes and mouth. The track marks on her arm made it clear that she was an IV drug user. They tried pumping her stomach and running a drug test; however, she ended up seizing, and no matter how hard they tried, she did not survive. She was only four months pregnant, and they were unable to save the baby.

He left the hospital and entered his apartment feeling defeated and disappointed in the world. After he showered and went to bed, he felt grateful that Tuesday was over and tomorrow was a new day. Now only one, short, eight-hour shift stood between him and seeing Elsie again.

As he lay awake, exhausted but with his mind fighting sleep, he couldn't stop thinking about the pregnant lady and her unborn child. He needed to find a way to get her off his mind before reminders of all the patients he had ever lost began to resurface. Today, the lady and her unborn child made eighty-nine patients in five years.

With the patient's face still haunting him, he turned and picked up the phone from his nightstand, hit the voice mail button, and clicked on the message from "Unavailable." Before he drifted off, he made a mental note to ask her for her phone number tomorrow.

He closed his eyes and listened to the message she had left him. He was grateful that for the first time in all his medical training, he was able to lie in bed and picture Elsie's beautiful face as a distraction from the haunting face of the patient he was unable to save earlier in the day. Yes, the day had sucked, but listening to her voice and picturing her sweet, innocent face reminded him that with all the crazy in the world, there was still good. He knew there was good in Elsie, and he was looking forward to learning more about her.

He had a bad habit of taking work home with him. Falling asleep to the haunting images of those who had died under his care was his form of self-punishment to ensure he'd do better the next time, to find a way to save the unsavable. This self-inflicted torture was the only way he knew to make up for the painful, fatal mistake he had made in his past. He shivered as he at once stopped his mind from drifting back to the most painful mistake he had made in his life. He wouldn't allow himself to go there—not tonight—not when he had Elsie to think about. No, tonight he would focus on the hope that he has earned something good in life instead of dwelling on the reality of all the bad he has done as a flawed human and witnessed as a doctor. Tomorrow was a new day.

Chapter 7

Elsie woke up with butterflies in her stomach. She was nervous and excited that it was finally Wednesday. She rolled over, looked at her clock, and immediately sat up. She had overslept. She cursed herself as she realized that amid all the anticipation, she had forgotten to set her alarm. She jumped out of bed and threw on a pair of shorts and a hoodie over the t-shirt she had slept in. She grabbed a pair of shoes and, instead of untying the laces, tried to slip them on as she pulled her long brown hair into a ponytail. Lastly, she grabbed her book bag and keys and raced out the door. There was no time to eat breakfast or brush her teeth. She never missed class.

The unexpected late start to her morning threw her off of her routine for the rest of the day. She wasn't used to being late and having to rush around campus. Since she hadn't had time to eat breakfast before she left her apartment, after her first class she had to fight the late morning crowd to get something to eat from the campus café. It was busy and loud, and the lines were long. By the time she ordered an egg and cheese sandwich, she didn't have time to sit and eat it; she had to eat it while rushing to her next class.

The day passed surprisingly quickly as she rushed around

from class to class. She hadn't had time to worry about her date with Auggie; she was too concerned with making it to all her classes. By the time her school day ended, she was exhausted. She made it back to her apartment by four thirty and was relieved that she had an hour and a half to shower and get ready for her date. Finally, she could stop rushing around and just try to relax as she got ready.

She felt uneasy when she realized Auggie had never called back. She had assumed he'd call her since she left him a message and didn't actually get to talk to him. She thought he might call to tell her what they were doing or where they were going, but he never did. She didn't want to seem too eager or desperate by calling him, so she was left wondering what she should wear.

She thought for a while about all the couples she saw out and about on dates and concluded that most college girls dressed up for dates. At least, Marie did. She looked in her closet; she only owned one fancy black dress and a handful of casual tops. She sighed. She didn't have much to choose from. She began to feel overwhelmed with trying to decide how to dress, so she closed her closet door and headed to the bathroom to shower.

After she showered, she put on her white robe and took the time to blow-dry her long, wavy brown hair. Once her hair was dry, she turned her attention to her makeup. She applied brown eyeliner, then put on a thin layer of light, shimmery eye shadow to each of her eyelids. Lastly, she added pink blush to her pale face and a clear shiny coat of lip gloss to her lips. She smiled into the mirror; she was satisfied with her makeup.

Next, she turned her attention back to her outfit. September in Cincinnati was warmer during the day and cooler at night. After much agonizing debate, she put on a pair of stretchy denim jeggings and a silky white sleeveless blouse. She grabbed her blue jean jacket out of the closet, put it over her blouse, and examined herself in the mirror, only to shake her head in disapproval. The collar from her jacket made her hair lay funny, and the denims were two different shades of blue. She looked through her closet, reexamining all her options, but she didn't have anything to wear that seemed date-worthy. If tonight's date went well and she anticipated more dates with Auggie, she would have to go shopping.

She looked at the clock on her nightstand. It was 5:35. Auggie would be here in twenty-five minutes. She began to panic and couldn't think straight. She wished Marie was home to ask her opinion on what she should wear. She tried to think back to the conversation they had had the other day when Marie was overloading her with all the dos and don'ts of dating.

Where is Marie anyway? she thought to herself as she took a deep breath in, then exhaled slowly trying to calm her nerves.

Suddenly she heard the front door slam shut, followed by footsteps running up the stairs, then her friend yelling "Elsie, are you still here?"

"Yes. And I'm freaking out! I don't know what to wear!" she yelled back. Just then Marie walked into her room carrying several shopping bags.

"Have no fear, my fashion-less friend! Your fashion expert is here!" Marie exclaimed as she tossed the bags on the bed and began to dig through them.

"Did you go shopping?" Elsie asked. "For me?!" She sounded surprised.

"Did you really just ask me that? Of course I did!" Marie said excitedly. "And trust me, you'll thank me later," she said as she smiled and pulled out a salmon-colored dress. She threw it at Elsie and said, "Put this on," then grabbed a pair of brown boots from another bag and said, "and these!" as she threw them at Elsie.

She didn't question Marie. Anything would be better than the outfit she was currently wearing. She turned away, undressed, and put the dress on. She turned back around and examined herself in the full-length mirror hanging behind her door. Although she didn't like wearing dresses all that much, she had to admit, it was cute. The chest scooped low, but not too low, and there was an elastic band at the waist showing off her figure, then it flared out. She had to admit, the dress fit her perfectly and looked like her style. It wasn't too flashy or too boring; it was plain but had a little character to it. Not to mention, it fit her body like a glove and actually ended where it was supposed to—at her knees and not her ankles!

"You actually found something in my size that's cute, and looks my age?!" she asked in disbelief.

"Of course I did! You just have to know how to shop. That's super cute on you!" Marie said, grinning.

"Not bad," Elsie complimented her friend.

"Now for the boots. Simple, but cute!" Marie said as she handed them along with a pair of boot-length socks to Elsie. "Did I mention they're kids'?" Marie laughed as Elsie sat on her bed and put on her socks and then boots.

Elsie stood up. She had always loved boots but had never found a kids' pair that looked old enough for her to wear. The ones Marie found for her had a small heel and zipped up the side.

"I like them!" she said with a smile, admiring her new outfit in the mirror. "Thank you, bestie!" Elsie was now feeling more confident and date-worthy than she was ten minutes ago, before Marie got home.

Marie walked up to Elsie with a pair of scissors and cut the tag off the back of her dress. Then she cut the tags off of an off-white cardigan and said, "You'll need this if you go to a restaurant, or if you're out later when it starts to get cold." Before Elsie could grab the cardigan, Marie moved it out of her reach and added, "Unless you want Hottie Auggie to keep you warm," she said in a flirtatious voice.

"Really, Marie?" Elsie looked at her smiling friend and grabbed the cardigan out of her hands.

"Geez, take a joke, Smalls!" Marie teased.

"I know, I'm sorry. I'm just a little on edge." Elsie explained.

"Now that you have this adorable new outfit, you'll be fine!" Marie joked, trying to lighten the mood.

"Oh, and the messenger bag that I bought you for your birthday will match perfectly," Marie said with a smile.

Elsie grabbed her purse from her closet and threw in all her essentials—her wallet, keys, ChapStick, and lip gloss. She threw the purse over her shoulder and reexamined herself in the mirror. This outfit was definitely different from the comfortable stretchy jeans and t-shirt she was used to wearing. As she examined herself, she decided she liked her new look. It was casual, not too fancy, and the boots gave her a country look. She had always identified with country music and loved writing it.

"Now you look like a college girl who is ready to go on a date!" Marie exclaimed in approval.

She nodded her head in agreement. "I think you're right!" Elsie said with a confident smile on her face.

It was six o'clock on the dot, and Auggie would be arriving any minute now. They made their way downstairs to the living room to wait. Marie sat on the couch while Elsie paced the room. Marie could tell how nervous Elsie was, so she tried distracting her with the story of how she had cut class today to go shopping for the outfit only to run into the professor from one of her morning classes having lunch in the mall cafeteria.

Elsie laughed as she took a seat next to Marie on the couch. As always, she found herself calming down and feeding off of

Marie's energy. Marie was excited for Elsie, so Elsie began to replace her nervousness with excitement. That was, until she looked at the clock and realized Auggie was late—ten minutes late, to be precise.

"Don't worry, he'll come," Marie affirmed as she noticed Elsie staring at the clock hanging on the wall behind her.

She just nodded, but her stomach started to tighten and her heart started to feel as if it was a balloon that was slowly deflating inside her chest. She'd never been stood up before. In the past she couldn't have cared less if a date didn't show up, but she actually wanted to see Auggie again.

At six fifteen, Elsie really began to worry. Marie tried to keep her spirits up by distracting her with stories about school and Brandon, but her stories were no longer working.

By six thirty, the minutes were slowly ticking away, and Elsie had a bad feeling that he had indeed stood her up and she might never see him again.

At six forty-five, Elsie was pacing the living room and fighting back the urge to cry. She couldn't believe she actually cared this much about a boy not showing up for their date.

She began to question her judgment. Auggie had seemed like a funny, caring guy. After all, he did take her and her drunk friend home. And he did bring her flowers the next day. She wondered how she could have been so wrong about him. He didn't even have the decency to call and tell her he wouldn't be coming!

She knew that in the grand scheme of things, a boy not showing up for their date really wasn't all that important, but upon their first meeting he had instantly felt important to her. She just couldn't deny the sinking feeling in her heart. She had actually opened up to someone other than Marie, laughed, talked, kissed, and now? Now she was standing in her living room in a dress, and he was forty-five minutes late, and she knew he wasn't coming.

Marie walked over to her, gave her a hug, and tried to reassure her. "I'm sure he has a good reason. I mean, guys don't leave flowers on a girl's doorstep only to stand her up. Why don't you try calling him?" Marie suggested.

She shrugged her shoulders in defeat. She wasn't sure why he'd ask her out only to bail on her, but sadly she was used to things not going the way she wanted them to go. Although she had only spent a couple of hours with him, her heart sank as she realized he was the first boy she had ever taken an immediate interest in. She wasn't used to looking forward to spending time with anyone other than Olive and Marie. Nor was she used to not being able to concentrate because all she could do was think about when she'd see him again and the way his lips felt pressed against hers. She began to feel annoyed with herself for having been so foolish in thinking that he felt the same as she did—because clearly, he didn't care enough for her to show up for their date.

"I'm not calling him." Elsie's disappointment was apparent in her voice. "Obviously, I'm not worth showing up for, so I need to just forget about him," she said as she left the living room and jogged up the stairs.

"Besides," she added, "I only spent a couple of hours with him. He doesn't owe me anything. That's how college boys can be, right?" she asked.

Marie nodded her head in agreement. Sadly, she knew from experience that college boys could change their minds about their feelings for a girl faster than they could run out of a lecture hall after their final exam. She followed Elsie to her room.

Elsie could hear Marie behind her, "Don't worry, Marie. I'll be fine," she said as she grabbed her guitar and carrying case and laid them on her bed. She unzipped her case and put her guitar inside. "I'll get over this disappointment. You know I always bounce back," she reasoned as she zipped the case and slung it over her shoulder. She was mad at herself for kissing and caring about a guy she hardly knew. She was raised better than that. Her dad had warned her about college boys and young men being disrespectful and had educated her on how to pick a good man. He explained to her that a respectful man would take the time to date her and not push her into moving too quickly into a relationship. A gentleman would open doors for her and hold an umbrella for her. He would always be on time and never leave her waiting. Most importantly, he taught her to listen to her gut and never wear her heart on her sleeve.

She shook her head as she replayed her father's advice in her head. Auggie wasn't a gentleman. He hadn't returned her phone call and had stood her up. Her gut had been wrong about Auggie. She had let his dreamy blue eyes; his perfectly straight, white teeth; and his witty, charming personality get the best of her. She would learn from her mistake, and she wouldn't let this happen again.

"I'm going to my studio. I'll be back later tonight," she informed Marie, avoiding all eye contact.

"You know, Els, you look like a country music star with that outfit on and with your guitar flung over your shoulder like that," Marie complimented her, trying to take her mind off having been stood up.

Elsie glanced at herself in the mirror. She really did look like a country singer. She allowed herself to give Marie a faint smile. Once again, Marie had somehow found a way to distract Elsie and make her smile when smiling was the last thing she felt like doing. She drew in a deep breath and then released it, willing the foolishness she felt inside to be released as well.

Lee and Olive had taught Elsie to always find the positive in every challenging situation. She silently searched for a positive and concluded that even if Auggie had turned out to be a jerk, she still had an amazing best friend. Not to mention, Marie had helped her to find a new clothing style—one that she didn't completely hate. She smiled at herself in the mirror.

"I really appreciate all you've done for me, Marie," she said as she glanced at her friend's reflection in the mirror.

"Anytime," Marie said. "And there'll be other guys and other dates, Els. This wasn't your fault," Marie said. Then, in a more upbeat tone she added, "And one day when you make it as a famous singer, I'll be your personal assistant and make you look this fabulous every day."

Elsie couldn't help but let out a small laugh, then said, "I wouldn't have it any other way," as she walked over to her friend, stood on her tiptoes, and reached up to give her a big hug. "Thanks, Marie," she said as she held back the tears she felt building up behind her eyes. No matter what life threw her, she knew she'd be able to get through it with Marie by her side.

She headed downstairs, grabbed her new purse and her keys, and walked out the front door. As soon as she had made her way to her Jeep and was unlocking the door, she heard the sound of squealing tires pulling into her driveway. She glanced over her shoulder to see Auggie's black Audi sitting in the driveway behind her Jeep.

Unbelievable! Elsie thought to herself as she shook her head in disbelief. "How dare he show up an hour late for our first date!" she said out loud as she opened her driver's side door and placed her Gibson on the passenger seat.

Auggie jumped out of his car and yelled to her. "Elsie, wait! I'm sorry I'm late!" And he jogged over towards her car. "Please give me a chance to explain."

"Don't bother, Augustus!" she said, infuriated, too mad to even turn around and look in his direction. He hadn't called to tell her he was running late, and then he just showed up asking for her to listen to him so he could explain?!

Who does this guy think he is? she thought to herself. "I'm sure you have a real good excuse," she said in a cold, flat voice.

As the frustration continued to build, she found the courage—or anger (she wasn't sure which)—to turn around and face him. "But whatever your excuse is, I'm sure it wasn't life or death!"

Normally, she was a very levelheaded person; however, tonight her emotions were getting the best of her, and there was no hiding the fire in her eyes or the pain and frustration in her voice. Until today, she had never cared if a boy blew her off. She wasn't sure which was bothering her most—the fact that he had left her waiting for an hour, or the fact that she cared that he had left her waiting.

He threw his arms into the air in defense and began to turn away. He mumbled something to himself then turned back around to face her. "Actually, it was!" he stated in a very matter-of-fact tone as he rested his hands on his hips. While driving to her house, he had debated about whether to tell her the truth or make something up. He had decided not to tell her the whole truth and to just blame work for keeping him late; however, now that he saw how upset she was with him, he knew he needed to be honest if he wanted another shot with her. It was now or never.

"Yeah, okay," she said in a disbelieving voice as she turned towards her car with every intention to jump in, drive away, and forget this terrible night ever happened. But just as she was trying to get into her car, she felt his body against her back as he gently put his hand on her shoulder, begging her to stop and listen to what he had to say.

She stopped dead in her tracks. He was standing so close behind her that she could feel his breath on her neck. No matter how hard she tried to stop it from happening, chills went up her spine. She was annoyed with herself for enjoying his touch when she was so angry at him. Her feelings for Auggie were so confusing.

"Look," he said in a pleading voice, "I normally don't tell

people I just met this, but the reason why I was late actually was life or death." He exhaled, relieved by his own honesty. "I'm not lying when I say life or death," he continued, with his hand still gently resting on her shoulder. "Please," he pleaded, "just give me a chance to explain; that's all I'm asking."

Despite how hard he tried, he couldn't control the desperation in his voice.

Elsie shook her head as she closed her Jeep's door. She then took one step closer towards her Jeep in an attempt to put some distance between the two of them and to release his hand from her shoulder. She turned around to face Auggie, her back pressed up against the driver's side door. She felt trapped and knew that he wasn't going to let her leave without hearing his excuse. She wanted to be able to look him in the eyes while he told her his excuse to see if he was lying or not, but she didn't know if she'd be able to. Every time he touched her or she looked into his blue eyes, some force she'd never experienced seemed to take over her entire being.

Even though she was avoiding eye contact with him, he could see the fire and hurt in her eyes. He felt terrible for having kept her waiting for an hour with no explanation. Two of his pet peeves were being late and disappointing people he cared about. Sadly, he had managed to do both of those things to her without even trying. It seemed that, despite how hard he tried, disappointing people was his strong suit. He shook his head, trying to erase all the memories from his childhood that were resurfacing and just focus on Elsie.

"I'm listening," she said in an annoyed voice.

"I'm a doctor," he said as he threw both his hands in the air and shrugged. Instantly he felt relieved that she knew the truth. He carefully watched her face as she processed what she had just heard.

At first, she remained void of expression. Then the corner of her lip turned up and she smirked as she rolled her eyes at him and sarcastically remarked, "Yeah, okay, good one! If you forgot about our date, then all you have to say is *I forgot about our date.* You don't have to lie to me!" Now Elsie was even more annoyed.

She began to turn back towards her Jeep when he placed his hand on the door, willing her to stay and talk to him. She turned and looked at him. He was so close to her that she really couldn't go anywhere, but she didn't feel threatened by his closeness. Instead, she only felt his desire for her to hear what he had to say. She knew he wouldn't leave until he had said his piece.

"I'm not lying to you," he argued, keeping his hand firming pushed up against her car door and leaning down towards her so that his face was close to hers. "I'm an emergency medicine resident at University Hospital."

She gained enough courage to briefly glance at his eyes; they were deep blue, pleading for her to listen. She looked away, trying hard to process his excuse, the tone in his voice, and the pleading in his eyes. He didn't look like a man who was lying. *He's a resident?* she thought to herself. She was fairly certain from all the *Grey's Anatomy* episodes she had watched that a resident was a doctor-in-training or something along those lines.

She shook her head and chuckled. "Nice try. You're too young to be a doctor," and she crossed her arms against her chest and looked down at the ground.

Auggie was somewhat intrigued. Typically, once a girl found out he was a doctor, she would become clingy and want to take advantage of "all his money." (And while yes, he was a doctor, he didn't have money to waste on buying girls expensive jewelry and taking them to pricey restaurants. His main priority was paying off med school!) He smiled as he realized he had been right about her. She was different, and that made him like her even more. It was obvious he had hurt her feelings by showing up an hour late for their first date, and even if she didn't want to proceed with their date, he knew he owed her a full explanation.

"I'm twenty-five years old and yes, I am a doctor. I was working today, and forty-five minutes before my shift's end, a guy came into the ER in cardiac arrest." He paused, waiting for her reaction. She didn't say anything or look up at him, so he continued. "We were able to revive him. I stayed late to talk to his family, to explain what had happened, and to answer all their questions. After I left the hospital, I rushed home to shower and change before I came here." He willed Elsie to look up at him. He needed to see her face to know whether or not she believed him.

Elsie looked up into his eyes searching for the truth. The fire behind her dark brown eyes had seemed to dissipate and was replaced with curiosity, so he continued with his apology.

"I'm sorry I was late," he said in a very sincere voice, "but it was for a good reason, and yes, it actually was for a life-or-death situation. I promise I got here as soon as I could. Last Saturday, I didn't tell you about my job because in my past, once people found out I'm a doctor, they treated me differently." He let out a sigh and removed his hand from her car door, giving her some personal space. He had said his piece; now it was up to her to either give him a chance or get in her car and leave.

She didn't move. He felt the need to continue. "I would have called to tell you I was running late, but you didn't leave your phone number in your voice mail. Not to mention, the hospital has terrible cell service. When you called me the other night, your number came up as 'unavailable' on my phone. I honestly had no way of contacting you." He pleaded for her to understand.

"So, you're a doctor?" she asked in disbelief as she looked up from the ground to his face. She was still trying to process everything he had just told her.

"Yes," he said, grateful she had listened to his explanation.

"Like a real-life, went-through-medical-school, can-order-prescriptions, and works-with-blood-and-guts kind of doctor?" she asked in both awe and disgust.

"Yes," he answered with a smile on his face.

"And you work in the emergency room at University Hospital?" she asked.

"Yes," he confirmed.

"And you didn't call me because you didn't have my number?" she asked, verifying all that he had told her.

"You didn't leave your number in your message, and your number came up as unavailable. I can even show you my phone if you don't believe me," he said as he reached into his back pocket to get out his phone, but she stopped him.

"No, that's alright," she said as she thought back to the message and realized he was right; she hadn't left him her number. Also, if he was willing to show her his phone, she knew he wasn't lying.

"Look," he began, "you have every right to be mad at me. I get it. From your perspective, I showed up an hour late for our first date without calling to explain. But now that you know the reason, can we consider this a huge misunder-standing and would you please, please, give me another chance?" he begged her as he took one step closer to her and reached for her hand. He felt the need to be close to her. The last couple of days, he had been going crazy longing to touch her again to confirm that the connection between them was something real, not something he imagined.

"If you give me your number, I promise I'll call you the next time I'm running late," he reassured her.

She wasn't sure how she felt about all the new information she'd just learned about Auggie a.k.a. Dr. Owens, but she knew exactly how she felt whenever he touched her. All the tingles and butterflies made it hard to concentrate on anything other than her physical attraction towards him. She had never experienced any of those feelings before and wasn't ready to end it just yet. She needed time to figure out how she felt about Auggie being six years older than her and already having a real-life, after-college job, but she knew she couldn't deny her feelings. Her instincts had been right about him; he was a gentleman. He could easily have left without telling her the truth, but he stayed to give her an explanation and an apology. She decided to give him another chance as well as give herself more time to think.

"You think there's going to be a next time?" she asked in a flirty voice as she looked up into his deep blue eyes.

He took a step closer to her. His face lit up with excitement. "There's still plenty of time for our date tonight. And yes, after tonight, I think there should definitely be a next time," he said in a smooth, confident voice.

Although she wasn't sure how she felt about dating an older guy, her gut was telling her to go and make the most of the evening. Marie was always telling her to live a little, and tonight she decided to take her friend's advice. She took in a deep breath and tried to remain as cool and confident as Auggie seemed. She shrugged her shoulders and playfully replied, "Well, I guess tonight's your lucky night. Some jerk didn't show up for our date or bother to call and cancel, so now I'm free for the rest of the evening." She wasn't used to flirting and didn't know if she was doing it well or not, but the smile on his face confirmed that she was doing it very well.

"Man, what a jerk!" he played along as he gently rubbed the top of her hand with his thumb. "His loss is my gain!" he said in a flirtatious voice as he gently pulled her away from her Jeep and towards his car.

As they walked towards his car he asked, "Are you sure you want to go with me? Five minutes ago, you looked pretty darn determined to go somewhere with that guitar." He gestured towards her Jeep.

"Oh, that old thing?" she said with a dismissive wave of her hand. "We're old friends; it can wait." As they continued towards his car, she began to think of her studio and her parents. Auggie had said it best earlier when he explained why he hadn't told her he was a doctor. Once people learned about his career, they tended to act differently towards him. She could relate. Whenever someone found out she was an orphan, they instantly treated her differently, and from that moment on, all she saw was pity in their eyes. Although she wasn't ready to divulge her past nor her dream of a career as a musician, she was beginning to feel as if they had more in common than she had thought. She needed to see if he was going to stick around and get to know the real her before she told him her whole life story.

"Thank you for giving me another chance," he said with a big smile on his face. "I know I can make it up to you. Shall we?" he asked as he opened the passenger door of his Audi and held it open for her.

"We shall!" she said with a smile on her face as she climbed into his car. She wasn't sure what he had planned for the two of them, but so far, she had learned that spending time with Auggie Owens meant expecting the unexpected.

"Where we headed?" she asked as she buckled herself in.

"That's for me to know and you to find out," he said with a mischievous smile on his face.

Elsie was filled with nervous excitement as he drove them to the spot he had chosen for their date. They made small talk during the car ride, but it was obvious that he was still trying to convince her that he was genuinely sorry for being late, and she was still trying to wrap her brain around the fact that she was on a date with a man who was not only older but much more accomplished than her. Discovering that Auggie was a doctor hadn't changed the feelings she had developed for him upon their first meeting; she didn't like him any more or any less. She could have discovered that he was still in college working at Target, or graduated and was a banker or an architect, and still she would have liked the funny, caring guy who had approached her last weekend. Her parents had taught her to make an honest living and not judge others by their socioeconomic level, so Elsie grew up seeing people for who they really were instead of determining what kind of person they were based on how much money they had.

She saw him for who he was—an attractive, smart, and caring gentleman who was the victim of a misunderstanding entirely out of his control. One thing his age and profession did make her question, though, was their compatibility to date. She was still in college, majoring in music. She wasn't sure where she'd find a job after graduating in a year and a half. She wasn't sure where life would take her. Auggie, on the other hand, must have started planning his future at a young age in order to accomplish all he had so far. She wasn't sure where his career would lead him either. Elsie shook her head. She had a bad habit of worrying about the future instead of focusing on the here and now. She took a breath and reminded herself that this was only their first date. She needed to relax and enjoy it before she started worrying about what would happen a year from now.

Her thoughts were interrupted by Auggie. "I saw these guys last summer. Amazing show," he said as the radio began to play "Keep the Car Running" by Arcade Fire. "Mind if I turn it up?" he asked her as he reached for the volume button.

"Not at all!" she said, relieved that he had interrupted her thoughts and brought her back to the present. She realized that she was in a car with a cute guy listening to music she liked. She smiled as he began to sing along and again she was glad that they shared a similar taste in music. She wanted to sing along with him, but wasn't ready to reveal her talent to him just yet. She needed to get to know him better before she felt comfortable opening up.

As the song came to an end, he drove up a long, curvy road, and right away she realized where they were going—Ault Park. Ault Park was one of her favorite parks. Not only was it full of beautiful greenery and flowers but it sat high up on a hill overlooking the city. This park had it all—playgrounds for kids, fields to throw a Frisbee or fly a kite, flower gardens every-where, walking trails, and in the center sat a huge pavilion perfect for outdoor weddings and events. Elsie smiled in approval of Auggie's choice for their first date.

He parked his car and said, "Wait here," as he jumped out. She could hear him opening his trunk and grabbing things. A few seconds later, he appeared holding a blanket and a basket. He opened her door and extended his hand towards hers, smiled, and said, "My lady."

She eagerly took his hand and smiled as she got out of the car. They held hands as they walked for several minutes before finding the perfect spot. Auggie spread the blanket beneath a huge oak tree that sat atop one of the highest hills in the park. As he unpacked their meal, Elsie was awed by the view of the city, which sat below them in the distance. Although it was still light out, the view of the river and downtown was breath-taking.

"I wasn't sure what foods you liked because we didn't eat the other night; we just drank beer," he chuckled as he continued to unpack the basket. She walked over to the blanket to join him. "So, I brought antipasto," he said as he laid out the sliced French bread, mozzarella cheese, a small bottle of balsamic vinegar, and a container of assorted olives, peppers, and mushrooms. "And in case you don't like anti-pasto," he added, "I brought brie cheese, pepperoni, and crackers," he looked at her and smiled, hoping she approved of his meal choice. He grabbed two small bottles of wine from the basket and said, "And if you don't like any of the food options, I have red wine and water!" he said.

"All of that sounds delicious! Thank you!" she said as she eagerly sat down next to him on the blanket. As she prepared her plate, he twisted open her bottle of wine and sat it down in front of her. "Sorry I'm not classy enough to bring a bottle of wine and wine glasses, but I blame it on not having a bigger basket!" he said, then laughed as he handed her a fork and a napkin.

"It's perfect! Thank you. Besides, I don't do fancy very well!" she said as she took a sip of her wine from the small bottle. Auggie smiled, relieved that she was pleased with his dinner selection.

"So," she said as she took a small bite of her antipasto—careful not to put too much in her mouth since she knew they'd be talking while they ate. "Why medicine? And better yet, why Cincinnati, of all places?!" she asked.

"Wow, you don't mess around, do you, Els?" He smiled at her. "Forget small talk." He winked, then added, "You go for the kill!" He chuckled.

She could feel her face turn pink, somewhat embarrassed, but when she looked him directly in the eye, she could tell he was amused by her. Those dimples . . . and the way his bright blue eyes danced when he smiled . . . she wondered what a man as handsome as him saw in someone as plain as her.

"Relax, I'm only giving you a hard time," he reassured her as he noticed her face turn flush. "Medicine kind of runs in my family. And I chose Cincinnati because many years ago, my mom graduated from UC's College of Nursing. Then, she worked at University Hospital. That's where she met my dad," he answered.

"Was he a nurse too?" she asked.

"No," he chuckled. "He's a plastic surgeon. He, um, lives in

California. That's where his private practice is," he said as he cleared his throat and avoided eye contact with her. His father was the last thing he wanted to talk about.

"Wow," she said, feeling somewhat intimidated by the fact that his family was also in the medical field. "A plastic surgeon," she said as she grabbed a bottle of water out of the basket. "That seems like a very challenging profession."

He laughed at her comment in between bites of his food.

"What?" she smiled nervously back at him. "Did I say something wrong?" she asked.

"No!" he reassured her, "Not at all. I agree with you. Giving someone their ideal image—that's not stressful at all," he teased, trying to lighten the mood while he talked about his father. "However, my world-renowned father would most likely brag about how easy his work is and how being the best isn't work at all; it just comes naturally to him," Auggie said with a disgusted look on his face as he took a sip of wine. "He thinks tummy tucks and nose jobs are child's play. He's known for doing major facial and body reconstructions after serious injuries."

"Talk about some big shoes to fill!" she said, full of admiration. She was impressed but could tell by his tone and comments that he was more annoyed than impressed with his dad. She could sense that his relationship with his father wasn't something he wanted to discuss on their first date. She made a mental note to find out more another time, already hoping there would be another time. "I think your job is amazing, by the way. It must be very rewarding, being able to help people the way you do. That's something to be proud of," she said in a sincere tone.

He smiled and nodded. "Thank you. How about you?" he asked as he placed a piece of pepperoni and brie on a cracker. "Did you always know you wanted to be a . . . music teacher?" he asked, steering the focus towards her.

"What makes you think I want to be a music teacher?" she asked with a smile as she swallowed her cheese cracker and took a sip of water.

"Part of my job is observing people and trying to put all the pieces of the puzzle together—in some cases before it's too late. Not every college girl drives around with a Gibson in her Jeep," he said as he popped an olive in his mouth.

"Well, aren't you observant!" she said as she stuck her tongue out at him like a schoolgirl would do to the boy she was chasing around on the playground. "But why did you guess a music teacher instead of, say, I don't know . . . a famous music performer?" she asked with a shrug.

"Easy. You're not an attention seeker," Auggie said as he shrugged his shoulders.

She couldn't help but chuckle. "Ha, this is true. I don't like being the center of attention. But," she began, "you're incorrect, teaching is more of a backup plan for me." She smiled shyly as she continued to eat her olives and mushrooms.

"Oh, really?" He was intrigued by her comment. "Sounds to me like my beautiful date is hiding a secret talent?" he said, grinning.

"Guess you'll have to stick around awhile to find out," she said flirtatiously as she took a sip of wine.

He couldn't help but smile at the thought of taking her out on another date. "I think that can be arranged," he said as he poured some balsamic vinegar on his bread. He looked over and noticed Elsie was staring out into the distance, taking in the view. Her cheeks were flushed pink, making her even more beautiful. As she smoothed her long brown hair behind her ear he noticed a jagged left scar on the side of her neck.

"What's the story behind that?" he asked as he gently caressed the scar on the side of her neck.

The soft touch of his fingertips sent chills down her neck. "And I'm the one who just dives right in to the questions, huh?" she teased, trying to draw attention away from her burning hot cheeks. Every time he touched her she couldn't help but turn red in embarrassment. "You're one to talk! You've been studying me closely!" she said as she laughed. She had always been self-conscious of the hideous scar, but for some reason she didn't mind that he had noticed it. As far as she could tell, he still seemed to like her, scar and all.

"That scar is my battle wound from attempting to go to my first junior high dance," she smiled as she recalled the memories from that day.

"What?" He laughed. "How did you manage to hurt your neck at a dance?" he asked.

"I didn't even make it to the dance," she chuckled as she explained. "Well, you remember my friend, Marie, from the other night, right?" she asked.

"Ah, puking Marie . . . How could I forget her?" He laughed even harder now that he knew the story involved her. "I have a feeling the two of you have plenty of interesting stories to tell," he speculated.

"You could say that again." She nodded her head in agreement. "Anyway, she was at my house curling my hair before the dance and got distracted talking about how she was going to ask Dustin to slow dance even though he was dating Kari. Needless to say, she kind of forgot what she was doing until my hair started to smoke," she said. "The curling iron got stuck in my hair and by the time she was able to get it out, not only had she burnt a good chunk of my hair off but she had managed to burn the side of my neck," she said as she rubbed her scar, remembering how badly it had hurt.

"Ouch!" he said. "That had to hurt!"

"Not only did it hurt but the smell was god-awful!" She scrunched her nose as she recalled the smell.

"Oh yes, one of my favorite smells of all time—the smell of burning flesh," he teased.

"And on that lovely note, I'm done eating!" she said as she placed the pepperoni cracker she was holding in her hand down on her plate and took a sip of her wine.

He laughed. "What? Can't stomach the smell of burning flesh? You wimp!" He chuckled.

"Um, no! I can hardly make it through an episode of *Grey's Anatomy*!" She laughed. "I don't know how you do it," she quipped.

"Eh, it's just like any other job really. You get used to it," he said with a shrug of his shoulders. "So, I think it's fair to assume you never made it to the dance?" he asked.

"Nope!" She laughed. "I spent the rest of the night in the emergency room with my dad and Marie," she said.

"That was nice of Marie to skip the dance and go to the hospital with you," he said.

"Yes, she felt awful. I told her to go, that I wouldn't mind, but she refused to leave my side." She smiled. "We've always been there for each other," she said.

"You're lucky to have a friend like that."

She nodded in agreement. "Yeah, she's pretty great when she's not almost puking in the back of your car," she teased.

"Ha!" He laughed. "How about the next dance? Did you let her do your hair again?" he chuckled.

"No," she shook her head, "but I didn't need her to. I—I never went to any of our school dances," she shamefully admitted.

"What?" he asked. "Not even in high school?" This caught his attention.

Elsie shook her head no as she took another sip of her wine and avoided eye contact with him.

"Not even homecoming or prom?!" he asked in a surprised tone.

"Nope," she answered. "I guess that makes me sound like a complete loser," she said, avoiding eye contact with him.

"No, not at all. I'm just surprised, that's all," he said. He could tell she was feeling a little self-conscious, so he added, "Man, that whole curling iron incident must have really scarred you for life." And then he added, "No pun intended," and smiled.

Elsie couldn't help but laugh out loud. "I didn't realize I was on a date with such a dork!" she said, rolling her eyes at him. She was glad Auggie was able to make her smile just as she was starting to feel self-conscious.

"But seriously, I'd just assumed it was every teenage girl's dream to go to homecoming with the hottest or most popular guy," he asked as he finished his bottle of wine.

"For most girls, I guess." She shrugged. "But no, not for me," she answered, feeling more at ease now.

"So, you've never danced with a guy?" he asked in disbelief.

"Besides my dad when I was little, no," she said.

"Man, what's wrong with you?" he said in a playful tone then winked at her again.

Elsie's heart skipped a beat as she marveled at how incredibly sexy his smile was when he winked at her. She wondered if he knew how charming he could be. She watched as he picked up his phone and began to search through his music playlist. He hit play and stood up, extended his hand, and said, "Elsie McCormick, may I have this dance?"

As "Bright" by Echosmith began to play from his phone, Elsie's face turned flush again. She smiled as she stood up, smoothed her dress, then eagerly grabbed Auggie's hand and said, "I guess, but only because you have good taste in music." She flashed him a sly smile, then focused hard on hiding her nervousness.

As he rested his hands just above her hips, her body began to tingle. She reached up to wrap her arms around his neck, but they didn't reach, so she rested her hands on his shoulders.

She took a deep breath in as they began to sway back and forth in time to the beat.

He smiled down at her in amusement. "Having trouble reaching my neck?" he teased.

She peered up at his bright blue eyes, chuckled, and playfully swatted his shoulder. "Maybe just a little."

"I like that about you," he said as he kissed the top of her head and pulled her in closer to him. Her head now rested just below his chest.

She was glad he couldn't see her face because her cheeks were on fire. As he held her close and they swayed back and forth to the song, she realized why she'd never cared about going to any of the dances growing up; because until this moment, she had never wanted a boy to hold her and dance with her the way Auggie was doing now. He had this power over her that she had never felt before. He had the ability to make her heart flutter with the slightest touch of his hand. When he looked at her with his blue eyes and flashed her his bright white smile, she never wanted him to look away, even if she felt as if she would explode with excitement.

As they danced to the music, the sun began to set in the background. She concluded that despite the unusual start of their evening, this was the best date she'd ever had. She took mental note of their surroundings, wanting to remember every detail of this night forever—the way her body tingled when he held her close, the sound of his heart beating in his chest, the smell of his cologne, and the way the lights were beginning to illuminate the city in the distance below. For the first time in a long time, in this moment, life felt right.

"Tell me more about yourself," he urged as he gently rubbed his hands up her back while they continued to dance.

"What else do you want to know?" she asked, having trouble concentrating with him touching her so intimately.

"Everything. Anything!" He laughed. "I have a feeling

you're holding back from me."

"Well, Doctor, I'm sorry to disappoint, but compared to all you've accomplished at such a young age, I think I'm pretty ordinary," she said.

"Ha! I doubt that! Something is telling me you might be a little . . . complex," he teased, then added, "And way to sell yourself short to the man you like," he smiled.

"Who said I liked you?" She playfully pulled away from his embrace and gently smacked his chest.

"You did," he said as he gently grabbed her hand and quickly spun her around, then pulled her back into his embrace and continued to dance. "The other night when you kissed me. Then tonight when you agreed to give me a second chance."

"Well, I guess you caught me!" Elsie confessed as she tried not to look him directly in the eyes for fear of blushing. "Smart, observant, hardworking, and a good dancer. What other talents are you hiding from me?"

He dipped her backwards, then playfully copied what she had said to him earlier that evening. "I guess you'll have to stick around long enough to find out." Then he gave her a quick kiss. She giggled as he returned her to an upright position and they danced until the song ended.

Their date continued with them eating, talking, and laughing as they listened to music and watched the sun set. As their evening together was ending, they sat on a bench overlooking the city below.

"This view is amazing," Elsie said as Auggie wrapped the picnic blanket around the two of them, put his arm around her, and held her close.

"Sure is," he agreed. "Nights like this remind me of my mom. She loved astronomy," he added with sadness in his voice. "She used to look at the moon every night before bed, rain or shine," and he held her a little tighter.

"Used to?" she asked in a solemn voice as she glanced over at Auggie, who was looking at the sky above. He avoided eye contact as he nodded his head yes.

"She's not in California with your dad?" she asked quietly.

He shook his head no as he glanced at her. Sadness filled his eyes.

Although their eyes met only briefly, Elsie instantly knew that look of pain and sadness in his eyes—the look of mourning a parent. The look of wondering what your life would be if that parent were still there. The pain of waking up every day feeling as though you were constantly looking for something you were never going to find. She knew that look because she saw it staring back at her every day when she looked in the mirror. So many unanswered questions haunted her daily. She knew better than to ask any more questions; he'd share when he was ready to.

Although her heart ached for him, she let out a sigh of relief knowing she had finally met someone who could relate to the pain she kept buried deep inside her. She squeezed his hand a little harder. "I know your pain. That emptiness that you feel, I feel it too. And I'm sorry. I'm sorry for the both of us," she said, holding back tears.

He looked at her with questioning eyes, but knew better than to pry; that conversation would be for another day—a time when they were both ready to open up about the past. He pulled her in a little closer and rested his head on top of hers. "I knew there was something about you. Something that simply understands me, without having to give any explanations," he whispered. "I wish it was anything but that though," he said as he gently kissed the top of her head.

"Me too," she quietly replied.

For some time, they silently held each other close as the sun set and the stars slowly appeared, mirroring the city lights below. With crickets chirping in the background, Auggie leaned in for a soft, gentle kiss, savoring her lips. She let her lips linger upon his, desperately hoping for more moments like this one in the future.

PRESENT DAY

Chapter 8

Choking back tears, Auggie ran into the small on-call room, slammed the door behind him, and locked the door. Exhausted, he put his back up against the door and held his head low. He was dripping sweat, and his blue scrubs were now stained with blood—her blood. He began to panic as he realized how much of her blood covered his entire body. He ran to the bathroom, tore off his scrubs, and threw them in the trash. He turned on the shower as hot as it would go and let the water wash away all of Elsie's blood.

He was mentally and emotionally exhausted. Somehow, he had been able to bring Elsie back to life and stabilize her for surgery. He rested his head against the shower wall and let the water hit his back. For the first time in a long time, he felt completely helpless as he realized her care was now out of his hands and out of his control.

He closed his eyes and pictured the haunting image of her being rushed out of the trauma bay and into the OR. Her once flawless skin was now bloodstained and ghostly white, making her barely recognizable. Her eyes, that once shone bright with so much life and happiness were now dark and lifeless. Even in the hot shower, he shivered at the thought of her eyes perhaps never shining again. Although he was able to stabilize her, several long, intense surgeries awaited her. As a doctor, he knew that her probability of surviving surgery was low, but he was going to do everything in his power to help her to live.

On his way to the on-call room, he called in a personal favor to the chief of surgery. When he explained that she was a close friend and a public figure, he didn't ask any questions and said he'd be in immediately. Auggie knew if Elsie made it through her abdominal surgeries, he'd need to make one more phone call—a call he dreaded but knew he must make.

He turned the shower off, grabbed a towel, wrapped it around his waist, and sat down on the edge of a small bed. He sat there for a long while, replaying the night's events. He had done what most people would call a miracle. He had brought her back. Suddenly, just as all the blood had rushed back through her heart again, all the memories of their time together rushed back into his heart and mind. He couldn't hold back the tears. He hung his head low and cried until he had no tears left to cry. He let years of buried memories resurface. He made a promise to himself that if she survived, he'd make things right. He'd do and say what he should have done and said six years ago.

SEVEN YEARS AGO

Chapter 9

After their date at Ault Park, Auggie and Elsie were practically inseparable. Despite their busy lives, they always found time for each other. Whether they were just lying around on the couch talking while the TV quietly hummed in the background or meeting for a quick cup of coffee in between Elsie's classes and Auggie's shifts, every free moment they had, they spent together. When they were together, it was as if no one or nothing else existed. They were in their own world, entranced with what the other was saying or doing. Whether they were laughing over something as minuscule as an inside joke or entrusting each other with personal secrets, when one of them spoke, the other hung on every word.

They seemed always to be in a battle with time. Whenever they were together, the hours would pass as quickly as a single kiss, a laugh, or a heartbeat. They didn't want to blink, because they knew if they did, hours would have passed and it would now be time to part. Whenever they were apart, they consumed each other's thoughts. It was as if time stood still and they could physically feel every second slowly passing as they yearned to be together again. It was a vicious but wonderful cycle. Although they hadn't said it aloud, the two were falling in love faster than either of them could control, and love was unfamiliar territory for both of them.

It was the Saturday before Halloween. Marie headed home for Marc's football playoff game. Auggie was working but would be off by seven. To pass the time, waiting for his arrival, Elsie made dinner and prepared some surprise activities for the night. If there was one thing Olive had taught her in life, it was how to cook. She loved to cook and bake, especially from scratch. Since it was fall, she was in the mood for homemade soup. She made chicken noodle soup and for dessert, pumpkin spice cake with cream cheese frosting.

When he arrived at her apartment, Auggie was starving, having just come off a twelve-hour shift. After eating two bowls of soup and a big piece of pumpkin cake, he smiled at her. "This cake is one of the best cakes I've ever had! Where did you learn to cook?" he asked with a huge smile on his face.

"Olive is one of the best cooks I know," she said. "She started teaching me when I was six with easy stuff like eggs. As I got older, she taught me all her secret recipes. This cake is one of them." She smiled at his compliment. Auggie was so good at so many things, but Elsie was a far better cook than him. Secretly she loved being better than him at something.

"Well, this is better than any Betty Crocker cake I've ever had!" he said as he leaned over and gave her a quick kiss. He still had some cream cheese frosting on his lips and she laughed when he pulled away and the frosting was now on both of their lips. They laughed and kissed again, continuing to spread the frosting, but neither of them seemed to mind.

After cleaning up from dinner, they covered the dining room table with newspaper and each carved a pumpkin. Auggie carved a very detailed sugar skull and Elsie stuck with the standard jack-o'-lantern. When they finished, Auggie's pumpkin looked as if a professional artist had carved it; Elsie's looked as if a fifth grader had carved it.

"It appears you've done this before?" she inquired.

"Have I mentioned I'm pretty darn good with a scalpel?" he teased as he looked at his pumpkin with pride. She rolled her eyes at him.

"But in all seriousness, I carved a few pumpkins as a kid," he said, and then in a more serious tone added, "a long time ago though, before my mom passed." He continued looking at their pumpkins and avoided eye contact with Elsie.

Neither of them had mentioned their parents since their first date. Elsie wondered if this was the right time for her to share or not. She opened her mouth to say something, but he beat her to it.

"I think I'm just a natural with a knife!" He winked and then asked, "What's next?"

Another time, she thought to herself then refocused on the evening ahead. "How 'bout a movie?" she suggested.

"Sounds good to me!" he said as they walked into the living room and sat down on the couch.

They searched the guide to see what movies were playing on TV. With it being Halloween weekend, every channel was playing horror movies. After much debate, they decided to watch *A Nightmare on Elm Street*.

"I have to warn you, I'm not big on scary movies," she said as the movie played and she inched closer and closer to Auggie.

"You'll be fine," he encouraged her. "I can protect you. I mean you just witnessed how skilled I am with a knife." He smiled at her as he put his arm around her and held her closer.

She could feel her face turning red. She wondered if he'd always have the ability to make her blush at any moment of any day.

By the time the movie ended, Elsie was practically on Auggie's lap clinging to him. He turned off the TV, looked at her, and gave her a smug smile.

"Not big on scary movies, huh? How 'bout, can't handle

anything scary at all?" He laughed.

She gave him a slap on the shoulder and said, "Shut it!" She tried to act upset but smiled back at him. "I tried to warn you," she said defensively.

"Can't take a little scare?" he teased as he flung her off his lap and backwards onto the couch.

She let out a squeal of excitement as he began to tickle her. She started to laugh as she tried to fight back, but it was no use; he was much bigger and stronger. They both laughed until it hurt; and then once the laughter stopped, she looked at him and said, "I'm never trusting your taste in movies again. Thanks to you and that stupid movie, there's no way I'll be able to sleep tonight."

He brushed a strand of hair from in front of her face and looked her in the eyes. "Yeah, you are pretty small. You'd be completely defenseless if someone were to break in and try to kill you," he said with a taunting smile.

She tried to lift her arm to play punch or slap him, but he had her pinned down. "Wow, thanks for bringing that to my attention!" she sassed.

He leaned in and stole a kiss before she could turn her head. "Anytime!" he continued to tease. "You know what you have that most small, defenseless girls in horror movies don't have?" he asked.

"Hmm . . . common sense," she answered, playing along with his game.

"Um, no, you definitely don't have that!" His eyes danced with excitement now as he held her down, leaned in very close to her face, and said, "You, my dear, have a handsome, strong boyfriend to protect you!"

Although they had never given themselves the official title of boyfriend and girlfriend, Elsie had assumed them to be an exclusive couple. Her heart fluttered at the sound of the word "boyfriend" escaping Auggie's lips.

She tried to play it cool as she playfully asked, "Oh, is that what you are?"

"Yup, sure am!" he proudly claimed. "And you know what?" he asked her as he leaned in a little closer so she could feel his breath against her lips.

"What?" she asked as her heart pounded in anticipation.

"I think I should stay the night. You know, to make sure you're okay in this big apartment all by your tiny, defenseless self," he said. And he leaned in even closer to kiss her. Although he had just been joking with her a moment ago, there was nothing joking about his soft, passionate kissing. Through his kiss, he politely asked to stay and continue kissing her all through the night. He gently pulled away and looked deep into her eyes, pleading for her to say yes.

"I guess you should stay. You know, just in case someone tried to break in and kill me," she said in a breathy voice, trying to play it cool. She was still trying to catch her breath from his kiss. She could feel her heart pounding against her chest as she contemplated what he was asking of her.

Auggie's eyes grew wide with excitement. Suddenly Elsie realized he might be wanting more than she was ready to give.

"You can stay if, and only if, we sleep next to each other and nothing more," she clarified with a nervous smile on her face.

"I'll behave myself," he said, a little too eagerly. He smiled and said, "You won't regret this," as he leaned in for one more long intense kiss. He slowly removed his mouth from hers, then gently got up from on top of her and pulled her up off the couch.

Although it was Elsie's apartment, Auggie held her hand as he led her up the stairs to her bedroom. Once in her room, it was obvious she was nervous. He sat on the edge of her bed while she leaned up against the door frame waiting for him to make the first move. The room was dark, but the light was on in the hallway, dimly lighting her room. From the expression on her face, he could tell she was hesitant. He knew he needed to make the first move for her to feel more comfortable. Slowly, he stood up, unbuttoned his pants, then unzipped his zipper and let his pants fall to the ground.

Elsie couldn't help it. Taken by surprise, her mouth felt as if it were hanging to the floor as she watched his every move. She'd never seen a guy in his underwear. Auggie was wearing boxer briefs like the ones she'd seen in the Hanes ads—although seeing a pair of underwear in an ad bulge in the crotch area and seeing a man she had very strong feelings for bulge were two entirely different things. Her entire body was taken over by the need to feel his body pressed up against hers.

Auggie could tell she liked what she was seeing but still needed a little more encouragement. So, after he stepped out of his jeans, leaving them on the floor beside his feet, he grabbed the bottom of his sweatshirt and undershirt and lifted them over his head and down his arms, and finally dropped them on the floor next to his jeans.

Elsie watched as her entire body felt as if it were on fire. Although her body was telling her to move closer to him—to jump on top of him and kiss him wildly and passionately—she was glued to the door frame in fear. When he had his hands over his head, something caught the corner of her eye. Instead of focusing on his perfect six-pack and biceps, she tried to calm her nerves by focusing on his left side.

She slowly approached him, trying to ignore his perfect physique and make out what she was seeing. She stopped several inches in front of him, unable to look at his face, and with trembling hands gently grabbed his left arm and lifted it. Beneath his arm, along his entire left side, from his nipple line, to hip, was a tattoo of a cross. The tattoo was done in what appeared to be black and gray ink, but it was hard to make out in the dim lighting. Although Elsie had never been a fan of tattoos, his looked like a piece of art on a perfect canvas. The cross was a very detailed Celtic stone cross. It was beautiful.

As she examined his tattoo, neither of them spoke. He was holding his breath as her fingers gently touched his skin.

Elsie was the first to speak, "When did you get this?" she asked in a soft voice.

"When I was nineteen," he said quietly.

"Is this the only one you have?" she asked.

"Yes," he said, barely louder than a whisper.

"It's beautiful," she whispered back as she ran her fingers over his ribs, down to his hip bone, tracing the full length of his tattoo. They had talked about religion before, and Auggie said he wasn't one for religion. "What does it mean?" she asked as she reached the end of his tattoo. There had to be a story behind his choice of artwork.

"We all have a cross to bear," he said in a sad and serious tone.

For the first time since they had gone upstairs, she found the courage to look him in the eyes. Even in the dim light, she could tell his blue eyes looked sad, and something inside her knew it had to do with his mom. Her heart ached for him.

"Your mom?" she asked.

His eyes widened and looked a little misty. He stood and pulled her in for a hug and said, "That's a story for another day," then he gently pulled her closer to him and ran his fingers through her hair.

She rested her head on his bare chest and she could feel the rest of his body pressed up against hers. Her heart was racing a thousand miles per hour; she felt as if it was going to pop out of her chest at any moment.

He gently released his grip on her, leaned down, and began to slowly kiss her lips. As they continued to kiss, he reached down and gently pulled her shirt up. They stopped kissing so he could take her shirt off. Elsie stood there, frozen in place.

She had always been self-conscious about her frail body. She could feel his eyes looking over her chest, stomach, and down to her waist. She found herself holding her breath as he examined her. She looked away, afraid he wouldn't like what he saw. He looked back up, turned her face towards his, smiled, and whispered, "You're perfect."

With those two words, she exhaled and felt a huge relief rush throughout her body. She smiled back at him, a shy but grateful smile.

"If you say so," she said shyly.

"You are," he said more assertively as he sat back down on the bed, grabbed hold of her leggings, and in one swift motion pulled them down to the floor, exposing her slender legs. He pulled her in closer to him, encouraging her to lie beside him in bed. And there they stayed throughout the night, holding each other, talking, laughing, and passionately kissing until the sun came up.

Chapter 10

Since that Saturday night, Elsie and Auggie made sleepovers part of their weekly routine. They were falling fast and hard and loving every minute of it. Thanksgiving passed with Auggie working and Elsie, disappointed but understanding of his schedule, spent the holiday at home with Olive.

Before she knew it, Elsie's favorite time of year had arrived—Christmastime! She loved everything about Christmas—the lights, the snow, the decorations, and especially how everyone seemed to be happier, kinder, and more loving at Christmastime. The first week of December, Elsie helped Olive decorate the house, and then she decorated her apartment. In the weeks that followed, she found herself telling stories to Auggie about some of the things she enjoyed doing with her parents when she was a child. One night the pair headed downtown to Fountain Square to ice skate. This is something Elsie's father took her to do every year. After his passing, she hadn't felt like going back. But this year was different; this year she had Auggie.

She surprised herself that she was still able to do a few spins, a simple jump, and skate backwards. It wasn't anything special really, but to Auggie she was practically a pro. After showing off a few of her moves, she spent the rest of the night skating next to him, holding his hand as he stumbled around the rink. Auggie laughed as he fell backwards and pulled her down with him. "I'm sorry I can't be as short as you and have a smaller center of gravity!" he teased.

The snow fell down around them as they lay laughing on the ice. Auggie tried to stand only to fall back down again, knocking Elsie over in the process. They were laughing so hard that neither of them could stand up. People stared as they skated around them, but they didn't seem to care.

Once Auggie was finally able to stand, he skated behind Elsie, placing his hands on her shoulders and using her as his guide. As she skated slowly in front of him, pulling him along, he said, "I never knew being so awful at something could be so fun." He tried to kiss the top of her head, only to lose his footing again and fall back down.

As she helped him up she noted, "You make everything fun."

He stood, pulled her in close, and kissed her passionately, not caring about the crowd around them. When he pulled away he said, "No, WE make everything fun, together." Elsie was glad her cheeks were already red from being out in the cold because she could feel herself blushing.

That night they laughed so hard they cried as Auggie repeatedly tumbled to the ice and pulled Elsie down on top of him. By the end of the night they were both covered in ice and snow and shivering in their wet clothes. They didn't seem to notice how cold they were until they got off the ice. They held each other close as they sipped their hot chocolate and walked the streets lined with red, white, and green Christmas lights. When they arrived at Auggie's car, the snow was still falling down around them. Auggie leaned down and kissed Elsie before opening the car door for her. She knew her father would be happy that after all these years she was finally able to enjoy one of their father-daughter traditions with a man she was uncontrollably and undoubtedly falling in love with.

The week before Christmas was finals week for Elsie. Elsie was fortunate to have only a few finals. On the Sunday before finals week, Marie and Elsie spent an entire morning baking all their favorite holiday goodies—peanut butter blossoms, chocolate chip cookies, and sugar cookies. They needed "stress food" to keep them motivated and to get them through exams. While Elsie was busy studying, Auggie was busy working, but each night he'd bring dinner to Elsie and Marie. Marie would eat in her room, too busy cramming to come down and join Elsie and Auggie. Elsie would take a break from studying to enjoy some downtime with Auggie.

"Thanks for bringing us dinner!" Elsie said gratefully as she watched Auggie place her sandwich down on the dining room table in front of her and then head into the kitchen. "You didn't bring one for yourself?" Elsie asked.

"Nope!" he called back from the kitchen.

Elsie could hear the sound of the refrigerator door opening and closing, Auggie pouring something into a glass, and something going onto a plate. Auggie returned to the dining room holding a big plate of cookies, a glass of milk, and a huge smile on his face.

"When you told me you were baking cookies this morning, I knew what I was eating for dinner!" he said as he shoved an entire peanut butter blossom cookie into his mouth. His blue eyes danced with excitement. He reminded Elsie of a kid in a candy store. "Seriously, Els, what do you put in these things? Crack?" he asked with a mouthful of cookie.

"Now I know the secret to keeping you around," she said. "Cookies!"

"Yup, keep making these, and I'll never leave you!" he teased as he dipped his chocolate chip cookie into some milk before taking a bite and sitting down at the table next to her.

"When are you heading home for Christmas?" he asked her after taking a big gulp of his milk.

"I'm not sure. Maybe after my exam on Wednesday. I wasn't sure what you were doing . . ." she said, leaving her sentence unfinished.

He didn't talk much about his family. But from what she had gathered, he wasn't close to his father and wouldn't be joining him for the holiday. She wanted to ask him to spend some time with her on Christmas but, being new to the dating game, she didn't know if it was too soon. Also, she knew that if he came to her house, that was opening the door to questions about her past. She wanted Auggie to know everything about her but had never made herself that vulnerable to anyone.

"I'm not doing anything this week," he said as he took a bite of his sugar cookie covered in green frosting. "And I don't have to work Christmas Day," he added nonchalantly.

She tried to summon the courage to ask him to spend Christmas with her. She hadn't asked Olive if he could join them, but she knew Olive would want to meet him. Elsie opened her mouth to try and ask one simple question, *Would you like to have dinner with Olive and me?*, but her throat instantly tightened, and instead she shoved another bite of her sandwich in her mouth, swallowed hard, and tried to clear her throat with a big drink of water. She avoided eye contact with Auggie as she realized her face must be bright red. She didn't understand how he could still make her this nervous after three months of dating.

"I'll probably just relax, watch some movies, maybe steal some of your cookies for dinner," he hinted.

She knew he was trying to make it easier for her to ask him what he knew she wanted to ask. Her heart quickened as she picked at her sandwich and shyly offered, "You could eat dinner with us. I mean, if you want to." She could feel her hands begin to shake a little as she waited for him to answer. This was a big deal. It was the first time she'd ever invited a boy home to meet Olive.

"Hmm," he said, pretending to contemplate her offer, "let me think about this. Eat cookies by myself, or spend time with my girlfriend, meet her grandma, and eat a delicious dinner." Elsie knew he was only teasing. When she looked him in the face to see him flashing that huge, toothy, playful grin, her hands stopped shaking and she started laughing. "I think I'll just stay home and eat cookies!" He laughed as she playfully smacked his arm.

"Oh, you're going to pay for that," he said as Elsie tried to get up and run, but it was no use. He was already out of his chair and swooping her into his arms. As she screeched with laughter, he carried her upstairs to her bedroom. There they lay next to each other kissing and laughing.

"I'd love to meet Olive," he whispered as he kissed her forehead and then added, "and I'd love to spend Christmas with you."

She looked at his bright blue eyes and gently rubbed his muscular bicep. She still wasn't sure how she'd managed to find a guy as perfect as him. Not only was he good-looking and smart, but he made her laugh, and he liked her for who she was. He never tried to change her. For once in her life, things were going well, and that realization made her uneasy. Trying to ignore the uneasy feeling, she kissed her boyfriend and concentrated only on how exciting it would be having him at her house for Christmas.

Exams came and went, and Marie and Elsie survived on coffee, cookies, and late-night study sessions. Before heading home, Elsie gave Marie her Christmas present—a coffee mug that said "Best Roomie" along with a tin of cookies to take home to her family. She hugged her, grabbed her Gibson and dirty laundry, and headed out the door.

As soon as Elsie got home, she headed down to her studio to finish Olive's Christmas present—a CD of her favorite Christmas music sung by her favorite singer, her granddaughter. Olive was Elsie's biggest fan and had been asking Elsie to make her a CD. She spent the rest of Wednesday night and all of Thursday in her recording studio, only taking a break to go grocery shopping with Olive to get all the groceries they'd need for Christmas dinner. When Elsie was in her studio, she always seemed to lose track of time. She realized late Thursday night that she hadn't called to talk to Auggie. Although it was late, she called to check in.

"Well, there's my *long*-lost girlfriend!"

"Hi, boyfriend," she retorted.

"I was wondering when you'd call," he said with a hint of frustration in his voice.

"I know, and I'm sorry," she said. "I got caught up in helping Olive get everything ready for Christmas," she explained.

"Well, I hope you didn't get me anything, because after going two days without hearing from you, I kind of assumed you'd changed your mind about spending the holiday with me. So today I returned your present," he teased.

"You did not!"

"I guess you'll find out tomorrow!" he continued teasing her.

"So even though I'm an awful girlfriend and haven't called you, you're still coming?" she asked as she bit down on her bottom lip, anxiously awaiting his answer.

"Wouldn't miss it for the world!" he said excitedly. "Now get some sleep, and I'll see you soon!"

"I'm looking forward to it!" she replied. "Goodnight, Auggie."

"Goodnight, Els."

As she hung up the phone, she could hardly contain her excitement. Less than five minutes ago, she was exhausted and could hardly keep her eyes open, but now, after talking to Auggie, she didn't know how she'd ever fall asleep. She felt like a kid eagerly awaiting Santa's arrival. But instead of waking up to find a tree full of presents, she was going to wake up to one of the best presents she never thought she'd receive— spending Christmas with Olive and the first man she'd ever loved. Although she and Auggie hadn't yet said the words *I love you* out loud to each other, she felt it in his kiss, in his touch, and in the way his blue eyes lit up when she made him laugh.

She closed her eyes and reminisced on Christmas Eves from her past. She remembered her dad coming in throughout the night to check on her to make sure she was sleeping because Santa wouldn't come if she was awake. He'd read and reread *'Twas the Night Before Christmas* until she'd finally drift off to sleep. She closed her eyes, and this time instead of visions of sugar plums dancing in her head, it was visions of Auggie replaying in her head. She saw them ice skating, eating cookies, laughing on the couch, and him holding her in his arms as they drifted off to sleep.

The next morning was Christmas morning. When she awoke, she could faintly hear the *Charlie Brown Christmas* album playing from the living room. This was something her mom and dad used to do for her when she was a child. She jumped out of bed, threw on her plush white robe and matching slippers, and bounded downstairs to the living room. There Olive sat in her blue recliner sipping her coffee. Next to the fireplace, the tree was plugged in and the white lights sparkled.

"Merry Christmas, Grandma!" She walked over to the recliner and leaned down and gave Olive a hug, being careful not to spill her coffee as she kissed her on the cheek.

"Merry Christmas, my sweet granddaughter," Olive said as she gently hugged her back.

"Thank you for playing my favorite Christmas music. It makes me feel like a kid again." She stared at the tree, admiring all the white lights and the childhood ornaments she had made.

"Being a kid at heart is the secret to living as long as I have," Olive mused. "You're only as old as you feel. Remember that, dearie," she said as she sipped her coffee.

Elsie smiled. Olive always had a way with words, and she always gave good advice.

"Looks like Santa left you a little something," Olive said as she gestured towards Elsie's stocking hanging by the fireplace. Although it was Elsie's third year of college, Olive still filled her stocking with her favorite goodies.

"You didn't have to get me anything," Elsie said as she walked over to the fireplace and took her stocking off the hook. "I know I didn't have to, but I wanted to." Olive grinned.

She brought her stocking over to the couch and slowly began pulling out its contents one by one. When she finished emptying her stocking, she looked at everything that lay spread out on the cushion beside her. Olive knew her well. Her stocking was filled with all her favorite candy—peanut M&M's and Reese's Pieces—along with pistachios, candy canes, and oranges. She also included a new pair of fuzzy purple sleeping socks and a dangling pair of sterling silver, heart-shaped earrings.

"All my favorites! And I love the earrings! Thank you!" she exclaimed. "I got you something too!" she proudly announced as she stood up and pulled a square-shaped package wrapped in green wrapping paper from the pocket of her robe and presented it to Olive.

"Whatever could this be?" Olive pondered with wonder

and excitement. She set her coffee down on the table beside her and gently unwrapped the present. Olive read the title on the CD case aloud: "*Christmas Favorites*," she said with a smile on her face, "by Elsie McCormick. How lovely, a CD of my favorite songs? Thank you, dear." Olive said.

Elsie realized Olive didn't understand that it was a CD of *her* singing her favorite songs. She walked over to Olive and said, "Here, Grandma, I'll play it for you," and she took the CD and walked over to the entertainment center next to the fireplace. She took out the *Charlie Brown Christmas* soundtrack and put in her CD. The first song was her acoustic guitar rendition of "White Christmas." As the guitar and Elsie's voice began to echo through the room, Olive's eyes instantly began to tear up.

"This is a CD of you singing?!" she asked with watery green eyes.

"Yes," Elsie nodded.

"This is the best present anyone could ever give me!" Olive said as she wiped tears off her face. "Your parents would have loved to hear you sing as well as you do now. They'd be so proud." She got up from her recliner and gave Elsie a big hug.

Elsie relished her sense of accomplishment. Throughout the years, Olive had always given Elsie amazing gifts and taken such good care of her. Elsie was happy to finally give Olive something in return. Olive insisted on listening to Elsie's CD over and over again while they ate breakfast and got ready for the day. Before they knew it, afternoon had arrived. The two headed into the kitchen to start preparing dinner. Although she was tired of hearing her own voice coming from the speakers throughout the house, she hadn't seen Olive this happy about anything in a long time, so she let the album continue on repeat.

Before long the doorbell rang. Elsie looked at the kitchen clock to see that it was nearly four o'clock. *Auggie!* she thought to herself as her hands began to sweat, and her heart began to race. She wiped her hands on her kitchen apron and smoothed her wavy hair back behind her ears. There was no time to check her appearance in a mirror. As the doorbell rang again, Elsie realized her CD was still playing. As Olive made her way to open the front door, Elsie raced into the living room to turn off her CD. She hit the power button just as Olive was opening the door for Auggie. "Well, you must be Auggie!" Elsie could hear Olive greeting him at the door. "Come on in," Olive said.

"Merry Christmas, Olive, and thank you for having me!" He brushed the newly fallen snow off his black dress coat while he balanced two presents in his other hand.

"Merry Christmas to you too! Elsie has told me so much about you. It's nice to finally meet you," Olive said with a grin on her face as she pulled him in for a hug and then led him into the house.

Elsie appeared from the living room, flushed from having run to turn off her CD and from the nervous excitement of having her boyfriend in her home for the first time. "Merry Christmas, Auggie," she said as she gestured towards the living room. "Come on in!" The excitement was evident in her voice.

He smiled when he saw her. "You look lovely, Els." She had curled her hair and was wearing a red cardigan on top of a cream-colored dress.

"I can clean up every now and then," she teased. "Here, let me take your things," she said.

"Thank you," he said as she reached for the presents in his hand, and he took off his coat and handed it to her as well. Elsie looked him up and down, once again reminded of how handsome her boyfriend was. He was dressed in a red and white gingham dress shirt and dark blue fitted jeans. Her thoughts were interrupted by Olive suggesting, "Elsie, why don't you give Auggie a tour of the house while I finish up dinner."

She set his things down, grabbed his hand, and said, "Follow me, sir," in her best impression of a tour guide. His deep blue eyes flickered with excitement as she pulled him into the house. "As you can see, behind us is the living room. To your left is the kitchen," she proceeded. Auggie looked around. All the ceilings were high with beautiful arches, and all the furniture was modern and white. Although the house seemed small from the outside, on the inside it was very spacious.

Next, she led him through the dining room and out the back door. She opened the shades and turned on the Christmas lights that lined the screened-in porch. "This is one of my favorite parts of the house," she said as they walked past the table in the middle of the porch and to the railing overlooking the backyard. The sun had started to go down, but they could still see how the backyard led into the woods surrounding the house. Most of the trees were bare with frozen branches, but there were still a number of pine trees covered in freshly fallen snow. It was a mix of wintry green and sparkling white. To the right was a brook that ran as far as he could see. It wasn't completely frozen, so he could hear a gentle stream of water trickling. The beautiful blue creek sparkled next to the brilliant white snow.

"Growing up I used to sit out here, do my homework, eat dinner, and play with Marie," she reminisced. "I love it out here; it's so peaceful," she said as she smiled and looked up at him.

"This is an amazing backyard." He looked down at her and gently reached for her hand. They stood there for several minutes overlooking the woods, watching the snow slowly fall and listening to the steady stream trickling.

"We'd better head back in," Auggie said as he noticed Elsie starting to shiver.

Back inside, she led him down the main hall. "Bathroom,"

she said as she gestured to her left. "Olive's room," she said as they continued down the hall. "And finally, my room," she said as they turned into the last room on the right.

She stood off to the side holding her breath as he entered, looking all around and taking it all in. Like the rest of the house, her furniture was white. Her plush bed sat in the middle of the room with a nightstand next to it and a dresser against the far wall. From the looks of the furniture, you'd think a refined, rich person grew up here—that is, until you looked at the walls. Every wall was covered with posters and album covers of her favorite bands.

"I know the posters are kind of . . ." she swallowed in embarrassment, ". . . juvenile," she said, and looked down at her feet, afraid to see the expression on Auggie's face. He walked across the room examining each poster, then started to laugh a little.

"Are you kidding me? I didn't peg you as a country fan!" he teased as he looked at a Tim McGraw poster.

Elsie looked up, "Hey now, don't make fun!" she said.

"I'm not, I love it!" he said. "Weezer, Jimmy Buffett, Radiohead, the Beatles, Kenny Chesney . . . All these bands make you who you are today—a music major and lover." Auggie was walking back towards Elsie when he noticed several framed photos sitting on her dresser and walked over to take a better look. There he saw younger versions of Marie and Elsie giving each other bunny ears and sticking their tongues out.

"Ha! You and Marie," he said, more of a statement than a question.

Then he picked up the one next to the picture of Marie and Elsie. He didn't recognize anyone in the picture—a thin, petite woman with dark hair and dark eyes holding a little baby, and a taller gentleman with dark hair and green eyes. He turned to Elsie. For a moment their eyes met, and she willed herself not to cry. She looked down at the floor and confirmed what

Auggie suspected. "My parents," Elsie announced sadly as she tucked her hair behind her ear and concentrated on controlling her emotions.

Respecting Elsie's privacy, he placed the picture of her parents back on top of the dresser and glanced at the other photos. There were more of Elsie and her dad throughout the years, but the photos of her mother stopped when she was a young child. He concluded that her mother had passed before her father.

Auggie could feel the tension building in the air and broke the silence with a quiet, sincere voice: "You look like your mom. She was a beautiful lady, and so are you," and he glanced back towards Elsie, who was still looking at the floor.

"Thank you." Her voice sounded weak and distant when she answered. For her, Christmas was the hardest holiday to celebrate without them. She let out a sigh of relief, grateful that Auggie wasn't asking questions. She wanted to save the hard questions for another day. She cleared her voice and looked up at Auggie. "We should probably head back out to Olive," she said as she turned to leave her room.

As they walked back towards the kitchen, Auggie pointed to the long staircase that led downstairs. "Basement?" he asked. Elsie had been avoiding the basement. She hadn't told Auggie about her parents or about her studio. In a way she felt deceitful for not having shared those things with him, but she felt justified in wanting to wait for the right moment to tell him. He knew she was a music major, but he had never heard her sing or play guitar. She knew the moment was tonight when she gave him his gifts.

"Oh, uh, yeah, that's our basement." She shrugged her shoulders and added, "It's fully finished with a guest room, bathroom, laundry room . . ." Her voice began to trail. "You know, normal basement stuff," she said.

He gently grabbed her arm and slowed his stride. Elsie

turned her head backwards to see his face as he leaned down and whispered in her ear, "Guest room? No male guests are allowed, I presume?" he asked flirtatiously as he raised his eyebrows up and down.

She laughed. "Augustus Owens! Behave!" she whispered back as she grabbed his arm and continued walking to the kitchen,

"I kind of like it when you call me by my full name, Elsie McCormick!" he confessed. They both laughed as she dragged him along.

Upon entering the kitchen, Auggie eagerly asked Olive, "Is there anything I can help you with?"

"Oh, you're finished with the tour already?" Olive asked.

"Sure are," Elsie said quickly, before Auggie had a chance to answer.

"I just thought you'd be downstairs longer," Olive added, looking confused.

Auggie looked perplexed. He knew Olive wouldn't be sending them downstairs to spend time together in the guest room.

"I'll give him the tour of the basement later tonight, when I give him his present," Elsie said, shooting Auggie a sly smile.

He was amused. "So, that's why you didn't want me going into the basement, you're hiding my gift from me."

Elsie and Olive both let out a small chuckle as Elsie said, "Something like that," then quickly changed the subject. "Shall we help you set the table before everything gets cold?" she asked Olive.

"That would be a big help. Thank you, dear," Olive answered with a smile.

The look on Olive's face told Elsie that Olive had figured out that she had been keeping her talent and aspirations from him this long, and that it was because she loved him and she wanted him to know the real Elsie before he knew her as a musician.

Ever since Elsie had decided she wanted to pursue a career as a musician, she struggled with how to tell people. Somehow saying, "I want to be a famous musician," seemed attention-seeking and very unlike her. She didn't care about being famous; she didn't care about making millions. Her desire was simple, to help better as many people's lives as she possibly could through her lyrics, her voice, and her guitar. She needed Auggie to truly understand who she was for him to understand her career choice.

The table was set, and they all came together at the dining room table. "I hope you don't mind eating a little earlier than what you're used to," Olive said to Auggie. "Us old folks like to eat earlier than all you young people," she said, smiling.

"I don't mind at all," he reassured her. "I'm grateful for a home-cooked meal and to be spending the holiday with you two lovely ladies," he said with sincerity. "And I'm thrilled to be eating something other than turkey or ham on Christmas!" he added.

Both Olive and Elsie laughed. "We started changing up holiday dinners a couple years ago," Elsie explained.

"One year we had a Mexican fiesta, and another year we had an Italian Christmas feast," Olive said, smiling. "Just something different to do," she added.

Auggie swallowed a bite of his homemade beef barbeque sandwich covered in homemade coleslaw. "This is delicious," he complimented them.

"Thank you!" Olive replied.

"No, thank you for teaching Elsie how to cook!" He grinned. "She made me some of your cookies last weekend, and I think she could be selling them, they're so good!"

Olive laughed at the compliment. "You're too sweet!"

As they ate their Christmas dinner of homemade beef barbeque and coleslaw on dinner rolls, mac and cheese, salad, and corn cake, they continued to talk and laugh.

"Tell me a little bit about yourself, Auggie. Where did you grow up?" Olive asked.

"Well, I was born in Texas, but my family moved to LA when I was a toddler. When it was time to apply for college, I knew I wanted to go to the same college my mom had gone to. She had graduated from UC's College of Nursing. When I received my acceptance letter, I packed up, left LA, caught the first flight to Cincinnati, and haven't looked back."

"Is your family still in LA?" Olive asked.

Auggie was silent for a moment as if he were carefully considering his answer. "My father still lives there. He's a plastic surgeon with his own practice. And my mom—" he paused again before continuing, "She passed away when I was eleven." And he broke eye contact with Olive and gazed down at the plate of food in front of him. He took a deep breath and continued. "I'm an only child. My grandparents have all passed, but I still keep in contact with my aunts, uncles, and cousins. Some live in Arizona, others in Florida," he said in a lighter tone.

"Oh, my, I'm so sorry to hear about your mother," Olive said sympathetically, as she reached across the table and patted Auggie's hand. "You and Elsie have a lot in common, losing your parents at such a young age."

As soon as the words escaped Olive's mouth, Elsie's and Auggie's eyes met. Neither one of them spoke, but they didn't need to; they knew how the other felt. From the moment they met, they knew there was something other than physical attraction that had drawn them together.

"And you're an ER doctor?" Olive asked, breaking the silence in the room and turning the solemn tone into something more upbeat.

"Yes, ma'am, I'm in my third year of a four-year residency program. Next year will be my last year at UC before I apply for jobs," he explained.

"Well, I just admire you for all you've accomplished at such a young age," she complimented him.

"Thank you, ma'am," he answered humbly.

"And I'm assuming your full name is Augustus, and my granddaughter gave you the nickname Auggie?" she asked.

He laughed a little. "Yes, Augustus Owens, but she thought my name was too 'formal,' " he said, and looked at Elsie.

"Too old-fashioned!" She laughed as she recalled the conversation from their first encounter.

They continued to talk throughout dinner. Olive and Auggie had hit it off, and Elsie enjoyed seeing her grandma's face light up with laughter as Auggie told stories and they both joined to poke fun at her. Elsie laughed back. She loved how well-mannered Auggie was, referring to Olive as "ma'am," listening to her when she spoke, and asking questions about her life.

After dinner, they headed to the living room. Auggie picked up a package and handed it to Olive. "I got you a little something, Olive," he said, "as a thank you for welcoming me into your home and sharing your granddaughter with me this Christmas."

"You didn't need to get me anything, Auggie," Olive said as she opened her package. "Esther Price Opera Creams, my favorite candy!" Olive said with a huge smile on her face. She was flattered that he had brought her something. "My granddaughter must have told you that these are my favorite."

Elsie was pleased; his attention to detail always surprised her. "I might have mentioned it once, Grandma, but that was all. I can't take the credit," she admitted. And she was reminded of how grateful she was to have such a thoughtful and caring boyfriend.

"Your turn," he said, as he handed Elsie a smaller, rectangular present.

She eagerly unwrapped the present, anxious to see what

he had picked out for her. When the paper was off, a small, white box with the Apple iPhone logo appeared.

"You bought me an iPhone?" she asked, beyond surprised.

"Now listen, Els, I know you don't like cell phones, but this way we can get ahold of each other whenever we need to. Not to mention, now Olive has better access to you as well," Auggie explained.

Cell phones were expensive, and Elsie hadn't spent half the money on Auggie's presents as he had spent on her. Suddenly, her presents seemed mediocre compared to his elaborate gift. Although she didn't like how society was constantly connected to their phones, she'd never had the need—or even want—to be able to text or talk to someone at the click of a button—that is, until Auggie came along. These past couple of months, with his different work shifts and her school schedule, it had been hard to find the right time to call him. She knew the cell phone was necessary for his work life, and now she'd be able to keep in better touch with him throughout the day.

"If you don't like it—"

"No," she interrupted, "it's very thoughtful, and you're right; it will be easier to get in touch with you and Olive." Elsie stood up, got onto her tiptoes, and gave Auggie a big hug.

"I believe I saw some packages under the tree with my name on them?" Auggie asked excitedly as he broke away from their embrace.

She couldn't help but smile at the excitement on his face. He was giddy, like a kid at Christmas. As she grabbed his two presents under the tree, her heart sank a little when she realized, he probably hadn't celebrated the holiday with his family in years.

She handed him the presents as they sat down on the couch next to each other. Auggie unwrapped his first present, a framed picture of the two of them skating at Fountain Square skating rink. Auggie was lying on the ice and Elsie was laughing and helping him up.

Instantly Auggie smiled and laughed. "One of my most favorite dates we've been on, thank you! Where did you get this?" he asked.

"From their website, you could scroll through and order them online," she explained.

"Did you see the picture, Olive?" he asked as he passed the frame over to Olive, who was sitting in the recliner next to the couch.

"Oh, you two look like you had a great deal of fun! I like seeing my granddaughter smile!" she said as she passed the picture back to Auggie.

Elsie smiled. Now that she saw the expression on Auggie's face, she realized it didn't matter how much her presents cost in comparison to his iPhone. Both of their presents had come from the heart, and that's all that mattered.

Next, he unwrapped a dark blue stethoscope with "Dr. Auggie" inscribed on it.

He laughed, "It's perfect, Elsie! I think I'll start going by Dr. Auggie at work!" He put his arm around her and held her close. He gently kissed her on the cheek, careful not to be too affectionate in front of Olive.

"Elsie, don't you have another present for Auggie? Downstairs, I believe." Olive said.

"As a matter of fact, I do!" she said, grinning ear to ear. She had waited months for the right opportunity to show him her studio. She had never felt this comfortable with any other guy she had dated before. She wanted Auggie to know all of her, and that meant opening up her home and studio to him.

"Follow me!" she said as she jumped off the couch and gave his arm a little tug.

"Wow, this must be a big present if you're hiding it in the basement. Is it a puppy? Because I don't want to hurt your feelings, but I really don't have time to take care of a puppy," he teased.

"It's not a puppy." She laughed. "But I think you'll love it," she said, a little nervous as she led him down the stairs and turned the corner. Then she opened the door and said proudly, "This is my studio!"

"Your studio?!" He was astonished as he walked through the doors and examined all her equipment and instruments.

"Yes, my studio. This is where I am when I'm not with you or Marie." She blushed a little as she began to open up. "This is where I record my music."

"Excuse me, record your music?" he asked, wide-eyed.

"Don't act so surprised! I mean, what kind of music major would I be if I didn't record my music?" she smiled.

"Don't act surprised?" he repeated. "Um, I knew my girlfriend was talented, but I didn't realize she was writing, playing, and recording her own music."

"Are you upset with me?" she asked, unable to read his face.

"Upset with you, no, not at all," he said, giving her a quick hug and kiss on the cheek, then said, "I just don't understand why you've waited so long to tell me," as he began to eagerly explore the room again.

"This is a very personal space to me," she explained. "My mom used to sing to me, and when she passed my dad taught me how to play guitar," she said, walking over to one of her favorite guitars and picking it up off its stand. Then she sat down on a stool and continued. "As the years passed my love for playing music turned into learning to write my own music, which then turned into wanting to record my own music. My dad wanted to make sure I had a place to do that so, here we are," she said as she began to strum her guitar.

"So, on our first date, when I asked your major . . ." he said.

"Music performance with a minor in audio production."

She smiled proudly.

"So, your goal is to be a performer?" he asked still trying to wrap his mind around how and why she'd kept all this from him for so long.

"Absolutely. After I graduate, I want to move to Nashville. It's only four hours from here, so I'll be close to Olive. Not to mention that so many famous musicians started their careers there, so I have faith I could too." She smiled.

"But, I needed you to get to know me, for you to understand that for me, performing isn't about wanting to be famous, it's about my roots. Who I am, who my parents were." She could feel her cheeks turning warm as she explained. She looked at him, and he nodded his head, encouraging her to go on.

"My reason for wanting to share my passion for music with as many people as possible is to help them, as music helped save me from, well, everything I've been through," she said, looking him in his eyes. She didn't have to say it out loud; he knew the pain she was referring to.

"Wow, Els!" He couldn't help but laugh a little as he ran his fingers across her keyboard. "Sounds to me like your studio is kind of like my ER."

"Yes, it's where I do all my best thinking, where I really come alive," she explained.

"Well, you've made me wait three months to share this with me," he said, sitting down on a stool across from her. "So please don't make me wait any longer. The suspense is killing me, play something for me!" he playfully demanded.

"I think you know this one," she said, blushing, and began to sing, "I think the universe is on my side."

He smiled, realizing the song was "Bright" by Echosmith, the song they'd danced to on their first date. As she sang and played her guitar, he was simply mesmerized by her voice. He couldn't wait for the song to end; he jumped off his stool and interrupted her singing with a passionate, wild kiss.

"You are anything but ordinary," he whispered.

With burning cheeks and a pounding heart, Elsie knew she had waited for the right time to expose her true self to him.

There they sat, in the place she loved the most, giggling and singing songs together. Any song he threw her way, she knew how to play. He was beyond impressed. After an hour, Elsie put her guitar back on its stand and picked up the copy of her Christmas CD she had made for him. "Your last gift," she said, handing it to him.

"I hope you don't get sick of hearing your own voice, because this is going to be on repeat in my car," he said, smiling as he took the CD and gave her a kiss. Then he looked her in the eyes and in a more serious tone said, "This is truly one of the best gifts I've ever been given and the best Christmas I've had since I lost my mom. Thank you." He pulled her in close.

"Mine too," she said, hugging him back.

Their embrace was interrupted by a buzzing in his back pocket. He grabbed his phone to check and make sure it wasn't anything important.

"Work?" she asked.

"Kind of," he said. "Just my friend Bob, wishing me a merry Christmas and then asking a work question," he said as he texted back. "Sorry about that," he apologized, putting his phone back into his pocket.

"No worries," she said. "We should probably head back upstairs to Olive anyway."

The two spent the rest of the evening cuddled on the couch listening to Elsie's CD and eating Christmas cookies. The more Elsie's CD played, the more she accepted the fact that Auggie now knew her—all of her—and from what she could tell, not only did he accept her hobby but enjoyed it as well. As Olive and Auggie talked, Elsie sipped her hot chocolate and fell into a trance as she watched the Christmas snow continue to fall. This Christmas had been one of the best Christmases she'd had in a long time. She felt blessed to have spent the evening with not only her grandma, whom she loved dearly, but also with the man who was quickly stealing her heart. Suddenly she felt a little guilty for considering this one of her best Christmases when her parents weren't there for them to enjoy it together. She shook her head; she was not going to let her guilty thoughts ruin this perfect evening. She knew that if her parents were here, they would like Auggie just as much as Olive liked him, and they would be happy to see their daughter happy. That thought made her smile. Her eyes started to tear up, breaking her concentration, as she brought her attention back to the living room and Auggie's and Olive's laughter at something one of them had just said. She knew this was exactly the kind of holiday her parents would want her to have, and she wished for many more Christmases just like this one.

Six days later, Elsie and Auggie brought in the new year at his apartment. As they watched the ball drop on TV, she could hardly contain her excitement. This was the first time she'd have a kiss at midnight from a man she loved. As the crowd began the countdown, they eagerly joined in, and when the clock struck midnight and the room filled with the roar of the crowd, Auggie and Elsie were already kissing. Oblivious to the celebration happening on TV, the two were lost completely in each other. Kissing and touching, they stayed in their own private bubble for quite a while before Auggie gently pulled away. His face was inches from Elsie's as he gently ran his fingers through her long, brown hair, then to the side of her neck, gently rubbing her jagged scar. She opened her eyes to see him staring intensely at her. No words were exchanged as they gazed deeply into each other's eyes and took this moment to catch their breath.

Auggie focused on her deep brown eyes and nothing else. In moments like this one, he felt as if he could see directly into her soul. He knew they shared something he never thought was possible with another person. He didn't know if it was perhaps a mutual understanding of a painful past, but whatever it was, it had been there since day one, drawing him to her. The need, the want, the desire to get to know her had always been there with no explanation. For a man whose life and beliefs were based on scientific explanation, this unexplainable pull towards her puzzled him. In the ER, he had complete control. He liked being in control. With Elsie, he had never been in control. From his first glance in her direction, it was evident that it was her gravitational pull that was in control, and that was unnerving.

He gently brushed his lips against hers and then pulled back just enough so that they could still look each other in the eye. As he slowly caressed her cheek and gently rubbed the small of her back, he whispered the words she had never thought she'd hear a man say to her: "I love you."

Elsie stopped breathing momentarily to process what he had just said and to find the courage to say it back. She had known for a while now that she was falling in love with Auggie, but had been wondering if he had been feeling the same. She wasn't smart like he was, or as good-looking, or as accomplished. In her eyes, he was flawless and she was socially awkward. She was both grateful and confused as to why someone seemingly so perfect would love someone so imperfect. Somehow, she found the courage to speak and claim this monumental moment in her life before it passed.

She breathlessly whispered back, "I love you," confirming her feelings for him. She'd never been so happy and yet so terrified to confess her love for another person. Every time things went well in her life, something terrible happened.

He smiled and then pulled her face back in towards his and

kissed her again. They brought in the new year as a couple in love and spent the rest of the night entangled in each other's bodies.

PRESENT DAY

Chapter 11

Auggie nervously paced as he watched the surgeons operate on Elsie from the observation window. He ran his fingers through his hair and rubbed his bloodshot eyes. It had been six long, stressful hours since they had started working on her. He hadn't slept, eaten, or even taken a bathroom break. He needed to watch their every move to make sure they did everything in their power to keep her alive. As the surgeons continued to work, he thought back to a conversation he'd had with Elsie.

They had been dating for nearly seven months. Once the sun came up, they would be forced to give their time to school and to his residency. But the night was theirs. No matter how tired they were, they refused to give in to sleep. They knew that as soon as they closed their eyes, a new day would come, and it would be hours or days before they would see each other again. They would talk for hours until the sun came up.

"What are you most proud of so far?" she had asked him.

"Besides landing you as my girlfriend?" he teased as he smoothed her hair away from her face.

"Yeah, I know, I'm pretty fantastic," she laughed, teasing him right back.

Her laugh—he could hear it now . . . she had the best laugh. Her laugh had always reminded him of a child's—so innocent, sweet, and full of pure happiness.

"No really, it's your turn to ask me a serious question." She gently rubbed his chest.

"Alright, alright, I'll play by your rules." He paused before asking, "What's your greatest fear?"

She went silent for a long time and stopped caressing his chest.

"Not being remembered." The playfulness had left her voice.

"What do you mean?" he asked as he pulled back slightly so he could look into her eyes.

"I'm sure you can relate," she said. "When you lose someone who was everything to you, after the funeral is over you realize everyone goes home to their families and their lives except for you. You go home to an empty house. Everyone else continues with their lives, but your life stops. Nothing matters anymore." She paused as she remembered her parents' funerals and then continued. "Eventually life catches up to you and forces you to live again, but you're never the same." She glanced at him, and he nodded. He could relate to what she was saying. "And for people like me, who have only one relative left, it's overwhelming to think that my family dies when I do. Once you're gone, people may think about you every now and then, but eventually your family will die, and your name, your life, will be forgotten. The only family I have now is Olive." She broke their embrace and rolled onto her back looking up at the ceiling. "So, I guess my biggest fear is not being remembered by anyone." He put his arm around her and squeezed her tightly. She continued, letting years of built-up thoughts that she had never shared with anyone pour out. "Some may grieve my death or cry over my grave, but the rest of the world won't even know my name. They won't know the life I lived or what defined me as a person. I'll be just another name in an obituary. My opinions, my advice, my voice, my songs won't be remembered by anyone." She stopped talking, and he could tell tears were forming in her eyes.

"That's not true, I'll remember you," he said as he wiped away a tear that had trickled down her cheek. "And I know I'm not the only one who will know and remember your name, Miss Elsie McCormick," he said as he gently kissed the top of her forehead. "Trust me, your talent will leave its mark on this world."

She gave a sad smile. "I sure hope so," she said as she snuggled up closer to him.

They remained silent for several moments in each other's arms. Then, trying to lighten the mood, she added in a dramatic tone, "But if I try, only to fail miserably, will you disown me?"

He couldn't help but chuckle at her theatrics. "I'm not answering that question, drama queen."

She laughed with him, then continued in a more serious tone, "For real though, if I try and don't make it, at least I'll still have you."

"Always," he softly whispered. "I won't ever lose or forget you. I love you, babe."

He had rolled on top of her and started to kiss her slowly and sweetly. Before long they were making love and the sun was starting to rise.

SIX YEARS AGO

Chapter 12

Winter came to an end, and spring arrived. Cincinnati was taken over by the smell of beautiful flowers, and an array of colors filled every yard, every garden, every park. Cincinnati was absolutely beautiful in the spring. In between class and work, Elsie and Auggie found time to enjoy the weather by riding bikes together, walking the streets of downtown that overlooked the Ohio River, visiting the downtown farmers' markets, spending time at the zoo and parks, and grilling out. Before they knew it, Elsie had finished her junior year of college and Auggie, his third year of residency.

It was one week until the Fourth of July. The rest of America knew this day as Independence Day, but it was also Elsie's birthday. This year she was turning twenty-two. Elsie had never cared too much for celebrating her birthday since it reminded her of how much she missed her parents. When she was growing up, her parents always made sure her birthday was not overshadowed by Independence Day. Nowadays, her birthdays were usually spent with Marie and Olive. This year, however, she had someone else to celebrate with—her first real boyfriend.

Three days before her birthday, Elsie and Auggie were

eating a late dinner at his apartment. They were eating grilled barbeque chicken and corn on the cob on his back patio. He had been two hours late getting off work that evening, which was nothing out of the ordinary for him. Elsie had grown used to Auggie not being home on time, and on some days like today, she didn't mind. Today she took a break from preparing for her senior year by researching potential job opportunities in Nashville and recording demos, and spent the entire day at the pool with Marie. Elsie liked the sun, but the sun didn't like her. She was one of those fair-skinned girls who only burned instead of tanned. So, while Marie sunbathed, Elsie covered up with her wrap and wore a big, floppy pool hat to shade her face.

"You seem distracted." Auggie interrupted her thoughts at dinner.

"No, I'm just tired from having been in the sun all day," she apologized as she rubbed her chlorine-burned eyes. Even with goggles on, she somehow had managed to get water in her eyes.

"I'm surprised that my vampire girlfriend lasted all day in the sun!" he said teasingly. She smiled, too tired to laugh. "It's good practice though," he added nonchalantly.

"Practice? For what?" she quizzed him, trying to wake herself from her sun-induced grogginess.

"For when we travel," he said, "to places that are sunnier than Cincinnati—so you won't burn and die on me!" He winked at her as he took a bite of his chicken and corn.

She laughed and continued to play along. "Well, I guess as long as I stay north of the equator, my vampire skin could handle it. I'm free all summer, so whenever is good for you!" she playfully offered, and then took a sip of her ice water.

"Fantastic! How does this weekend sound?" His bright blue eyes sparkled with anticipation.

"Works for me!" she said as she took another bite of her

chicken. She was having fun with the playful banter.

"So, it's settled. I'll call work, tell them I'm sick with some horrible disease, and we'll catch a flight to Hawaii!" He schemed aloud between bites of food.

"Sounds good to me! But Hawaii is a long way, so you might need a week off, and you do work with doctors, so whatever disease you come up with has to be believable and last at least a week," she reasoned.

"Now you're thinking! How about something like malaria?" he asked very solemnly, with a grave, terrified look on his face as he said the word malaria.

She laughed at his expression. She didn't know much about medicine, but she did know that malaria was awful to get, and she was pretty sure you could get it from mosquito bites. "You're awful, Auggie!"

"I have a better idea!" he said as he wiped his mouth with his napkin.

"Oh really, better than faking being sick with malaria?" she continued, playing along.

"How about I work Thanksgiving instead of Fourth of July and take my girlfriend to Hawaii for her birthday?" Auggie's blue eyes were wide with excitement as he told Elsie his plan. At first, she thought he was joking and simply said, "Sounds good to me!" Then she looked into his eyes and realized he was serious. "Wait, are you being serious right now?" She stopped eating, put down her fork, and concentrated on his eyes.

"As serious as a heart attack!" he said as he reached under his plate and retrieved a long white envelope. Smiling, he handed it to her and said, "Happy birthday!"

What had he just said?! she thought as with shaking hands she opened the envelope and saw two plane tickets—one for Elsie McCormick and one for Augustus Owens. A third piece of paper had the words "Travel Itinerary" at the top of the page.

He leaned in closer to her and spoke quickly. "We leave Thursday night at nine! Our first flight is to California, and our second flight is to Maui. How does waking up in Hawaii for your birthday sound?" He was grinning ear to ear. She'd never seen him so excited.

She was still in shock and unable to speak. She stared at the plane tickets and then at Auggie, whose face was lit up like a Christmas tree, and then back to the tickets.

"Well . . . ?" he prompted as he nudged her shoulder as if to shake her out of her stupor. "Do you like your birthday present?" he asked, keenly aware that she had said nothing.

Her mind was racing. She had never been to Hawaii but had always heard it was a magical, tropical paradise, and she longed to go. Never in her wildest dreams had she imagined that a man she loved would surprise her for her birthday with a trip to Hawaii. She knew it had to have taken a great deal of planning on his part to switch holidays and get off work for a trip like this. Furthermore, it had to have cost him a decent chunk of money as well—money she didn't have but wanted to repay him. She was feeling guilty that he had spent so much money on her. She wasn't poor. She had money that she had inherited from her parents after they passed; however, she and Olive had managed it in such a way that Elsie wouldn't have to work while going to college and could concentrate solely on getting an education. She had a monthly allowance, but a trip to Hawaii was not in the budget.

"Els!" He gently prodded for a second time.

"Auggie," her voice cracked, "this is an amazing trip, and I am in shock that you went to this extent planning for my birthday!" She knew she was only seconds away from crying. "But . . ." she began.

"No!" he interrupted. "There are no buts, Els," he insisted. "I know you're thinking about the money, but don't!" he instructed her.

She looked at him, flattered that he understood her so well but at the same time curious as to how he knew that was her concern.

"When I asked Olive about this trip—" he began.

"You asked Olive?!" she interrupted. The fact that he had asked Olive made her love him even more.

"Of course! I needed to make sure it was okay if I stole you on your birthday." He smiled as he tucked a strand of her long, wavy hair behind her ear and continued. "She said she was more than excited for the two of us but knew you'd try to turn down the offer because of the cost. I've been saving to travel for years now, but before you came along, I had no one I wanted to travel with. So, think of this as not only a gift to you but a gift to the both of us!" He smiled. "Besides," he added, "the trip is nonrefundable, so if you don't come with me, think of it as throwing away my hard-earned money!"

She placed the envelope back down on the table and jumped out of her chair and into Auggie's lap. She wrapped her arms around his neck and gave him a big kiss.

"Thank you!" she said. "I can't believe we're going to Hawaii!" she screeched in excitement.

He gave her a big, sloppy kiss and then threw his head back and yelled into the hot, humid summer sky, "We're going to Hawaii!" Elsie joined him, the two yelling like little kids wild with excitement.

The moment the pair arrived on the island of Maui, Elsie was filled with awe. No matter which way she turned, there were bright, beautiful colors and tropical flowers. The ride from the airport to the hotel was short. Upon arriving, they were greeted with a friendly "Aloha!" from a beautiful hotel worker with long black hair. The girl placed leis around their necks, offered them some fresh guava juice, and directed them to check-in.

As Auggie checked them in, she walked around the hotel entrance. It was amazing. Just inside the main door was a huge koi pond filled with orange, red, and white fish. There were flowers everywhere, and the smell alone was heavenly. In some of the larger floral displays were giant cages filled with brilliantly colored exotic birds. Elsie walked down the main flight of stairs to get a better look.

As she descended the huge, white marble staircase to the lower level, she was surprised to discover the hotel had no side walls! At first, she found it odd, but then a warm breeze wafted alongside her. She inhaled deeply the scent of saltwater and tropical flowers and realized exactly why the hotel was so open.

By now Auggie had finished checking in and was standing next to her. "Well, what do you think?" he asked as she sniffed the warm, fragrant air.

"This place is amazing!" she shrieked.

"I know! I can't wait to see our room," Auggie added with sparkling eyes and raised eyebrows.

Auggie led her to their room, slid the key card in, and unlocked the door. When the door was opened, Elsie stood speechless. The room was spacious, with an enormous plush all-white bed in the center of the room facing two floor-to-ceiling glass doors. The curtains were drawn back, and even though it was close to sunset, she could see that all she had to do was open these doors and walk about a hundred steps to the beach.

She turned around and jumped into his arms. He wasn't expecting her to jump on him, so he stumbled a little as he laughed and fell back onto the plush white bed with Elsie on top of him.

"This place is paradise!" she said, smiling as she kissed his lips. "Thank you, thank you, thank you! A million times thank you!" Her face hurt from smiling so hard.

"I'm glad you like it." He smiled an approving smile as he swept Elsie off her feet and carried her to the door. "Come on, let's check out the beach before sunset."

They jogged to the beach, as if they couldn't get there fast enough. Once they reached the sand, they kicked off their flip-flops and ran to the ocean. Wading in only ankle-deep, Elsie screeched a little. She had expected the ocean to be much warmer, but with it being close to sunset, the water was quite cool.

They playfully splashed, kicking up their feet and spraying cool ocean water on each other. Although they were still in their clothes and not their swimsuits, neither of them seemed to mind. They continued with this playfulness until Auggie pointed to the sky. The sun was starting to set.

They worked their way back up to the dry sand and found a good place to sit and watch nature show off. Elsie sat between Auggie's legs and rested the back of her head on his chest as the sun disappeared and the sky turned dark blue. He held her close and kissed the top of her head. She sighed and thought about how perfect this moment was. This place, this moment was magical. She closed her eyes and wished for a thousand more moments just like this one.

The next morning, Elsie woke to the golden sun beaming through those big glass doors. It took her a minute to remember where she was as she rubbed her eyes and looked out to see a Hawaiian paradise. Instantly a grin spread across her face. Auggie was already awake. He leaned over and gave her a big kiss.

"Happy birthday!" he said, smiling.

"Thank you!" She smiled back.

"I got you a little something," he said as he sprang out of bed and headed to the closet.

"No, you didn't," she said. "This trip was expensive enough," she lectured as she sat up.

Auggie grabbed something out of the closet, then turned around holding a dark koa wood ukulele. He started to sing happy birthday to her as he attempted to play the ukulele. Elsie couldn't help but laugh at his failed attempt to play one of her favorite instruments and sing.

When his song was over, she applauded his efforts, chuckling.

"My plan worked," he grinned, "You can't be upset with me when I'm making you laugh," he teased as he handed her the gift.

"You're right, I can't." She smiled as she took the ukulele from him. "It's absolutely beautiful," she said admiringly. "Thank you so much!" she said as she leaned in for a hug and a kiss. "I could play this all day," she said.

"I'm glad you like it, but first, let's get the birthday girl some breakfast," he said.

The resort's restaurant overlooked the beach. Elsie feasted on eggs, fresh pineapple, mango, and guava juice while Auggie went the Hawaiian route and had Portuguese sausage and rice. Hardly a word was spoken as the couple enjoyed their meal and were mesmerized by the soothing sounds of waves sloshing onto the beach and birds chirping as they flew through the fresh, salty air.

After breakfast, they walked the beach, holding hands and laughing. Elsie was delighted to spot several sea turtles basking on the beach. Careful not to get too close, they used their cell phones to snap pictures of these magnificent creatures. Back at their hotel room, they decided they'd put on their swimsuits and spend the day relaxing on the beach and at the pool.

The Hawaiian sun was so warm and relaxing compared to the Cincinnati sun. Summer in Cincinnati was hot, but along with the heat came the humidity. Some days were too humid and muggy to relax by a pool. The pool water would feel like lukewarm bathwater, and the air would be too thick to breathe. Here, even during midday when the sun was at its hottest, there was always a soothing ocean breeze to keep you cool. Whenever Elsie started to feel too warm, they'd soak in the ocean water for a while and then go back to their beach chairs.

Since they were on the beach and it was Elsie's birthday, they decided to celebrate in typical vacation fashion—by sipping fresh fruity mixed drinks from the beach bar and snacking on delicious appetizers. Elsie had never been that big on drinking and had never drank for an entire day; however, there was something about being on a beach with an ice-cold beverage and no responsibility that just made it seem like the thing to do. These drinks weren't like any sugary cocktail Elsie had ever tasted before. They were full of fresh fruit with a splash of alcohol—just the right combination of tasty, smooth, and refreshing. For Elsie, they went down easy—a little too easy—and Auggie laughed as he advised her to slow her drinking and bought her a bottle of water in between each cocktail.

On the beach, in their lounge chairs, drinking, talking, laughing, listening to music, and Elsie strumming along to the music with her brand-new ukulele . . . this was how they'd planned on spending their afternoon. Auggie had created an entire beach tunes playlist on his phone. Being the music lover that she was, Elsie was surprised she hadn't heard of some of the bands Auggie was playing.

"What band is this?" she asked when a particular tune caught her attention.

"HAPA," Auggie answered as he sipped his drink.

"I like them," she said, smiling as she strummed along, matching the song chord for chord. She began to sing along when the chorus kicked in. When it ended, she hit repeat, this time singing and playing a little louder.

He sipped his drink and admired his beautiful girlfriend, in her red and white polka-dot bikini and floppy white hat, playing her ukulele and singing along with HAPA. Happier than ever and without a care in the world, she sounded amazing. He didn't say anything. He just watched and looked around. Slowly more and more people sitting along the beach began to notice Elsie.

When the song ended a few people applauded her performance. She smiled and teasingly said, "Thank you, I'm Elsie McCormick and I'm here all day if you have any requests."

Almost as if on cue, the beach bar server arrived with a tray of two fruity drinks.

"I must say, miss." He spoke with a slight accent. "You can sing!" He smiled.

"Why thank you, kind sir." She smiled back.

"As luck would have it, our entertainment for the day canceled. What would you say about coming and having these drinks," he said, motioning to his tray, "at the bar? If you play some songs for the other guests, in return we will let you, and your gentleman friend, drink for free," he proposed.

She looked to Auggie, who gave her a smile and a nod of approval.

"That sounds like a perfect birthday present," she said, grinning in excitement.

"Wow, happy birthday! If you please the crowd, I'll see what I can do about a free lunch, too," he said, laughing.

As Auggie gathered their belongings, Elsie pulled her hair back into a messy bun and put on her dress over her suit. At the bar, Elsie took her place on a stool by a microphone on a stand and Auggie sat at the table beside her.

"Happy Fourth of July, everyone!" she said into the microphone. "I'm Elsie McCormick, here all the way from Cincinnati, Ohio. Any other mainlanders here?" she asked.

The crowd all began shouting back: *Texas! Cali! Nevada! Florida!*

"Nice! Hope you all are enjoying your time in paradise! I'll be taking requests soon, but first, let's kick this party off, island-style," she said, then began to play "Over the Rainbow" by Israel Kamakawiwoʻole.

As she sang and played, Auggie watched in admiration. After he discovered her talent on Christmas, she shared it with him daily. Whether it was singing along in the car with him, or working on compositions on the weekends in her studio, or even on her bedroom floor, every time he heard her sing, he knew she was destined for success. Her love for music was pure, and her voice was simply flawless. As he watched the crowd react to Elsie, he knew they were just as impressed as he was. It was only a matter of time until someone in the music industry discovered her.

As the crowd erupted in applause, she graciously thanked them, then took her first request of Bob Marley's "Three Little Birds." Several couples gathered around the stage area and began to dance. Auggie couldn't let this moment go without documenting it. He began to record Elsie's performance and texted the videos to Marie, who immediately Facetimed to see her best friend's impromptu jam session.

It didn't take long for more guests, who were passing by, to stop and see what all the commotion was at the bar and for guests lounging on the beach to join in on the fun. Before Elsie realized it, the bar was completely packed. The hours passed with Elsie taking requests while some sang along and others danced. As she watched the crowd, including Auggie, enjoy themselves, drinking, dancing, and singing along with her, she couldn't help but think, *this is the best birthday I've had since my parents were alive!*

To Elsie's dismay, the afternoon passed much too quickly and her jam session came to an end. The crowd cheered for her as she left the stage and Auggie gave her a big sloppy wet kiss on the cheek. He couldn't stop complimenting her on how well she had done as they laughed their way back to their room.

An hour later, they were both showered and ready for her big surprise birthday night out. Auggie was wearing khaki linen shorts with a Hawaiian print shirt and brown flip-flops, and Elsie was in a white sundress with a bright orange, red, and yellow floral print. She wore her long brown hair down and just let her natural curl rule. Her skin was rosy from having sunbathed that day, and to Auggie, she'd never looked more beautiful.

He gently kissed her on the cheek as he led her out the door and along a path to the other side of the hotel grounds for their dinner destination. As they walked the tiki torch-lit path, Elsie could hear music and people chanting in the distance. They turned a corner, and Elsie's eyes opened wide with excitement. Hundreds of white tables and chairs lined the open green hotel ground, with a stage set up in the middle.

She gasped as she took in the scene—at least fifty beautiful Hawaiian men and women dancing, twirling fire sticks, and talking to guests while music played in the background. The men were shirtless, wearing only small flaps of fabric to cover their fronts and backs. The women, all with long, beautiful black hair, wore grass skirts and colorful flower-print tops. The chairs were filled with hotel guests, and the luau circle was lined with tiki torches. Auggie and Elsie approached the entrance, where a man and woman in native Hawaiian dress greeted them.

"Aloha!" the beautiful woman said as she placed a lei around Auggie's neck.

"Aloha!" the man said as he placed a flower lei around

Elsie's neck.

Another woman then handed them each a cold mai tai and a seat number. Auggie grinned at Elsie. "Do you like your birthday surprise?" he leaned over and asked.

"Do I ever!" She got on her tiptoes and gave him a big, wet kiss, and then laughed.

The two worked their way through the crowd and found their seats. They sipped their mai tais and talked for several minutes until an announcer got up on the stage and advised everyone to find their seats. After everyone was seated, he described the dining menu. A variety of fresh seafood was being set up to the right, a variety of chicken and beef to the left, and along the back were the dessert tables. After he finished explaining the food options, he left the stage. Each table was instructed individually to get up and fill their plates as the many men and women danced on stage.

They were so fixated on the show, they almost missed their chance to get food when the woman came and told their table it was their turn. All the food looked and smelled so delicious. Once the aromas awakened Elsie's senses, she realized just how hungry she really was. All she had done all day was drink. Fresh fruits, bread, salads, meats, seafood, pastries of every sort—there was too much to choose from, and they wanted to try it all! They decided to fill their plates with different foods so they could share and try as much as they could.

They returned to their seats, continuing to watch the show as they ate. A beautiful waiter kept bringing cold mai tais and mixed cocktails to their table. Before tonight, Elsie had never tried a mai tai, and just like the freshly mixed drinks from earlier in the day, they went down quite smoothly.

Elsie was mesmerized by how quickly the women per-forming could move their hips and how strong the men were as they swung around fire sticks and chanted loud tribal chants. The hours passed quickly, and the show was like nothing she'd ever seen.

The happy couple was sad to see the luau end; however, the mai tais and long hours of soaking in the sun were catching up to them, and they both were feeling tired. As they walked the long path back to their room, they laughed over their day. Auggie even found a stick on the ground and began twirling it like one of the luau performers. He kept dropping the stick, making Elsie laugh hysterically. The night was dark. Just as they were arriving back at their lanai, they heard a loud pop in the distance and turned to see the black night sky light up with brilliant red fireworks.

Auggie grabbed Elsie's hand, and they quickly jogged towards the beach as more fireworks continued to light up the sky. They sat down on the cool sand. He held her close as they watched the fireworks explode and the sky dance with red, white, and blue sparkles. Elsie had never seen fireworks over water before. The way they reflected off the dark ocean was spectacular.

Giving her a soft kiss on the forehead, he pulled her in closer and whispered, "I love you." Elsie turned her head as far as she could to look him in the eye and whispered, "I love you," and then gently kissed him on the lips. They fell backwards onto the cool, damp sand, and although the sky was dancing with vibrant colors, all Elsie saw was the deep blue of Auggie's eyes as they kissed.

After the fireworks ended, Auggie and Elsie lay on the beach watching smoke clear from the sky. Within minutes most of the smoky haze had cleared, revealing what appeared to be a million sparkling diamonds in the night sky. The stars were seen so much more clearly here on the island than back on the mainland. Auggie smiled as his thoughts took him back to his childhood and to memories of his mother.

"I told you before that my mom had a thing for astronomy," he began in a solemn tone. Until this evening, he had never felt the urge to talk to another person about his mom.

She didn't say anything, but instead nestled her head a little on his chest and began to gently rub his hand. Auggie closed his eyes, pulled Elsie in a little closer, and listened to the waves quietly crash onto the shore. The beach at this resort was so long and so spacious that it felt like they were on their own private beach.

"My mother would have loved seeing the stars tonight," he found himself openly confiding in Elsie. "We had a telescope that we kept in the garage. Almost every night we'd open the garage door, take that telescope out to the driveway, and see what we could see." He chuckled a little. "LA's air wasn't as clean as Hawaii's. We certainly could never see the stars as clearly as we do now."

"Your mom sounds like she was a good mom," she whispered just loud enough to be heard over the ocean waves. "I would have liked to meet her."

"She was," he reflected. "And she would have loved you." He let out a loud sigh. "It's all my fault, you know."

His voice sounded weak and distant.

She tried to understand what she had just heard. He rarely mentioned his mother, and he never spoke of his father. She propped herself up on her side, placing one elbow in the sand and resting her head on her hand so she could see his face. "What's your fault?"

He rubbed the corner of his eyes then massaged his forehead. Every time he thought back on that dreadful day, he found himself with an instant sinus headache. He knew it wasn't just the rum from the mai tai that was making him feel like he could trust Elsie with his hideous past. He'd waited a long time for someone like Elsie to come along—someone who would understand the pain of losing a loved one and who wouldn't judge him for the mistakes he'd made.

"Her death . . ." He let out a long, drawn-out sigh. "It was all my fault," he said in a shaky voice.

Even in the dim moonlight, she could see the pain on his face and hear the heartache in his voice. Her heart ached for him. Although the cool ocean breeze wasn't blowing at the time, she shivered as she remembered the countless nights she had cried herself to sleep asking God to forgive her. For years she blamed herself for being a bratty kid while her mom was suffering. It wasn't until she was a teenager and watched her dad suffer and die that she truly understood how difficult it was to handle at any age. Before he passed, Lee reassured her that she hadn't been a difficult child, but a typical child who was scared and confused and dealing with too much too soon. Her mom knew that, and she loved Elsie dearly. She knew that his mom had passed away when he was a child; it couldn't possibly have been his fault.

"You were young," she paused, trying to find the right words to encourage him. "I'm sure it wasn't your fault," she said confidently.

"It was," he snapped as he sat upright and brought his knees in towards his chest.

"I was old enough to know what I was doing, and I could have saved her," he said as he wrapped his arms around his drawn-up legs and stared blankly into the distant ocean.

"Tell me," she urged him as she moved in beside him and gently stroked his back.

"I was eleven, and summer was coming to an end. My dad had a conference in Michigan, and my mom and I had decided to tag along—one last getaway before I started back to school." He rubbed his forehead, willing the pressure in his head to go away.

She sat quietly beside him, rubbing his back and listening to his story.

"We stayed in a cottage in the woods about thirty minutes

from the hospital where my dad was presenting. There was another family in the cottage next to us with a son, Mike, who was around my age. One day we decided to explore the woods, but my mom told me I needed to be home by dark." He removed his hand from his forehead and glanced back up at the stars. He could feel her looking at him but didn't have the courage to look at her. He continued, "I was having a blast. Growing up in LA, I never had the opportunity to come home dirty from wading in the creek and playing in the woods. We lost track of time, and before I knew it, it was almost dark, and we were lost and trying to find our way back." He stopped talking for a minute. It had been years since he had thought about that dreadful day. Having to say out loud what happened next terrified him.

"You can tell me," she whispered as she placed her head on his shoulder. "You can tell me anything, and I wouldn't think any less of you."

He could feel his body tingle. He closed his eyes and continued. "While we were trying to find our way back, I heard her screaming . . ." He paused. ". . . crying out in pain." He paused longer this time, unsure of how to describe in words the horrid event that followed.

"My mom had come looking for me. We're not sure what happened—if she knocked into a beehive, or accidentally stepped on it, but she was stung hundreds of times. By the time I made it to her," he shook his head in disgust, "her face was swollen. She was gasping for air. My mom, she was allergic to many things, and I searched her pockets for an EpiPen." He buried his head into his knees and stared at the sand, willing the tears not to come. "But I couldn't find one."

Elsie didn't know what to say as she pictured a younger version of Auggie seeing his mother the way she must have looked. She thought back on her own experience with her parents' passing. She never liked it when people would tell her how sorry they were for her. It just felt as if it was something people were programmed to say.

"That must have been awful for you to see your mom that way," she said sincerely as she gently wrapped her arm around his lower back, focused on the moonlight shining off the ocean waves, and willed herself to be strong for him and not cry.

After a while, he finally spoke again. "There's more." He paused and took a deep breath before continuing. "I sent Mike to get help, and I—" He paused and took another breath of fresh ocean air, and reminded himself that he was here on the beach and not an eleven-year-old in the woods fighting for his mom's life. "I stayed and did CPR on my mom until help finally arrived."

Elsie's head lowered in pain. To be so young, to feel so helpless and responsible for your mom's death and yet to be so brave in trying to save her . . . she now understood why he never spoke of his mother's death.

"You tried your hardest," she attempted to reassure him.

"I didn't try hard enough," he said in a frustrated voice, wiping tears from his face.

"You're a doctor," she said matter-of-factly. "You must know by now that your mom needed more than CPR to survive."

"Yes, I know that. But I was old enough to know I was out too late and should have returned on time. If I had, she wouldn't have had to come looking for me, and she would be alive today." He picked up a small rock in the sand and threw it towards the ocean.

She realized that like herself, Auggie had been holding onto guilt for years with no one to talk to who understood. "I was awful to my parents before my mom died and mean to my dad after she passed," she confessed. "Kids make mistakes. You can't know what would've happened if your mom had lived. I tortured myself for years thinking that way. You can't do that to yourself. You just can't. It'll drive you crazy."

"It did drive me crazy," he blurted out as he ran both his hands through his hair. "After my mom passed, my dad grew distant and pushed me away." He looked out over the ocean and thought of those dark times. "He never said out loud that he blamed me, but he didn't have to. I could feel it in his glare, I could hear it in his voice. After the funeral, he started leaving pre-med books on my desk and hardly spoke to me about anything other than medicine. He even went so far as to sign me up for CPR classes. My childhood ended at the age of eleven when I was instructed to spend all my free time preparing for medical school and life as a doctor. I was miserable and lonely."

"Wow, Auggie," she said before she could even fully comprehend everything he had just said. Her heart sank as she pictured a little boy with bright blue eyes spending all his time alone, reading to himself in his room. "That's so unfair. I didn't know," was all she could bear to say as she shook her head in anger. She was instantly grateful that hers had always been such a kind, fun, loving father. Her dad had always encouraged her to follow her dreams and just be herself. He often spoke of her mom so as to never let her memory fade away.

"He didn't stop there." Auggie could feel the anger growing inside him as he thought about his father and the way he neglected him in the years that followed. "He'd force me to go to all his conferences and take notes on his lectures. In his free time, instead of spending time with his son as most parents do, he would bring home random women he had met at work. I stopped learning their names. Stopped even coming out of my room to meet them by the time I was thirteen. What kind of person does that after his wife dies, Els?!"

She could see the tears welling up in his eyes. She wanted to say something to comfort him, but she couldn't find the words. The way his father had treated him was selfish and cruel. She couldn't imagine a parent taking all their hurt, anger, and frustration out on their child the way his father had done. Tears of anger filled her eyes. She pulled Auggie in close. He put his arm around her, and she rested her head on his shoulder.

"Anyway, I tried to rebel and choose a different career, but when it came down to it, medicine is in my blood. It's all I've ever known." He shook his head in disgust and added, "It just figures, doesn't it? When UC College of Medicine made me an offer, I accepted and moved to Cincinnati the first chance I got. I haven't spoken to my dad or been back to LA since." He let out a huge sigh of relief as if a heavy weight had just been lifted. His arms were shaking as he pulled Elsie in tighter and kissed her on the forehead.

She felt the hand that was resting on her back shaking and knew how relieved he must be that he had told her everything she needed to know about his past. She had never felt closer to him than she did at this moment. He had laid out his life story and was now sitting emotionally naked and vulnerable at her side. She willed herself to look for the appropriate comforting words. Elsie always struggled when it came to saying the right thing at the right time. She had always been better at writing her thoughts down after she had time to process everything and was left alone with her thoughts. She knew he had said all he wanted to say about his father, and although she was furious with what he had done to Auggie, she knew this conversation had been brought on by his memories of his mom. She didn't want to dwell on his loss but rather bring back into perspective the love he had for her.

"I think your mom led you to me," she whispered. "If she hadn't gone to UC, you wouldn't have wanted to come here. Think about it. You could have gone anywhere—Harvard, Duke—but you chose UC because of her. If you hadn't, we wouldn't have met."

"I think you're right," he said as he pulled Elsie back onto the sand and gazed up at the moon. "Without the sun, there would be no new beginnings; without the moon, there would be no new dreams."

"I like that," she said as she put her arm around his chest. "What's that from?" she asked.

"Something my mom used to say," he said.

"She was a wise woman," she noted.

"Yes. Yes, she was," he agreed.

No matter how hard she tried, she couldn't shake the mental images of a young Auggie finding his mother fighting for her life. Or of a young, lonely Auggie being shut off from his friends by his father and forced to study so he could learn to perfect all that his father felt he had done wrong. That thought made her cringe. She shoved those thoughts aside and tried to focus on the positive. He had opened up to her in a way he had never done before. She was both grateful and terrified at this—grateful because he had entrusted her with the truth surrounding the most painful event he had ever endured; terrified because she'd never felt as close to anyone as she now felt to Auggie. She was afraid that someday she might lose this handsome, smart, sweet, good man whom she loved dearly, and she knew that she'd never love anyone else the way she loved him.

She lifted her head from his chest and looked him in the eye. His eyes appeared distant, filled with pain and sorrow. For a very long time, the two simply sat in silence and held each other as they listened to the waves crash onto the shore. After a long while, she started to shiver. Auggie stood up, pulled Elsie up, and without speaking a word, the two headed back to the hotel.

Once in their room, they lay quietly in bed. Elsie very gently kissed Auggie, as if she was trying to heal his wounds from the past. Slowly his eyes began to focus on her. The pain and sorrow that had filled his eyes disappeared. Now she saw only love and desire in his eyes. That night they made love more passionately than ever before. Neither could get enough of the other, and by the time they were too tired to move or to fight sleep any longer, the sun was beginning to rise. They fell asleep naked in each other's arms, tangled in the plush white sheets as day broke outside.

The rest of the week was spent relaxing by the pool, lounging on the beach, playing in the ocean and indulging in all the delicious food and fresh fruit drinks. Most mornings they'd wake up early to walk on the beach and watch the sun rise, and every evening they would hold each other close and watch the glorious Hawaiian sunset over the vast blue ocean.

With the island band, Ka'au Crater Boys, blaring from the radio and the fresh sea salt air blowing through her hair as they navigated the long, winding roads towards the airport, Elsie was overcome by the natural beauty of the island. On this, their last day in Hawaii, they decided to take a brief detour in order to hike to the top of an overlook. The view was absolutely stunning. If they hadn't had a flight to catch, they could have stayed there all day. A fortress of beautiful blue lay before them, making it impossible to tell where the ocean ended and sky began. Elsie inhaled deeply, taking mental note of how fresh the air smelled and how she could taste the salt in the air. As she stood at the top of that cliff, she felt so close to the heavens. She knew that her parents and Auggie's mom were smiling down on them.

They hardly spoke on the car ride to the airport, both sad for such a magical, romantic vacation to have to come to an end. Once on the plane, although they were traveling through the night, neither of them could sleep. They tried to pass the time by flipping through photos on their phones and watching movies. As Elsie looked through all the photos on her phone, she realized that their vacation had been the most consecutive days they had ever spent together.

She thought back to something her dad used to tell her: "The two most important things you can give someone are your unconditional love and your time." She looked at Auggie sitting in the seat next to her. She realized now that her father was a wise man. Yes, Hawaii was amazing and breathtaking, but her favorite part had been the uninterrupted time with Auggie. She wondered when they'd have that much time together again. This year was going to be busy with her finishing college and him in his last year of residency. She reached over and grabbed Auggie's hand. "Promise me something," she said.

"Anything," he replied, looking at her with nothing but admiration.

"This year is going to be crazy busy for both of us. Promise me we'll always make time for each other," she pleaded with him longingly.

"Always," he promised. And he sealed it with a sweet kiss to her forehead. But for some reason, Elsie was battling a sick, sinking feeling inside.

After arriving home, Elsie and Marie sat up for hours eating cake and ice cream to celebrate Elsie's belated birthday and talking about her Hawaiian vacation. She showed Marie all the pictures and videos she'd taken on her phone and tried to find the words to describe Hawaii's beauty. Of course, no words did it justice.

Marie was in awe as her friend spoke and she skimmed through her pictures. Elsie was disappointed to learn that Auggie's week-and-a-half vacation had earned him second shift for the next two weeks, forcing them to only see each other for a couple of hours in the morning before it was time for Auggie to head into work. Although they were making time for each other, it wasn't nearly as much time as either of them would have liked.

When she wasn't spending time with Marie or with Auggie before or after his shift, Elsie found herself at home in her recording studio working on songs inspired by their vacation.

One night in mid-August, as Elsie and Auggie sat in Auggie's dining room finishing dinner, Elsie surprised Auggie by reaching into her purse and pulling out a thin, square-shaped present wrapped in light blue, hula girl-print wrapping paper.

"What's this?" he asked, intrigued. "A present for me?"

"I don't know," she teased with a sly smile on her face. "Why don't you open it and find out?"

He smiled as he tore into the wrapping paper to find a plastic CD case with the title "With You" written at the top and "by Elsie McCormick" across the bottom.

She was blushing as she began to speak. "I could never thank you enough for our trip to Hawaii." She suddenly felt sick wondering if Auggie would like his present. "So, I— um . . ." she stuttered as she searched for the right words to say. "I wrote you a song." She couldn't bring herself to make direct eye contact with Auggie as she finished her sentence. She'd never written a guy a song before. She only hoped he wouldn't be disappointed with her feeble attempt to thank him.

"Are you blushing?" he asked. "The talented Elsie McCormick never blushes when she sings to me," he said, intrigued, as he put the CD in his CD player.

"Shut up!" she said, laughing as she tossed a couch pillow at him. "I've never written a song about the man I love, for the man I love before, so yes, it's a little embarrassing." She chuckled.

He tossed the pillow back at her, grabbed the remote, leaned over and kissed her on the cheek, then hit play and anxiously waited to hear his song.

When the music started he recognized the unique sound,

smiled at her, and proudly said, "I knew you'd love your ukulele!"

As the music played, he put his arm around Elsie and pulled her down so they were sitting side by side on the couch. By the second time he heard the chorus, he was humming along to Elsie's catchy beat.

> *Fill me with summertime*
> *Drinking margaritas*
> *I'll be beachside*
> *Sunbathing with you.*
> *It's a good time, listening to HAPA*
> *Baby, beachside bumming,*
> *I just wanna be there with you.*

When the song ended, he jumped to his feet, pulled Elsie up off the couch, picked her up, and swung her around. "That was amazing!" He beamed.

"I'm glad you liked it," she said as she let out a sigh of relief. She had been on pins and needles the entire time her song played and was glad it was over. The room was then filled with Elsie's voice for a second time. This time she used a guitar instead of the ukulele.

"Two versions?" he asked as he listened.

"I couldn't decide which one I liked better," Elsie explained. "The ukulele gives the song a more Hawaiian feel, but the faster pace with my guitar sounded more like my style." She shrugged her shoulders. "So, I recorded both for you."

He gave her a big, sloppy, wet kiss and smiled proudly. "I love them both, just like I love my talented girlfriend." He set her down so that her feet touched the floor and kissed her again, this time a little less sloppy and more meaningful. After he pulled away, he looked her in the eyes and said, "Thank you. This is the best present anyone has ever given me." His eyes shone with sincere gratitude.

They sat on the couch listening to her song play over and over as they reminisced on their vacation. Two weeks later, Elsie started her senior year at UC and Auggie, the fourth and final year of his residency. They were both nervous and excited at the thought of finishing their schooling and training and starting their lives together.

PRESENT DAY

Chapter 13

Elsie had survived surgery. Dr. Owens found himself repeating this over and over again in his mind. If he hadn't watched the surgeon's every move, he wouldn't have believed that she could still be here. But she was still here. She was alive! She had a long road of recovery ahead and would need plastic surgery for facial repairs, but for the first time since he had set eyes on the unrecognizable Jane Doe ten hours ago, he was filled with hope that she just might have a chance of recovery, a chance to live her life again.

One thing remained that Dr. Owens needed to do—something he would never do for anyone else in the world but Elsie. With shaking hands, he picked up the phone and dialed.

"Dad?"

"What's wrong? Why are you calling at this hour?" he asked.

"It's Elsie," Auggie answered as tears began to race down his cheeks.

"McCormick?" He sounded confused.

"Yes. She—" Auggie paused trying to gain his composure before finishing the sentence. "She was in an accident. Her face—" He swallowed hard. "It's unrecognizable," Auggie said, wiping the tears from his eyes.

"Say no more, son. I'll be there soon." And with that, he hung up the phone.

Auggie hated having to ask his dad for a favor, but he knew he was the only doctor in the world who could make Elsie as beautiful as she once was. He reminded himself that it wasn't for him; it was for her. Everything he'd ever done had always been for her.

SIX YEARS AGO

Chapter 14

Every year, the University of Cincinnati Hospital hosted a charity event to raise money for research, and every year, Auggie skipped it—not because he didn't care about raising money for cancer research, but because he never had a date he cared enough about to take to such an event. This year, when Auggie received an invitation to the event, he immediately pictured Elsie in a fancy dress standing by his side. The theme this year was Vegas. A $150 ticket would cover unlimited drinks, food, and a thousand dollars' worth of play money.

At first, when he asked Elsie to come with him, she was apprehensive. The thought of being in a room full of doctors all night as they talked about things that were way over her head made her stomach feel queasy. Auggie promised her that if the conversation got too work-related, he'd either change the subject or they'd find something else to do. Auggie was always convincing. With his eyes as blue as the sky, a body built like a model, and a million-dollar, heart-melting smile, how could she say no?

Every day after they finished class, Marie and Elsie would make the fifteen-minute drive to Kenwood Mall to shop for the perfect dress for Elsie. Elsie hated shopping, but as always Marie made it a fun experience. Marie reminded Elsie that it was the season for homecoming dances, and that meant that junior departments would have an abundance of formal dresses to pick from. Elsie's petite frame would fit perfectly into a junior-size dress; the trick would be to find one that was age-appropriate.

After hours of scouring through rack after rack of dresses, Marie grabbed one and smiled at her friend. "This is it!" She beamed. "It will look amazing on you!"

At first glance, Elsie couldn't imagine what it was about the dress that would look so amazing on her. It was a deep purple velvet with an empire waist and light, shimmery beading on the straps.

"You sure?" she questioned Marie.

"Trust me, Smalls. Go try this on," she commanded as she handed the dress to Elsie.

She slipped on the dress and examined herself in the mirror. She wasn't used to seeing herself in such fancy clothing. Marie was right, as usual. The dress did complement her small figure really well. The beaded straps were beautiful and gave the dress character. It was tight-fitting down to her hips, and then it fanned out to the floor, swaying when she walked.

Without warning, Marie opened the dressing room door.

"Good thing I was dressed!" Elsie playfully snapped at her friend.

"Oh, please, it's nothing I haven't seen before! And it's your own fault for taking so long," Marie snapped back. Her tone changed as she looked her friend up and down. "Dang girl!" She beamed. "This dress was made for you!"

"You really think so, Marie?" Elsie asked.

Marie walked up behind her friend and gently gathered her long, brown hair into her hands, twisted it around the back of her head, and held it there. "Look how elegant your neckline is when you wear your hair up," she said as Elsie looked at herself and could hardly believe her eyes.

"You're right," she agreed.

"Of course, I'm right," Marie said. "I should know a thing or two about fashion design, considering I'm graduating with my degree this May! You won't even have to wear a necklace," she observed, "just some small but nice earrings. And I have just the pair for you to wear!" She beamed at her friend. "And don't worry about the length of the dress, Smalls. Throw on a pair of heels, and it will rest just above the floor. Perfect."

Elsie sighed. "Marie, I don't know what I'd do without you."

The big night had arrived, and Auggie waited anxiously at the bottom of the stairs for Elsie to make her appearance.

"What's taking so long?" he jokingly called up from the bottom of the stairs.

"Hold your horses, Dr. Auggie!" Marie called back down to him from Elsie's room. "Beauty takes time!" she added in a playful tone.

Ten minutes later, Marie came down and said, "You can thank me later," as she gently patted Auggie on the shoulder and headed to the living room to be out of their way.

Elsie used the handrail to steady herself as she carefully walked down the stairs. She wasn't used to wearing heels— and certainly not while walking down slippery wooden steps. She looked below to find Auggie waiting for her. As soon as he saw her, his eyes lit up. She let out a sigh of relief. The look on his face told her that he was pleased. It was a look she'd seen in the movies whenever a woman had captured the attention of a man from across a crowded room—the kind that made it seem as if they were the only two people around. Elsie couldn't stop the butterflies in her stomach. Although they'd been together for more than a year now, in moments like this she still found it hard to believe that someone as handsome as Augustus Owens had chosen her. She had never seen anyone look as handsome as he did tonight. He was wearing a gray suit, a white shirt, and a dark purple tie. As soon as she saw the tie, she smiled. She knew that Marie must have told him to wear a purple tie to match her dress. Her stomach tightened as nervous excitement consumed her.

Auggie stood speechless as Elsie descended the stairs. When she got to the bottom, he reached out and took her hand, brought it to his lips, and gently kissed it. Then he looked her directly in the eyes and said, "You are stunning."

"You really think so?" she asked nervously. "The makeup, the hair? It isn't too much?" she asked breathlessly. Marie had spent an hour curling and then pinning up Elsie's hair in a messy bun. After she was satisfied with her hair, she moved on to makeup, using products Elsie had never even heard of. She was worried it was a little over the top.

Auggie took a couple steps closer to Elsie, closing the space between them, took both of her small hands into his, and leaned in so that their eyes were locked. "I have never seen a woman look more beautiful than you do right now," he whispered. And he gently kissed her on the lips.

She could feel her knees wobble and her heart soar as his lips caressed hers. She wondered how it was that he had this kind of power over her—the kind of power that made her heart skip a beat every time they kissed or her skin tingle at his slightest touch. At this moment, Elsie felt like she was living in a fairy tale. She didn't know how long this love story would continue, but she was glad to be able to call this her life right now.

Auggie was the first to pull his lips away. "Shall we?" he

asked as he offered her his arm.

Elsie grabbed her dress coat and took his hand. "We shall."

Before leaving, she called out to Marie, who she knew had probably been eavesdropping from the other room. "Bye, Marie!" she said.

"You crazy kids try not to have too much fun now," Marie called back.

Elsie walked out the door expecting to find Auggie's Audi parked in the driveway. To her surprise, a black limousine was parked on the street in front of her apartment. She looked at the limousine, then back at Auggie, and then to the limousine again, making sure it was truly there.

"Is that for us?!" she asked, squealing with excitement.

"Yes! Your chariot awaits, my dear," Auggie announced, grinning ear to ear.

Elsie had never been in a limousine before. The back seat was huge—unnecessarily large for just two people—and it was heated leather! There was a mini-fridge with wine coolers and chilled champagne. Sitting in the large back seat with tinted windows, she felt as if they were important people hiding from the paparazzi. Auggie poured two glasses of champagne. As they sipped their bubbly, they sat close to each other talking quietly, smiling, and laughing. Every now and then, one of them would lean in for a kiss. Once the limousine stopped, Elsie was sad that their private ride had come to an end, but she was excited to see what else the night had in store.

The Duke Convention Center had been transformed to look like a real-life Vegas casino. At least a hundred tables were set up around an enormous ballroom. In the middle of each table stood a long, metal pole with a sign attached to it indicating which game was being played at that table. Poker, craps, roulette, blackjack—they had it all. Elsie had never seen such elegance and extravagance—women with gorgeous gowns and expensive-looking jewelry, men in suits and tuxedos. Hundreds were gathered around the tables laughing and drinking; some shouted in excitement as they won while others cursed their bad luck. She had to give it to the hospital; they sure knew how to throw a party.

"Would you like a drink?" A blonde waitress dressed in a frilly, red dress with large dice printed on it interrupted her thoughts.

"Yes, please!" she said, her voice full of excitement, and Auggie took two glasses from her and handed one to Elsie.

He raised his glass and said, "Cheers to a night to remember."

Elsie raised her glass too and expressed cheers with a small *clink* of her glass against his. She took a sip and giggled as bubbles fizzed up and tickled her nose. Even the champagne tasted expensive. She knew this was definitely going to be a night to remember.

"We better get some food before we play games," he said. "I know you need to eat every two hours, or you'll start to feel shaky. I swear someday you're going to be diabetic."

She nodded in agreement as Auggie led her towards the back wall where a table full of delicious foods sat. There was a chocolate fountain with all kinds of fruit for dipping, an assorted cheese and veggie tray, several varieties of finger sandwiches, and just about any dessert you could think of.

Before they had a chance to make a plate of food, a good-looking middle-aged man approached them from behind. He placed his hand on Auggie's shoulder, startling him, and said, "Fancy seeing you here, son. Long time, no see." He smiled at Elsie and then added, ". . . or no talk, for that matter."

Instantly the happiness in Auggie's eyes vanished as he turned to face him. "Father," he said flatly, and nodded in acknowledgment.

Auggie's father extended his arm for a hug only to have Auggie take a step backwards and place his arm around Elsie's back. He took a long sip of his champagne. It was obvious he was trying to avoid physical contact with him.

"I didn't think you had any free time, much less time to attend events like this," Auggie said coolly.

Although Auggie had rejected his hug, the man still smiled and said, "Well, son, someone from Owens Plastic Surgery Group had to make an appearance. After all, we are the research center's largest donor." He took a sip of his whiskey and then added, "I've been here every year hoping to run into you. Looks like this pretty young lady standing next to you had something to do with tonight's attendance." He smiled a warm smile at Elsie. "Excuse my son. It seems he's forgotten his manners. I'm Dr. Bruce Owens, Augustus's father," he said as he extended his hand to Elsie.

"I'm Elsie—Elsie McCormick. I'm pleased to meet you, sir," she said as she shook his hand. His bright blue eyes captured her attention, and it was then that she realized that whether Auggie liked him or not, he was the spitting image of his father.

"Do you work with Augustus?" Bruce asked.

"No, Dad," Auggie answered before Elsie had the chance to. "Unlike you, I don't mix work with pleasure," he snarled.

Elsie stared at Auggie in disbelief. She'd never seen him act this way or speak to someone the way he'd just spoken to his father. And from what he had told her about Bruce's actions in the past, she didn't blame Auggie one bit for being upset. But she also knew that Bruce had been reaching out to Auggie for years via phone calls and messages, and Auggie had been ignoring him. She tried to calm Auggie down by gently rubbing his back and politely responded, "No, sir, I'm studying music performance and audio production here at UC."

"Well, well. Beautiful and talented." Bruce smiled back at her.

"Ah, I don't know about that," she answered reticently.

She knew Auggie and his father had their differences, but still she wanted him to like her. After all, his son was the first man she'd ever loved.

"You're unbelievable," Auggie said in disgust as he shook his head.

"Excuse me?"

"Showing up here looking for me, talking to Elsie and me like you know us . . ." Auggie took a huge sip of his champagne, finishing it off, and instantly wanted something stronger.

"I told you, son, that I was invited—which you would have known if you had bothered to return any of my calls," Bruce stated plainly. "And on that note," he finished his whiskey and then said, "I was on my way out. I have a flight to catch. Son, it was good to see you after all these years." He placed his empty glass on a tray as a waitress passed them. "Elsie," he said with a sincere smile, "I know a few very important people in the music industry. If you ever need me to put in a good word for you, Augustus has my number."

Elsie looked at Auggie, who seemed annoyed, and then back at Bruce. "Wow! That's very kind of you. Thank you," she said.

"Augustus, don't be a stranger." Bruce patted his son's shoulder and then turned and walked away. As soon as he left, Elsie felt the tension dissipate.

Auggie let out a loud sigh of relief. "Sorry about all that," he apologized as he pulled Elsie in and gave her a kiss on the forehead. "I never wanted to put you in the middle of my family drama."

"Don't worry about it," she said, knowing there was a time and a place to discuss this further, and this was not it.

"I'm not going to let that ruin our night," he resolved. "Now, where were we?"

"I think we were going to get another drink and eat lots of

that delicious, expensive-looking food," she said with a smile, trying to remain upbeat. She wanted nothing more than to make the most of this truly magical evening.

Hours passed, and Elsie was thankful that Auggie had been able to brush off the run-in with his father and still enjoy their evening together. He held her close as they worked their way through the crowd talking and laughing and stopping every now and then to take a chance at winning. They won some and lost some, but it was all fun and games. Auggie kept his promise to Elsie. He made a point to introduce her to everyone he knew but kept the conversation light and avoided talking about work. Before they knew it, the fundraiser was quickly coming to an end. It had been a night full of smiles and laughter, and neither one of them wanted the night to end. Auggie stayed close by Elsie's side the entire evening, always touching her in some way, making it obvious to everyone around them that they were inseparable.

The crowd was thinning as casino night was drawing to a close. They were on their way to the dessert table to get one last treat before leaving when Auggie spotted one of his friends in the bar line.

"I see someone I want you to meet. Come on, let me introduce you," he said enthusiastically, and he took Elsie's arm and redirected them from the dessert table to the bar.

Elsie looked over to see a tall guy with shaggy brown hair standing next to a pretty woman wearing a long, tight, black dress.

"Bob!" Auggie said as he extended his arm out and bent down to hug the *girl*.

"Gus-Gus!" she said as she eagerly hugged him back.

Elsie stood at Auggie's side confused. Because of her inability to listen to Auggie's work stories involving blood and guts, he only occasionally mentioned his friends from work. He had told stories about his friends Jim and Bob, but she always assumed Bob was male. Now she was standing there dumbfounded to learn that one of Auggie's best friends—one with whom he works nights, weekends, and holidays—was a girl! Not only was she a girl but a very attractive one at that! And one who knew him well enough to call him "Gus-Gus." Elsie watched as Auggie's and Bob's hug seemed to last a little too long.

Elsie took the opportunity to look her up and down and discretely size her up. She was of normal build, around five foot five, slender but busty, which seemed so unfair to Elsie. Her sandy blonde locks hung down in big, bouncing curls that rested on her shoulders. Behind her brown, plastic glasses, her eyes were bright green. Elsie swallowed hard. Until now she'd never seen a girl be able to pull off glasses in an I'm-sexy-and-smart kind of way. Not only was she pretty, but she was a doctor, which meant she was also smart. *Well, shit*, Elsie thought to herself.

"Bob," Auggie said, "I want you to meet Elsie," and he proudly put his hand on the small of Elsie's back. Elsie didn't fully hear him since she was still processing everything, so she momentarily missed her cue to shake Bob's hand. Auggie nudged Elsie forward a little bit, snapping her out of her trance.

"Hello, Bob," Elsie began, her voice feeling a little weak. "It's nice to finally meet you," and the two shook hands.

"Likewise," she said in a perky tone and smiled as she shook Elsie's hand. "But please, please don't call me Bob; it's Bobbie. Gus just likes to call me Bob to annoy me," she said as she rolled her eyes at Gus.

"Well, you're practically one of the guys," he laughed.

"So funny," Bobbie said in a sarcastic tone. "I'm going to be paying for my parents' mistake my whole life," she laughed.

"I, uh—" Elsie was still trying to wrap her brain around the fact that in all this time Auggie had never mentioned that Bob was a girl. "I think you're the first girl Bobbie I've ever met," she said as she looked up at Auggie, hoping he would pick up on her subtle way of saying *Why the hell didn't you ever tell me Bob was a girl?!*

Bobbie laughed. "Yeah, I don't think it's all that common—not unless you had parents like mine—hippie stoners who idolized Bob Dylan," she replied, and then turned her attention to her date.

"Gus, you remember my friend Ryan," she said as she gestured towards the guy standing next to her.

"Of course," he said. "Good to see you again, buddy," Auggie said as he shook Ryan's hand.

Ryan was about the same height as Auggie with a nice head of shaggy, curly, brown hair and brown eyes. He shook Auggie's hand. "Always a pleasure, Gus." Then he turned his attention to Elsie, shook her hand, and said, "And a pleasure to meet you, little lady," in a cheerful, polite voice. He dropped her hand and then addressed the entire group. "Is this party a killer or what?"

"Besides seeing my jackass father, it's been a pretty damn good night!" Auggie said as he put his arm around Elsie and looked down at her, smiling. She looked up at him and gave a slight smile back.

"He's here every year," Bobbie said. "Last year he was the keynote speaker. Didn't you know that?" Bobbie asked.

"Of course he was," Auggie said as he shook his head in disapproval. "And no, I didn't know that. You know I don't speak to the man."

Elsie took a quick sip of her champagne to make sure her jaw didn't drop to the floor as she angrily thought to herself, *Not only does she know my boyfriend's dad; she knows they don't speak to each other?!*

Auggie spoke again. "That's enough about him. I thought you had to work tonight," he asked.

"I did. I brought my stuff to work and got ready in the locker room. Ryan picked me up, and we came straight here," Bobbie explained. "So, we only missed the first hour or so."

"Well, you look nice," Auggie said, smiling.

Elsie noticed Bobbie perk up at Auggie's compliment.

Bobbie shrugged her shoulders and laughed, "This is how I always look out of scrubs."

Auggie laughed. "Was work busy?" he asked.

"Eh, you know," she began. "The typical Saturday night— a little bit of this, a little bit of that," she said with a smile. "Did you see Dr. Meyers here?" Bobbie asked Auggie.

As Bobbie—the girl—continued to talk, Elsie stood by Auggie's side feeling lost and confused. She still couldn't wrap her mind around the fact that Bobbie was an attractive girl with an obvious connection to her boyfriend. She tried her hardest not to be concerned, but having Auggie leave her out of the conversation wasn't helping. Elsie took a deep breath. Mindful that her face must surely show her hurt and confusion, she did her very best to smile and join in, but the more she watched and listened, the more she found she didn't even want to join in. Until now, Auggie had kept his promise not to talk about work, but as soon as Bobbie came along, Elsie was left feeling lost and alone. She knew she needed to divert her attention to something other than them.

"So, Ryan—" Elsie spoke up. "Do you work at the hospital too?" She tried to sound as if she didn't care that her boyfriend was ignoring her.

"Nope!" he said proudly, "I could never deal with sick people. And I'd put money down on me passing out at the first sight of blood and guts," he said, laughing.

Elsie smiled. She could totally relate.

"I know what you mean," she said in agreement.

"I work at Great American," he said.

"Oh, very nice. The ballpark or the insurance company?"

Elsie asked trying to remain interested and engaged in their conversation.

"For the insurance company, in the workers' comp department," he said. "How about you?" he asked.

"I don't have a quote 'real job'—" she said, using air quotation marks. ". . . yet. I'm in my last year of studying music at UC," Elsie explained. Out of the corner of her eye, she could see Auggie and Bobbie smiling and heard bits and pieces of their conversation. They were now discussing some "unusual case of an intussusception" (whatever that was) on a thirty-year-old man. It was clear to Elsie that their conversation wasn't going to be over anytime soon.

"Ah. You're still a youngster," Ryan smiled as he teased her. Elsie smiled back although she was distracted. "Ryan, I'm going to go get a dessert. Do you want to join me?" Elsie asked, not wanting to stand and watch Auggie and Bobbie ignore her and Ryan any longer.

"Yeah, sure, I'll walk over with you," he said to Elsie.

"Bobbie, Gus, you need a drink or want anything? Elsie and I are going to grab some more desserts and drinks before it's too late."

For a moment Bobbie and Auggie stopped their conversation to say no thanks, but then they carried on.

As the two of them walked to the dessert table, Elsie felt compelled to find out more about Bobbie. When Bobbie introduced Ryan, she had referred to him as her "friend."

"So," Elsie began, "you and Bobbie—how long have you known each other?"

"Bobbie and I met in college when she was in med school and I was in grad school. We both went to UC," he explained.

By this time, they had reached the dessert table. Ryan grabbed a small clear plastic plate and began filling it up with chocolate chip cookies.

"We started dating after she and Gus broke up."

With those words Elsie felt as if her stomach had dropped to the floor and her heart stopped beating. Initially she was shocked that Auggie had failed to mention that he had dated his friend Bob, who was a smoking hot girl.

"But there's not really much time for a personal life when you're in graduate and medical school." Ryan continued to talk. "Then once she started her residency and I started my job, things got even more hectic." He paused, took a bite of his cookie, and said, "Mmm, these are some darn good cookies." He smiled at Elsie as he devoured the rest of his cookie.

Elsie continued to pile desserts on her plate while avoiding eye contact with Ryan. She could feel her cheeks burning with frustration as the initial shock was starting to turn to anger and insecurity, feeling as if Auggie had been hiding Bob from her all along.

She tried to compose herself as she asked, "So now you and Bobbie just date every now and then?" she asked.

"We're trying to keep things casual until the end of this year when she finds a job," he said between bites of another small cookie. "Who knows where she'll end up," he said nonchalantly with a shrug of his shoulders.

Elsie was taken aback by how calm and collected he seemed. She could tell he cared for Bobbie, but it also seemed like he didn't mind if she took a job elsewhere. "Would you move," Elsie asked, "if she got a job out of state?"

Ryan shrugged his shoulders. "Maybe—if it's within driving distance of Cincinnati. You know, somewhere close, like in Kentucky or Indiana. But other than that, no, I wouldn't." He had finished one plate of cookies and was starting to fill another.

"Do you mind if I ask why not?" Elsie quizzed him.

"Why wouldn't I move?" Ryan asked.

She nodded her head yes, confirming her question.

He shrugged his shoulders and said, "My family, my life—

they're all here in Cincinnati," he continued. "I come from a family of seven. I already have ten nieces and nephews. This is where I want to raise a family of my own one day," he said confidently.

Elsie looked at Ryan and gave him an understanding head nod, trying to focus on him and not Auggie and Bobbie.

"I know what you're thinking," Ryan said to Elsie. Elsie could feel her eyes widen as she sipped her drink and thought to herself, *That I can't believe my boyfriend didn't tell me he dated one of his best friends a.k.a. your on-again-off-again girlfriend*?! But she shrugged her shoulders and said, "Oh? And what's that?"

He continued. "That it's unusual for a goofy twenty-seven-year-old guy to be talking so openly about wanting a family," he said.

Elsie shook her head. "No, actually I wasn't thinking that at all. I think it's great that you know want you want."

"Well, that's what Bobbie thinks," he said as he looked over in her direction. "I mean, don't get me wrong, I'm crazy about that girl," he said, smiling, "but I've always known that I want a big family just like the crazy, fun-loving, sometimes obnoxious, family I grew up in." He smiled and shook his head as if he was reminiscing on his childhood. Then he looked back at Elsie and asked, "Do you know the divorce rate for doctors is ridiculously high? It's like seventy-five percent higher than for any other career."

Elsie looked at him wide-eyed, thrown off by this fact. For once she shifted gears from being upset to being fearful about the statistics of her and Auggie's future together.

"No, I didn't know that," she said in a sad, shocked tone as she glanced towards Auggie and Bobbie. She could feel her blood pressure rising as she watched them laugh about something, then Auggie gave Bobbie's shoulder a playful shove. He looked over to Elsie and gave her a wave. She tried to smile as she waved back.

"Anyway," Ryan interrupted, "I'm not trying to be a Debbie Downer or anything, but when you're in our shoes—you know, the doctor's significant other shoes—there's a lot to consider. Things like are we willing to move to wherever they find a job or can we handle their crazy hours and different shifts." Ryan's voice started to trail a little as if these questions had been weighing on his mind. Then he looked at Elsie and patted her on the back. "I'm sorry. I don't mean to burden you with any of these thoughts. It's just nice to have someone to talk to who's on my side," he explained as he looked down at Elsie and smiled apologetically.

"No, no, it's alright," Elsie said. Her mind was swirling with thoughts about all the points Ryan had just made—things she hadn't considered, things she and Auggie hadn't discussed, things about their potential future, and things about Auggie's past.

"I'm going to grab another drink. Want one?" Ryan asked.

Elsie was staring at Bobbie and Auggie again without realizing it. After discovering they used to date, she couldn't take her eyes off of them. Suddenly she felt sick to her stomach, overwhelmed with all of Ryan's points and fearing that there might be something more than friendship between her boyfriend and Bobbie. "Um, no thanks. I need to hit the ladies' room. I'll meet back up with you guys in a bit," she said as she felt the sudden urge to be as far away from Auggie and Bobbie as she could get.

"Let me take your plate, and I'll give it to Gus," Ryan offered and took her plate from her.

"Thank you, Ryan." Elsie smiled. He really did seem like a kind, thoughtful person.

As Elsie made her way to the bathroom, her mind was racing. She could feel a headache coming on as she replayed the last thirty minutes in her mind: discovering Bobbie was a girl with a strong connection to her boyfriend; the way Auggie acted around Bobbie—all relaxed and happy; how he had basically ignored her in front of Bobbie; the conversation she'd just had with Ryan; and now realizing that she and Auggie had a great deal to discuss by the end of the year.

As she walked into the restroom, several women had finished drying their hands and were on their way out. Elsie's head was pounding. She didn't need to use the restroom; she only wanted to be left alone with her thoughts for a few minutes before rejoining the group. She walked over to the powder area and sat down in the plush chair in front of the mirror. She looked in the mirror. She didn't even recognize herself with her hair all curled and pinned up and all the makeup she was wearing.

While looking at herself in the mirror, she looked directly at her eyes. Her dark brown eyes danced wild with an array of emotions—confusion, hurt, and worry. Mostly she was confused and hurt wondering why Auggie hadn't mentioned that his best friend from work was a girl whom he was obviously close to. She took a deep breath and tried to consider his side of the story. Maybe they really were just work friends, and she was overreacting. Even if that was the case, she didn't like how friendly the two of them were. It made her feel uneasy. Or maybe she was just jealous. She had never really cared enough about a boy before to know what being jealous felt like. She knew she needed to talk to Auggie to figure it all out. She took in a deep breath and then exhaled. She decided to try not to stress over Bobbie until she talked to Auggie and had more information.

Another emotion she saw in her dark eyes was sadness. She felt sad when she thought about Auggie and their future— if there even was a future for the two of them. Now she wasn't so sure. They hadn't talked about what was to come of them after she graduated in May and he finished his residency. Ryan had some valid points about dating and marrying a doctor. There was no telling where Auggie would ultimately live and work. Once he did get a job, what shift would he be assigned? Would he work nights, weekends, holidays? None of those were conducive to raising a family. A family. Elsie shook her head. She wasn't even ready for a family; why was she thinking about a family? She needed to focus on her career before she could even think about starting a family. And what about her career? Where would it lead her? Would Auggie be willing to follow her? If their careers took them in opposite directions, could their relationship survive the distance?

Elsie thought back to their vacation in Hawaii. Having Auggie's undivided attention for a week was the best gift she'd ever been given. She couldn't remember a time when she'd ever been so happy. She realized that it was his time that she needed most to feel his love—not jewelry, chocolates, flowers, or cards, but his time—time to talk to each other and open up the way they had that night on the beach; time to make each other laugh, goof off, and just be themselves. Her dad's words rang true: time is the best gift you can give to or receive from someone you love. She knew that a long-distance relationship would never give them the time she needed.

Elsie reached into her wristlet and grabbed a peach lipstick Marie had given her. She freshened her face a bit and then let out a deep sigh. What had started as a fun, relaxing evening had turned into a stressful evening spent worrying about a future she wasn't even sure existed. She had a bad habit of letting things consume her and worrying unnecessarily. She knew it was because of what she'd been through—losing both parents—that had taught her that life was full of uncertainties. She told herself to relax and give Auggie a chance to explain his relationship with Bobbie. When she got home, she would pull out her writing book and work through her feelings and fears in the best way she knew.

Just then she heard the bathroom door open and saw a woman walk into a stall. She wasn't sure how much time had passed, but she knew she'd probably been in the restroom for far too long. Did Auggie even realize she was missing? She got up from the plush chair, smoothed her dress, and walked out of the restroom. As soon as she walked out the bathroom door, she heard, "There you are!" Auggie was leaning up against the wall across from the women's restroom.

"Oh, hey," Elsie stammered, caught a little off guard. She had expected Auggie to be in the other room still talking to Bobbie, but she was secretly relieved he wasn't. Auggie walked towards her, leaned down, and gave her a kiss on the cheek.

"It's time to go, lovely," he said, and then kissed Elsie on the lips. His breath smelled and tasted like alcohol.

"Did you get another drink?" Elsie asked.

"Yes, Ryan and I had a drink of Scotch while Bobbie went to the restroom to look for you," he said.

It took a moment for Elsie to respond to what Auggie had just said. "Bobbie came looking for me?" Elsie sounded confused.

"Yeah, she wanted to talk to you and get to know you a little before they left," he said.

"Oh. Well, I didn't see her," she said, and instantly realized that Bobbie had actually never come looking for her. From where she had been sitting in the bathroom, she could see everyone entering and exiting. Why would Bobbie lie to Auggie about something so trivial?

Elsie was starting to feel herself get frustrated with the whole Bobbie situation and didn't want Auggie to know. She immediately steered the conversation away from Bobbie. "When did you start drinking Scotch?" Elsie asked.

Auggie shrugged, "It's a special occasion," he said, "and I'm here with the prettiest girl in the room." He smiled at Elsie and pulled her in a little closer to him.

She couldn't help but smile back. Even now—the first time she'd ever been upset with him—he still had the ability to make her feel all light and fuzzy, like she was floating on clouds.

"It's time to go," Auggie said. "Your limo awaits." He took her hand and led her out the door to the front of the convention center. Their limo pulled up, and Auggie opened the door for Elsie. She climbed in. The leather seats were nice and warm.

A chilled glass of champagne was waiting for them in the back seat. They'd already eaten and drunk much more than usual, but it was a special occasion, after all. How could they not partake?

"Cheers!" Auggie said. "To one of the best evenings I've ever had with the prettiest woman I know," and he clinked his glass to Elsie's.

She took a long sip trying to clear her mind, when Auggie asked, "So what do you think of Bobbie?"

Elsie coughed as she choked on her bubbling champagne. She had not anticipated Auggie bringing up Bobbie after he had just toasted to the prettiest woman he knew. Elsie took another sip and swallowed hard to try and get the choking feeling out from the back of her throat.

She wanted to say, *I hate that she's pretty and smart and gets to work with you at all hours of the day and night!* But instead she answered, "Honestly, I was kind of surprised to meet *her*." She said, stressing the word "her." Elsie paused before she continued. She was buzzed from all the drinks, but she knew she needed to choose her words wisely. "Every time you mention Bob and Jim from work, you talk as if they're both guys." Elsie stared into her champagne glass, avoiding eye contact with Auggie.

"What?" Auggie looked surprised. "I'm sure I've mentioned it before. But honestly, she's practically one of the guys." He chuckled then added, "Bobbie, Jim, and I, we've been through a lot together in med school and during our residency. We're all just trying to survive—to make it through this residency."

Elsie avoided eye contact with him and tried to stay calm as she added coldly, "Apparently you've been through a lot more with Bobbie than you have with Jim."

"What are you talking about?" Auggie asked, confused.

"How come you never told me you two dated in college?" she said in a stern voice, trying to keep her frustrated tears at bay.

He shrugged and said. "Because I didn't think it mattered. It was years ago, in med school, and it wasn't serious—at all," he said. "Did Bobbie say something to you in the bathroom?"

"No, Bobbie said nothing to me in the bathroom, because she never came into the bathroom looking for me. She lied for some reason, probably to try to make it look like she actually gives a damn about me, when she doesn't; she clearly only cares about you!" she snapped.

"Wow! Where is all of this coming from?" Auggie asked defensively; he'd never heard Elsie talk this way before. "Are you mad that, years ago, I dated Bobbie? For a very short period of time, I might add!"

Elsie's body immediately began to tense up and her stomach was in knots. Her mind began to run wild with thoughts again as she gazed out the window. She couldn't look at Auggie. She was hurt that in a year of dating he had failed to mention that he had dated one of his coworkers and best friends. She took a huge drink of her champagne and reached for some more.

"Yes, Auggie, I am. I mean, no, I'm not mad that you've dated other girls before me. I'm upset because we've been together over a year. And in all our time together, you have *never* mentioned that your best friend *and* coworker, who you call Bob, is not a dude, but actually a very attractive girl that you used to date!" Elsie stated coldly as she choked back the tears.

"Because it was a long time ago, Els. I didn't think it was important." He tried to reassure her. "And I probably never mentioned that Bobbie is a girl because I honestly only think of her as one of the guys." Although he was tipsy, Auggie could sense the tension between them. "When we dated, we were both so focused on school." He paused. "We agreed we were better off as friends," he said as he put his arm around Elsie and tried to pull her closer to him, but she resisted. Her body was stiff with tension.

She needed time to process everything the evening had uncovered. First, the drama with his dad; now all this with Bobbie. She was feeling overwhelmed.

"Hey!" Auggie could feel Elsie's frustration. "Bobbie and I are just friends," he reassured her as he gave her a sloppy kiss on the cheek. "You're the girl I'm crazy about," he said. "Believe me when I say this, I have *never* had the kind of connection, or chemistry, that we have, with anyone, including Bobbie, before," he said in a serious tone.

Elsie didn't want to look Auggie in the eyes. As stubborn as it sounded, she was still upset with him and knew as soon as she looked him in the eyes, she'd start to forgive him. She wanted time to process her feelings.

"I was so embarrassed tonight," she said, still staring out the window. "I mean, it was an awful feeling to discover that the guy I love used to date his best friend. And to find out the way I did, from Ryan, a guy I had just met." She wiped away a tear trickling down her face and sniffed. "Can you understand why I'm mad and hurt?" she asked as more tears began to form.

"Yes, I can. And I am so sorry you feel that way. I would never intentionally do something to hurt you, or upset you," he said, scooting in closer beside her, resting his hand on her back, urging her to look at him.

"I thought I knew everything about you, Auggie," she said. Finally feeling ready to look him in the eye, she turned towards him.

"Telling you that I dated Bobbie never crossed my mind, honestly. I think it's because I simply don't look at her the way I look at you," he said. "I'll tell you anything you want to know, you just ask. I'm not intentionally hiding anything from you," he said, pulling her in close.

She gave in to his hug and rested her head on his chest. She knew he was being sincere in his apology, but still was feeling uneasy about Bobbie. The way Bobbie looked and acted around him made her feel uneasy.

"I believe you," she said, then added, "but, I don't know, there's something about the way she was looking at you, and then at me, that made me feel very uneasy. You may be over her, but I don't think she's over you," she argued.

"Trust me, you have nothing to worry about," he assured her as the limo pulled into her driveway.

As much as she wanted to believe him, a small voice inside of her was telling her otherwise. Elsie shook her head trying to erase all the negative thoughts creeping into her mind.

Auggie opened the limo door and put his arm around her as he walked her into her apartment. They both walked quietly up the stairs and into her room.

Once ready for bed, they held each other close. "This really was one of the best nights I've had," he whispered. "Despite seeing my father and having the whole Bobbie argument, I've never wanted to go to any of those events before, because I never had anyone I wanted to share that side of my life with, until you," he said, pulling her in close and giving her a kiss. "I love you."

"I love you too," she said as she kissed him back.

After a night of partying, it didn't take Auggie long to drift off into an alcohol-induced sleep, leaving Elsie alone with her thoughts. As hard as she tried, she knew she wouldn't be able to fall asleep without putting her thoughts down on paper. Slowly and quietly she snuck out of bed, careful not to wake him. She grabbed her journal and headed to Marie's room, who was nowhere to be seen. *I guess she's not coming home tonight,* she thought to herself as she climbed into Marie's bed. Without holding anything back, she let her thoughts flow through her pen and onto the blank white sheet of paper. She knew she could say whatever she wanted without having to worry about being judged or fearing what anyone else thought. Here, in her composition book, her thoughts and feelings were hers and hers only. Things she had never even confided to Marie lived in this book. Happiness, sorrow, all of her life's struggles filled the pages, front and back. She let the tears fall from her eyes as she openly worked through her frustration, anger, and fear. She wrote about Bobbie and wondered whether or not she and Auggie had a future together. Although she was alone in the quiet, dark apartment, her room seemed to echo with the steady stream of screaming thoughts.

After about an hour of writing, she crept back into her room, grabbed her guitar off of its stand and headed back to Marie's room. In the midst of venting, she had managed to transfer her feelings into lyrics. After the lyrics came to her, the music didn't take long to follow. She could hear the tune in her head; now all she had to do was find the right series of chords. As soon as she began to play, she could feel the hurt and confusion working its way from her mind and heart and out through her voice and fingers. Her music was her stress release, her joy, her own form of therapy. Music was how her dad had taught her to communicate, to connect with herself and work through her emotions.

She played until she was physically and emotionally

exhausted—until her fingers could no longer strum. She gathered her stuff, headed back into her room, set down her guitar and notebook, and climbed into bed next to the man she loved, feeling a sense of satisfaction.

She reassured herself that tonight was the first argument they had had in over a year. In any relationship, conflict was bound to happen, and she had been satisfied with the way Auggie handled the conflict. As far as their future was concerned, they had a full seven months to come up with a plan for after residency and graduation. Her brain was exhausted. Wanting to fall asleep to a good, positive thought, she snuggled up next to Auggie and smiled as she thought back to how much fun they had that evening and how reassuring Auggie had been when she confronted him with her feelings. And this worked right up until she was drifting off to sleep, when one last dreadful thought crept into Elsie's mind—the divorce rate among doctors of which Ryan had informed her. And just like the boogeyman haunting a child trying to get to sleep, this thought would make her toss and turn in a terrified state all night long.

PRESENT DAY

Chapter 15

Three of the longest days of his life had passed since Auggie's dad, *the* Dr. Bruce Owens, the best plastic surgeon in the US, had arrived to repair Jane Doe's face. After Auggie discreetly identified her as Elsie McCormick, the hospital attempted to contact her next of kin, Marie, but unsuccessfully. While the staff praised Dr. Bruce for his generosity, Auggie could barely bring himself to mutter the words "Thank you" out loud to his father. He reminded himself, however, that it was for Elsie, and he somehow found the wherewithal to give him a hug.

Before operating on Elsie, his father asked Auggie to provide him with a photo of her that portrayed her true face and smile. He rushed home and raced to his bedroom closet where a shoebox full of pictures, letters, and souvenirs from his time with Elsie sat on the top shelf. He picked one where Elsie looked the happiest he had ever seen her. Looking at the picture took Auggie back to the night it had been taken.

Wanting to make up for hurting Elsie's feelings the night of the casino party, he had asked her over for dinner where a surprise awaited her—something he'd received in the mail earlier that day. As they ate, he sensed Elsie was annoyed.

"I can tell something is bothering you," he said as they ate.

"Are you still upset about what happened at the casino night?" he asked.

"Not upset, more like hurt," she said, putting her fork down. "Honestly, I felt left out. Not knowing about your past, and you and Bobbie talked the entire night, practically ignoring everyone around you," she admitted.

His heart sank as he realized he had disappointed her. The expression on her face was similar to the expression she had every time he got stuck at work late or had to work a holiday or weekend. He hated disappointing her.

"Before you, Bobbie was my best friend," he began to explain.

"You're not making me feel any better," she said as she folded her arms across her chest.

"I'm not done. I said *before* you." He hoped she'd really listen to what he had to say. "Then you came along, and everything changed. Once we started dating, I stopped hanging out with Bobbie outside of work. And when we're at work, all I talk about is you. You're not only my girlfriend; you're my best friend." Elsie could tell he was sincere. He got up from his chair and walked to where she sat, urging her to stand. Reluctantly she stood to her feet. "Casino night was the first night I had seen my old friend outside of work in over a year, so I guess I got a little carried away," he told her.

She looked up at him, her deep brown eyes filled with pain.

"I'm sorry. I didn't mean to ignore you," he apologized, "and it was never my intent to keep anything about Bobbie from you. I promise."

"I don't know, Auggie," she said as she tried pulling away from him, but he only held her a little tighter. "I mean, the way she looked at you . . . She made me feel uncomfortable, like she wants you all to herself."

"No," he shook his head, "not a chance. We broke up for a reason. If we wanted to be together, we've had all these years to do that. And even if she wanted to be, which she doesn't, I'd tell her no. You're the girl I want to be with, Els."

"Are you sure?" she prodded.

"Yes, I'm sure," he said as he gave her a quick kiss on the forehead. He broke their embrace and led Elsie over to the living room couch.

"If I wasn't sure, would I have done this?" he said as he picked up an envelope from the coffee table and handed it to her.

The outside of the envelope read "Vanderbilt Medical Center."

"What's this?" she asked.

"It's a letter confirming my interview. It's scheduled for December seventeenth at Vanderbilt Medical Center in Nashville," he said proudly.

"Nashville?" she repeated in disbelief as butterflies began to fill her stomach.

"Vanderbilt is one of the best hospitals in the country to work for." He smiled proudly. "Not to mention, it's my talented girlfriend's dream to move there after graduation," he added nonchalantly as his eyes danced with excitement. "So, I figure why not start our careers there, together," he said with a shrug.

"You want to move to Nashville together?" She couldn't believe she was saying those words out loud.

"Yes! I'd follow you anywhere, Els." He smiled, pulling her in for a passionate kiss.

After several moments of kissing, she gently pulled away. Still in shock by all that he had just laid on her, she felt as if she could hardly breathe.

"Oh my God, Auggie, are you serious?!" she squealed.

"Yes, you're the reason I chose Nashville; it's all for you," he said, grinning ear to ear.

Elsie couldn't contain her excitement any longer. She

threw her head back and shouted, "We're moving to Nash-ville!"

"We're moving to Nashville!" Auggie repeated, just as overjoyed as Elsie.

Hours passed with them smiling and laughing as they discussed their future together in Nashville. At the end of the night they held each other close and took a selfie to remind them of the night they decided to move away and start a life together outside of Cincinnati. Auggie never imagined that six years later he'd be handing his father that selfie in order to reconstruct the most beautiful face he'd ever laid eyes on.

SIX YEARS AGO

Chapter 16

As fate would have it, several weeks following Elsie and Auggie's decision to start a life together, after months of receiving rejection letter after rejection letter, one day Elsie received a very large envelope in the mail that read "Country Rock Studios." With shaking hands, she tore open the envelope and began to read the letter.

Dear Ms. McCormick,

We were impressed with your demo "With You" and would like to set up a meeting at your earliest convenience . . .

Elsie's hands were trembling. A combination of disbelief and excitement overcame her as she reread the first sentence twenty times before its magnitude finally set in. All her years of playing, writing, and singing, the countless hours of perfecting her demos, all had led her to this monumental life moment. This letter could pave the path to her career in the music industry in Nashville.

"OLIVE!" she finally screamed. "You're not going to believe this!" Her legs couldn't move fast enough as she ran towards the kitchen.

Olive took one look at Elsie and knew something important had happened. "You're as giddy as a schoolgirl. I don't think I've ever seen you in such a state," she said.

"They were impressed!" she beamed as she handed her the letter. "With MY demo!" she said, jumping for joy.

To say that Olive was proud would be an understatement. They hugged, laughed, and cried tears of pride and happiness.

After leaving a voice mail on Auggie's phone asking him to come over immediately after work for some exciting news, she grabbed a box of Oreo cookies, hopped into her Jeep, and headed north on I-71. About twenty-five minutes later, she arrived at Gate of Heaven Cemetery. Even though the ground was cold, she sat down beside her mother and father's headstone, opened up the box of Oreos, and began to tell them about her letter.

"Can you believe it?!" Her voice was full of elation. "Country Rock Studios wants to interview me, your daughter! Dad, I bet you never thought teaching me how to strum your beat-up old guitar would lead to this moment." She laughed as she set two cookies on the ground for them. When she was young, her parents would talk and tell stories to her over milk and cookies before bed. Now, anytime she came to visit, she brought cookies.

"What if they really like me! Can you imagine me, up on a stage? In front of thousands?!" She was so overjoyed that she couldn't even eat her cookie. "I'd pass out from pure excitement for sure," she chuckled.

"I'm getting way ahead of myself." Her tone changed. "I mean, what if they interview me and only want to give me an offer for my song?" She began to get lost in dismal thoughts. "Or if they only want to use me as a songwriter and not a performer, or worse what if they meet me and decide I'm not a good fit for their company at all?" She began to feel stressed.

"I really wish you two were here to talk to in person," Elsie said as tears began to fill her eyes.

Elsie looked around at the surrounding headstones near her parents' grave. She didn't recognize any of their names. She focused on a fresh mound of dirt that didn't even have a headstone yet. She wondered what kind of life the person had lived. Was the person old or young? Did they live a happy, short life or a long, miserable life? Did they follow their dream and become who they wanted to become, or did they play it safe and settle for a satisfactory job that offered stability but sacrificed happiness? All the graves had a story to tell. Then she wondered, what would her story be? Would she have any regrets? Life was full of unknowns and things we can't control, but the one thing she could control was how much effort she put into pursuing her career.

She realized then, as scary as rejection was or the company criticizing her songwriting, her voice, or maybe even her lyrics, what scared her the most in life was not doing everything in her power to turn her dream into her reality. She knew she needed to set up the interview and leave all nervous thoughts and inhibitions at the door. During the interview she needed to be as authentic as possible.

She said her goodbyes to her parents and headed home to share the news with Auggie and celebrate together. When she proudly showed the letter to Auggie, he couldn't have been more elated. He picked her up and swung her around in a circle as he kissed her wildly, only stopping to say, "I knew you could do it, Els!"

Everything continue to fall into place as Elsie was able to schedule her meeting with Johnny, from Country Rock Studios, the same week as Auggie's interview in December. Not only would they have each other to lean on for moral support, but after their interviews they'd be able to spend a few days exploring the town together.

The big week arrived and Auggie and Elsie packed their bags and headed to Tennessee. During the four-hour drive they passed the time at ease, singing along to music and planning their week.

When the day of her interview finally arrived, Auggie walked her to the door, kissed her good luck, and reassured her that this wouldn't be the last time she'd step foot into Country Rock Studios. He reminded her that he believed in her, but most importantly she believed in herself and that was what was going to make her successful. She smiled; he always knew how to calm her nerves. As she walked through the door, she looked back to see Auggie giving her a thumbs-up, and she couldn't help but chuckle.

Johnny reminded Elsie of her father. He had kind green eyes and was easy to talk to. From the moment she shook his hand, she felt as comfortable as she did in her studio back at home and the interview took off and passed easily and in a blur. To her surprise, when asked to play her demo, she was eager to play with no inhibitions.

Hours later, she was celebrating with Auggie over drinks and dinner, smiling and laughing as they toasted to a promising future together in Nashville. Both seemed confident that their interviews had gone well, and everything seemed to be falling perfectly into place.

The next day they headed back to Cincinnati, where Elsie celebrated Christmas with Olive and Marie while Auggie worked. Although she was disappointed that she wouldn't be able to spend her favorite holiday with the man she loved, he reassured her that in their future, they'd have plenty of holidays to spend together.

On January first, the two kicked off the new year in love and eager to start a future together. January was cold, with numerous ice and snow storms. Elsie and Auggie spent their nights holding each other close to keep safe and warm.

However, nothing would keep Elsie safe from the storm that awaited her. In February, Auggie received a phone call that would change the course of their future—a phone call he would keep secret from Elsie.

FIVE YEARS AGO

Chapter 17

Elsie could hardly believe that this was her life. She expected to wake up tomorrow to learn that it had all been a dream. She and Auggie had traveled two hours to see one of their favorite bands playing in a small outdoor pavilion—their present to each other for Elsie having graduated and Auggie having finished his residency. It was a perfect spring night for a concert, despite the lovely Ohio humidity. The sky was slightly overcast, and there was a cool breeze. They sat in the front row just to the right of center stage. She knew all the words to every song and had been singing along for hours. Her throat was raw and her feet hurt from jumping up and down. The last hour of the show, it began to rain, but the audience didn't care and neither did The Killers. The energy from the crowd was electric. She smiled and looked at Auggie as the rain began to fall. They both started laughing as he pulled her closer to him and yelled into her ear so she could hear him above the music. "I never want to forget this night."

She smiled and yelled, "Me neither." She was having the time of her life. Auggie stayed close by her side but didn't seem to be as into the concert as she was. Rather, he seemed to be taking it all in as if he was trying to store it in a memory box.

When she smiled, his eyes traced the outline of her lips. When she laughed he closed his eyes, listened, and smiled a satisfied smile. Looking back now, it all made sense. He had a secret.

On the long drive home, they rolled down the windows and let the hot, humid air dry their damp clothes. She stuck her arm out the window, letting the warm air flow through her fingers. She smiled as she rested her head on her arm, stared up at the dark night sky, and reminisced about the concert. She had finally gotten to see one of her favorite bands perform live, and in the company of her favorite person. The storm clouds had passed, leaving a clear view of the star-studded sky. Driving through the country, she could see so many more stars than in downtown Cincinnati.

"Tired?" he asked, interrupting her thoughts.

"Exhausted, but it was so worth it," she said in dry, raspy voice. Her voice was tired from screaming above the band.

"Why don't you try to sleep? I'll wake you when we get to your place," he said as he patted her leg.

She glanced over to the driver's seat and squeaked, "We're not going to your house?" as she rubbed her throat, hoping she wasn't going to lose her voice.

He paused slightly before he answered. "If we go back to your place, you'll have clean, dry clothes in the morning," he answered without looking over at her. His eyes were glued to the dark, winding road ahead of them.

She thought about it for a minute and then nodded okay. She rolled up her window and laid her head against the cool glass, turning her attention to the country that surrounded the highway. It was so much darker in the country. She shuddered. It was almost spooky dark. You couldn't tell where the dark fields ended and the sky began. Suddenly her eyes began to feel heavy and exhaustion set in.

She faintly remembered being half-awake as Auggie carried her up the stairs and laid her in bed. Her bed had never felt so warm and comfortable. She was sore from standing and dancing for four hours straight. As she started to slip into sleep again, she felt a gentle kiss on her forehead and Auggie's fingers gently tracing the outline of a heart on her hand. Their own little personal way of saying "I love you." She fell asleep with a smile on her face, having no knowledge of what tomorrow would bring.

She woke up to the spring sunlight shining through her window, dancing on her face. She rubbed her eyes and turned to her side, reaching out for Auggie only to feel nothing but empty blankets and sheets. She opened her eyes a little more and saw that Auggie wasn't on his side of the bed. She turned to the other side to look at her alarm clock sitting on the nightstand. It read eight thirty-eight. On her nightstand was a glass of water and an Advil. She smiled. It was the little things Auggie did that proved he was always looking out for her. She sat up and reached for the Advil and glass of water. To her surprise, the water was warm.

He must have gotten up early to get a head start on his day, she thought to herself.

She took several savory sips of water to help ease her scratchy throat. Even though her body was sore and her throat a bit scratchy, she smiled as she replayed the previous night in her head. It was such a great show. Nothing put her in a better mood than seeing a good band perform live. There was always something so magical and energetic in the air during the show. She stretched, hopped out of bed, and worked her way downstairs to look for Auggie. Marie was lying on the couch watching TV.

"Good morning, sunshine! How was the concert? You're looking a little rough, so it must have been good!" Marie winked at her.

"It was awesome!" she answered in a raspy voice, a little surprised she could talk. "Definitely worth the trip and getting caught in the rain." She was scanning the kitchen and living area for Auggie. "Have you seen Auggie?" she asked.

"Nope, only McDreamy's face from last week's *Grey's*. I assumed he was in bed with you," Marie said as she turned her attention back to the TV.

"No, he wasn't upstairs," she sighed. "Hmm. I bet he's already back at home getting an early start on packing." Auggie's lease was up, and they had only two months before moving to Nashville. Instead of renewing, he was going to put most of his stuff in storage and stay at Elsie and Marie's.

"You still okay with him staying here?" Elsie asked. "I know it's our last month together before you move to New York."

"I'd rather keep you all to myself before we go our separate ways, but I guess I'll share." Marie winked.

Elsie grabbed her phone and dialed his number as she started back up the stairs. It went straight to voice mail. *He must have forgotten to charge it*, she thought to herself. *I'll just head* over there and figure out our plans for the day.

Elsie got dressed, jumped in her Jeep, and headed to his apartment. When she reached Auggie's place, his front door was locked. She knocked and stood there for a minute, but Auggie didn't answer. She reached into her purse, grabbed her key, and put it into the lock, but something wasn't right. The key wasn't fitting in the keyhole. She looked at the key to make sure she had the right one. Yes, this was Auggie's key. She tried again. The key wasn't fitting.

She reached for her phone and dialed his number. Again, it rang once and then went straight to voice mail.

Why isn't he answering? And why isn't my key working? Elsie thought to herself. She dialed Auggie a third time and knocked on his door. This time when the phone went to voice mail, she left a message: "Hey, you! It's me. I'm outside your house, and for some reason, my key's not working." She paused, cleared her scratchy throat, and went on. "Are you home? Call me back. Love you." She hung up her phone and put it back in her purse.

She walked around the apartment to the side window where she would be able to see if he was in the kitchen listening to music too loudly to hear her knocking. Once she got to the window, she cupped her hands over her eyes and looked inside. What she saw was a sight so terrifying she temporarily stopped breathing as she stood frozen in place. Auggie's kitchen was empty. Completely empty. How this could be? She walked over to the next window where she would be able to see into his living room and looked in. Nothing. No furniture, no bookcase, no books, no TV. No signs of Auggie or anyone else living there.

She could feel her heart pounding in her chest. Her breathing quickened and tears quickly began to fall from her eyes. With shaky hands, she reached for her phone. Again, she tried Auggie, only this time nothing went through. Instead of going to voice mail, Elsie heard an automated voice recording: "We're sorry. The number you have dialed has been disconnected or is no longer in service. Please hang up and try your call again."

Elsie dropped to her knees and cried hysterically. Her heart was pounding so hard and fast. She didn't understand what was happening. She had just been with Auggie less than eight hours ago. Where was he? Why wasn't her call going through? Why was everything gone from his house when she was supposed to be helping him move into her apartment this week?

When she calmed down enough to drive home, she allowed herself to fall apart all over again as she ran into the house screaming and crying for Marie. By the sound of Elsie's voice, Marie knew something was terribly wrong. She immediately came running down the stairs, asking Elsie if she was alright and what had happened. Elsie couldn't respond. She stood with her back up against the door, trying to catch her breath as the last hour's events raced through her head. She felt dizzy and lost in confusion, wanting to wake up from this awful nightmare that she was living.

Marie ran to her friend. She took one look at Elsie's bright red, tearstained face and knew something awful had happened. Elsie could hardly breathe from crying so hard.

"Oh, my God, Els! What's going on?" Marie's voice was full of panic.

Elsie started to collapse to the floor, but Marie swooped her small friend into her arms and carried her to the couch. She ran to the kitchen, grabbed a towel and ran it under cool water, then twisted it to wring out the excess water. She brought tissues from the bathroom and returned to the couch, where Elsie was lying curled up in the fetal position.

Marie smoothed Elsie's tear-soaked hair off her face, then gently dabbed the cool, wet towel on her forehead and cheeks. "Shh, it's okay," Marie cooed. "I'm here for you. Calm down, breathe," she instructed Elsie. "Take a breath in, now out," she instructed Elsie over and over again. "Good," Marie said as Elsie's breathing began to slow.

Once Elsie started to regain control of her breathing, she slowly untucked herself out of the fetal position and sat up. She began to tell Marie bits and pieces of what she had seen at Auggie's house—how his house had been empty, and how her key wouldn't unlock his door. Marie listened quietly as her friend painfully relived the past hour. As Elsie continued, she began to breathe heavily again, and tears started to fall faster and harder.

Marie managed again to help slow Elsie's breathing and

calm her down. In between sobs, Elsie told Marie how she had tried to call Auggie. The first few times she called him, it went to voice mail; now when she called, there was nothing; the call didn't even go through. Elsie was afraid something was terribly wrong with Auggie. Marie, however, was worried about Elsie.

When she finished telling Marie everything, she felt heavy and exhausted. She lay back down on the couch, resumed the fetal position, and continued to cry.

Marie got up from the side of the couch, grabbed her computer from the coffee table, and searched her and Elsie's Facebook pages.

After several minutes of investigating, Marie thought she had an idea of what might have happened to Auggie but wasn't sure how to break the news to her friend. She saw Elsie's phone hanging out of the back pocket of her jeans, picked it up, and searched through her photos. She sighed as she realized her suspicions were being confirmed. She placed Elsie's phone on the coffee table, picked up her computer, and then sat down on the couch next to her friend.

"Els," Marie said, "I think Auggie is fine." She started with the only positive she could find in this situation.

"What? How do you know?" she asked as she sat up.

"Well, I don't think he's hurt, but I'm not sure where he is." Marie's voice was shaky.

"What?" Elsie cried.

"I love you, and I don't want to show you this," she paused, "but I think it's important for you to see."

Marie turned her computer towards Elsie. On the screen was Elsie's Facebook page. Elsie's profile picture used to be a picture of her and Auggie making goofy faces at each other. It had been replaced with the blue outline of a person and a question mark in the middle. Her eyes filled with tears as she scrolled down the page. Where her relationship status used to read, "In a relationship," it now read, "Single." She felt sick to her stomach. Was this someone's idea of a sick joke?

"I don't understand," she cried to Marie. "What's happening?" She sniffed as she continued to cry.

Marie moved closer to her friend and put her arm around her back trying to comfort her, although she knew nothing she could do would take away the pain.

"Elsie," she explained, "I think Auggie has moved on." She paused. She could hardly manage to say those words to her friend without losing it herself. Elsie seemed to be smaller and more fragile than ever before.

"But why? Where is he?" Elsie placed Marie's computer next to her on the couch and lowered her head into both her hands. She began to cry even harder. Her head spun with confusion. Her heart ached, longing for Auggie to walk through the front door and give her a hug and a kiss and tell her it was all just some misunderstanding. But deep inside, she knew this wasn't going to happen.

"I don't know. I checked my page too," Marie answered. Elsie turned her head hoping that her friend had found something—anything—to help explain what was happening and where Auggie was.

Marie couldn't bring herself to look her best friend in the eyes. She turned her head and looked towards the wall. "He's not on Facebook anymore. He's not listed as my friend or yours." Marie stopped as the pressure started to build in her eyes. "I think he's ghosted you, Els." She paused. "Like to the extreme. Not just broke up with you without telling you but moved away and left without a trace!"

"No!" Elsie sobbed harder. "He would never leave me!" She was sobbing even harder now, close to hysteria.

Auggie had left her without giving an explanation or saying goodbye. She slowly processed everything she was discovering and lost herself in her tears. She felt as if she could actually feel her heart breaking. Something inside of her was shattering into a million tiny pieces. Auggie had left her, leaving no trace of himself having ever been in her life. He had deleted her photos from her phone and hacked into her Facebook account and erased all the photos of them together. He had deleted all evidence of his existence, both electronically and physically. He made certain that she'd never be able to contact him again. He had even taken the box she kept tucked away in her closet that contained all the notes and things they'd collected throughout their relationship. In less than twenty-four hours, he had successfully managed to delete all evidence of his existence and all evidence of their relationship. She had no idea where he was going, what he was doing, or who he was with.

She cried so hard she began to puke. Marie carried her into the bathroom, where Elsie lay on the floor crying until she had no tears left to cry.

PRESENT DAY

Chapter 18

How do you leave the person you love? Especially after planning a future together? It was the hardest decision Auggie had ever made in his entire life. For two long and agonizing months he had tossed and turned over the decision.

As he stared at Elsie through the ICU's glass window, he thought back to the bitterly cold February day when he had received word from Vanderbilt Medical Center. He was leaving for work when his phone rang. Recognizing the number, he eagerly answered, expecting to hear good news; however, that wasn't the case. They had called to regretfully inform him that after much consideration he was not selected for the job. When informed who they selected over him, his heart ached in utter betrayal.

"Open up, Bob!" he screamed, letting twelve hours of pent-up frustration out as he pounded on her front door.

"I was wondering when you'd show up," she said as she opened the door and let him in.

"How could you do this to me?" he said, storming into her apartment.

"How could I what? Accept a job that I *earned* at one of the *best* hospitals?" she sassed, closing the door behind him.

"How could you go up against me for any job? Especially this one, when you knew how badly Elsie and I were depending on me getting that job!"

"I can apply for any job I want, Gus! And believe it or not, I actually want to work there. Unlike you, who's just following around some girl like a lost puppy dog!"

"Some girl? You know she's not just *some girl* to me." He could feel his face turning red in frustration. "I wanted that job so badly that it was the only job I applied for!" he proclaimed.

"Well, that was a stupid thing to do! Everyone knows you're supposed to apply for at least five jobs!" she lectured.

"I realize that now!" he snapped. "At the time I thought it would show them how committed I was to working there. Now I'm going to be stuck with whatever crappy job I can find."

"You know you could always call in a favor from your . . ."

"Don't you dare finish that sentence," he interrupted, then glared angrily at her. She knew better than to mention his father during a time like this.

"You're right, I'm sorry," she agreed.

Feeling defeated, he sat down on the couch and hung his head low, running his fingers through his hair in exasperation, and continued, "I don't understand. Can you please explain to me why my best friend of almost ten years is intentionally trying to ruin my life?"

"I'm not trying to ruin your life, I'm trying to protect you!" she defended herself as she sat down next to him.

Confused, he asked, "Protect me from what?"

"Think about it—what do you think is going to happen if Elsie makes it in the music industry? Do you think you're going to be able to travel, to be by her side every weekend for every show? You're not going to be able to support her when we practically have to sell our souls to get a weekend off. It won't work, Gus," she said, patting him on the back as if he was a child who needed calming.

"You don't know that!" he argued as he stood up from the couch, annoyed by her touch. "And who do you think you are to say that my relationship won't work when it's between Elsie and me—not you!" he yelled, throwing his hands in the air in frustration. "What kind of friend are you?" he continued, looking her dead in the eyes. "You didn't even want that job until I told you I was going to move there with Elsie. Dammit, Bobbie, that was my job! My way to make it work with Elsie, and you ruined it for me!"

"Oh, forgive me for wanting to work for one of the best hospitals in the country!" she said sarcastically as she stood up. "And I'm not going to apologize for getting the job over you." She waved her finger at him and then continued with her lecture. "There's a reason they chose me over you! It's not my fault. And I'm not apologizing for trying to keep you from making a mistake."

"A mistake?" He was fuming with anger now. "What mistake would that be? Being with Elsie? Being happy? Having a great job? How are any of these things a mistake? Please, Bobbie, tell me how any of these are mistakes!" he shouted.

"Not being with me!" she yelled. "That's the mistake! You should be with me, Gus, not with Elsie!" she cried.

"You can't be serious!?" He threw his hands up in the air. "We haven't been together for years. And I'd like to remind you that you broke up with me, not the other way around!"

"You're a smart guy. You honestly didn't see that I never stopped loving you?" Bobbie said, wiping tears from her eyes.

"Why would I think that you still love me when you're the one who dumped me? And I can't be too smart because I was stupid enough to consider you to be a real friend—my best friend—but real friends don't intentionally go behind your back to sabotage their personal relationships!"

"I only broke it off with you because our grades started slipping from spending too much time together and not studying. You knew that, you idiot!" She wept.

"Unbelievable!" he uttered.

"Can't you see? Ryan and Elsie are just filling the void. It's only a matter of time until we end up back together," she said with pleading eyes.

"I don't even know what to say right now." His head was pounding in anger, disappointment, and disbelief. "You mean to tell me, you've kept your feelings hidden from me all these years while you've dated Ryan? What is wrong with you?" he asked, shaking his head in disapproval.

"No, I've always been honest with Ryan. Do I love him? Yes. Am I in love with him? I don't think so, but he and I both knew our relationship was temporary from the start, and he accepted that. We want different things out of life. He wants a big family; I don't. He needs time and attention that I can't give him because I have accepted that my job is my life. You used to accept that fact too. And now it's only a matter of time before you open your eyes. I won't let you throw away everything you've worked for, for a girl!" she argued.

Feeling overwhelmed, he shook and remained silent, shaking his head in disagreement. Everything he cared about and loved was crashing down around him. He didn't get the job, and now he wouldn't be moving with Elsie. He feared what a long-distance relationship would do to their relationship. Not only would he have to break that to her, but he'd also have to tell her how Bobbie, his best friend of ten years, had applied for the job just to selfishly keep Elsie and him apart; and as if that wasn't enough, he needed to tell her that she was right, Bobbie was still in love with him.

"Think about it, there's a reason why most doctors end up married to other doctors or nurses. It's because we understand that missing holidays comes with the job. That long hours are expected, and we can't feel guilty if we're not home on time. We understand that we took an oath that comes before our own lives. We've been there for each other through college, med school, and residency. It's only a matter of time before we're back together."

He was trying not to listen to her but as much as he wanted everything she was saying to be completely wrong, something inside of him was wondering if there was some truth behind her words. *Would Elsie remain happy even if she came second to his job?* He quickly pushed the doubt out of his mind. He knew they could find a way to make it work.

"You're wrong," he said confidently.

"If I'm so wrong, then why'd you come here—to my apartment this late at night?" she asked, taking one step closer to him.

"I came here because I thought we were friends. I needed to know why my best friend would stab me in the back the way you did," he defended himself.

She closed in the space between them. "Are you sure that's the only reason you came here?" she asked, her eyes filled with desperation.

"Don't be stupid, Bobbie, you know the only reason I'm here this late is because I came after work," he said, feeling as if he were backed into a corner.

"Are you sure?" she said, taking another step closer, leaving practically no space between them.

"Don't do this," he begged her. But for some reason he was feeling more vulnerable than ever. He was filled with confusion, desperation, anger, and sadness.

"If you don't love me anymore, then I could kiss you right now, and you wouldn't feel anything," she said hopefully.

"Don't," he pleaded, but was interrupted as she grabbed his head and pulled him in close for a kiss.

He was filled with so much anger and confusion as she

kissed him. As much as he hated to admit it, there was some truth behind Bobbie's argument about how hard his career would be on his relationship with Elsie. Not to mention, if she did make it in the music industry, things would be even more complicated. He allowed himself to kiss her back but only to see if she was right, to see if he had any residual feelings for her—but he didn't. He was immediately filled with over-whelming guilt and gently pushed her away.

That night when he said goodbye to Bobbie, he said goodbye for good. What she did was unforgivable. There was no going back to the way they once were.

When he went home, he couldn't sleep. All he wanted was to see Elsie and tell her everything that had happened, but she wasn't home, she was at Olive's. This was a conversation he needed to have with her in person, not over the phone.

The next day, he headed to Olive's, planning on telling Elsie everything that happened between Bobbie and him, kiss and all. Little did he know what was in store for him.

"Auggie! What a surprise," she smiled, greeting him at the door.

"Morning, Olive," he said, leaning in for a hug. "Elsie around?" he asked as his eyes scanned the living room search-ing for her.

"She's out running some errands for me. She shouldn't be too much longer," she said. "How about a cup of coffee while we wait, huh?" she offered. "No offense, but you kind of look like you could use one." She patted him on the shoulder as she directed him into the kitchen.

He rubbed his bloodshot eyes and laughed, then said, "I look that bad, huh?" as he followed her into the kitchen and sat down at the table.

"No, not bad, just tired and stressed. A penny for your thoughts?" she asked as she poured him a hot cup of coffee.

"Thank you," he said, taking the cup from her. "I don't want to bother you with my problems," he said, stirring some creamer into his coffee.

"Well, I hate to break it to you, young man, but your problems end up being Elsie's problems, and she tells me everything, so I'm going to find out one way or another," she said, patting him on the hand.

"You have a point there," he chuckled. He let out a loud sigh, then added, "I have some disappointing and difficult news to tell Elsie." He paused, embarrassed to tell her the truth, but knew he needed to, "I, um, I didn't get the job in Nashville," he shamefully admitted.

"Oh, I see," she said, taking a long sip of coffee as she thought for a moment. "Well, Auggie, I am sorry to hear this and you're right, Elsie will be upset," she sympathized. Then she said, point-blank, "I know you probably don't want to hear but, I think it's a good thing you didn't get the job."

"You do? Why?" he asked, shocked by her response.

"You and Elsie are different from other folks your age. You two are gifted, with extraordinary talents of your own, and you both have worked tirelessly to perfect your talents. And this is just the beginning, this is where you finally get to start seeing the results of your talents. You, by helping to save people's lives, and Elsie by changing lives through her music," she explained.

"So, what does that have to do with me not getting the job in Nashville?" he asked confused.

"Sometimes you have to give the people you love some space to grow in order for them to reach their full potential," she said.

He stared at her, not understanding what she was saying.

"I'm asking you to let her go, Auggie," she said plainly.

"I don't understand. Why would I do that when we love each other?" he asked defensively.

"Let me tell you a story," she said. "When I was young I attended college in Texas and did quite well, so well that I had the opportunity to further my education and work on my PhD. This was a big deal for women my age, you see, times were different then. More and more women were attending college, but women professors were far and few between." She smiled, reminiscing on her past. She continued, "I was young and had fallen in love with one of my cohorts, Hank. We shared the same love for education and hoped to teach at the same university, and heck, maybe even become department co-chairs one day." She chuckled. Her tone changed as she continued. "But all of that changed with the draft," she said, misty-eyed. "Hank was one of the many unlucky men who left for Vietnam and never came home," she said, patting her eyes dry.

"I didn't know any of that, and I'm truly sorry to hear it," he said sincerely. Then he added reassuringly, "But I'm not going to leave Elsie."

"I know you're not going to war, but my point is life is unpredictable and we can't control what comes our way," she said. "Shortly after Hank went to war, I found out I was pregnant with Elsie's father, Lee—Hank Lee Jr.—and my life was forever changed. Being a single mom, I had no other choice, I had to stop working on my PhD and move back home to be close to family. I needed their help and support raising Lee. I took the first job I could find as an elementary music teacher. Don't get me wrong, I loved being Lee's mom and loved being a teacher, but, something deep inside of me always craved more out of life. Not a day goes by where I don't wonder what my life could have been like if I would have found a way to follow my dreams. If I would have completed my PhD and accomplished everything I wanted to accomplish." Her voice filled with remorse.

"Olive, I'm truly sorry for all you went through and that you didn't get the life you wanted, but believe me when I say that I want Elsie to have everything she wants in life," he pleaded.

"I know you do, but my experience taught me that there's a time in life that should be devoted solely to yourself. A time dedicated to following your passions and becoming a person you are proud to be and love, before you end up giving a part of yourself away as a partner or a parent. After you give a part of yourself away, you won't have the time for yourself ever again. So many women my age never got to do what they wanted to do, whether it be from losing their loved one in the war or not having the resources available to them. I don't want that to happen to Elsie. I won't let that happen to her," she said, shaking her head.

Auggie remained silent, reflecting on everything Olive had said.

"There's an old saying; if you love someone, set them free; if they come back to you, it was meant to be. I want you to let her go. Give her the space and time to let her accomplish everything she was born to do before you both settle down for good," she said, staring into his eyes.

He looked away, shaking his head, not knowing what to say, shocked and heartbroken by her words.

"I don't think I can do that," he finally muttered, holding back tears.

"Well, you need to because she needs you to," she firmly stated.

Auggie sat silently in disbelief, not knowing what to say to Olive's request. Not only did he have to break the disappointing news to Elsie about not getting the job, and Bobbie still being in love with him and kissing him, but now, he also had to tell her Olive wanted them to break up so that he wasn't in the way of her future. He felt completely defeated. All cards seemed to be stacked against them. He had no idea how he was going to make things right, or if Olive would let him make things right. His thoughts were interrupted by the sound of the front door.

"I'm home!" Elsie shouted. "Auggie, I saw your car out front; what a nice surprise," she said, smiling ear to ear as she rushed into the kitchen to greet them both.

Placing her bags on the counter she looked at Olive and said, "There better not be any sugar in that coffee! The doctor warned you your diabetes is getting worse and to limit your sugar," she lectured.

"No sugar for me, dear, but thank you for looking out for me." She smiled at Elsie.

Elsie walked over to Auggie and said, "No offense but you don't look so good." She gave him a quick kiss on the cheek. "Rough night?" she asked.

"You have no idea," he said, glancing towards Olive, still in disbelief from their conversation.

"Want to tell me about it?" she asked as she took a quick sip of his coffee and then handed it back to him.

He looked at Elsie, her hair pulled back in a messy bun, her cheeks still pink, flushed from the cold wind outside; and just like the first time he saw her, he was at a loss for words, struggling to know the right thing to say.

Avoiding all eye contact, he took a long sip of his coffee, then replied, "Just, a bunch of blood, guts, and sad stories you don't like to hear about." Until that moment, he had never lied to her. No sooner than the words escaped his lips, he regretted it. With the unpredictable turn of events that had transpired within the last twenty-four hours, he feared one lie could quickly lead to another and then another until there was no turning back. Suddenly he felt sick with regret.

"You're right." Olive interrupted his thoughts. "We don't

need to hear about any of that gross medical stuff. How about I make you two some brunch?" she offered.

"Actually, I'm sorry to cut this date early ladies, but suddenly I'm not feeling well," he said, setting his coffee down on the table, then standing up.

"You're probably exhausted," Elsie sympathized as she rubbed his back.

You have no idea how emotionally exhausted I am, he thought to himself as he walked to the front door and Elsie followed close behind.

"I'll call you later," he said as he hugged and then kissed Elsie goodbye.

When he left Olive's house that day, nothing would be the same for him again. From that moment on he'd struggle with knowing what the seemingly right thing to do was. Having to tell Elsie about all the events that took place at Bobbie's apartment was one thing, but Olive not wanting them to be together because he might hold Elsie back from her career, well that was an entirely different story on a whole other level. Olive was everything to Elsie, her only living family member and her connection to her parents through stories of her past. There was absolutely no way he could come between the two of them.

If he were to tell Elsie about the conversation he had with Olive, he had no idea what Olive would say. After all, if she wanted Auggie out of the way of Elsie's future career, why didn't she have the conversation with Elsie instead of him? That's when the truth hit him like a ton of bricks; Olive knew exactly what she was doing the moment she told him what to do. She didn't want to hurt Elsie or be the bad guy, instead, she wanted him to take the fall for it all. She wanted Elsie to have everything she never did and didn't want anyone or anything holding her back; and according to Olive, he would be holding Elsie back from the future she deserved.

He felt he had been put in an impossible situation. A game he didn't want to play, because one way or another, in the end, he knew he would lose.

The night of the concert, he tucked her in, placed a glass of water and some Advil on the nightstand, and then sat on the side of her bed and watched her sleep for an hour before forcing himself to leave. Following through with Olive's request to leave Elsie was the most difficult decision he'd ever made. As tears dripped off his face and onto her nose, he gave her one last gentle kiss goodbye. Although he knew she wouldn't see it this way, he really was leaving her out of love and respect. Causing her any amount of pain was the last thing he ever wanted to do. He cried as he walked out of her room and out her front door for the last time.

He made one last stop at his cleaned-out apartment to grab the last of his belongings and then hit the road; he had a long night of driving ahead of him. Throughout his drive, as tears trickled out of his eyes, he kept repeating to himself, *It's for the best. I love her too much to get in the way of her success.*

He couldn't let himself think of how confused and heartbroken she'd be once she woke up, started connecting all the dots, and began to understand that he was gone and wasn't coming back. Elsie would be devastated; but since this is what Olive wanted, he knew between Marie and Olive, Elsie would be well taken care of and encouraged to live again. After all, a clean break heals the fastest—at least that's what they taught him in medical school.

His iPhone buzzed in his lab coat pocket, interrupting his thoughts and bringing him back to the present day. He sighed realizing that his visit with Elsie was coming to an end, and he entered her room.

When he looked at her, he didn't see an injured woman; he saw happiness, light, and love. A person whose presence had the ability to energize a room with just one smile. He looked around. The room was filled with flowers, balloons, and cards, but still no sign of Marie. He knew that would soon change.

Before this evening's visit, he saw in Elsie's chart that the nurses were finally able to reach her next of kin, Marie. She had been unreachable on her honeymoon in Paris due to having her phone turned off. As soon as she turned her phone on and received word of Elsie's accident, she booked the first flight home. She would be arriving tomorrow. Auggie knew Marie's arrival would put an end to his visits. If she were to see him, anywhere in the hospital, especially anywhere close to Elsie's room, she'd probably cause a huge scene and call security in a heartbeat.

He quietly walked over to her nightstand where a purple vase sat. He looked around to see if anyone was watching, then reached inside his lab coat and pulled out a white calla lily and set it in the vase. He had brought one every night he came to visit her. Tonight made ten. Before leaving her, he noticed her sheets were resting high on her chest, too close to her face. He smiled slightly, remembering how she never liked sleeping with the sheets touching her face, and knew if she were awake, the sheets would be driving her crazy. He gently turned the sheets down, resting them below her chest.

He didn't say anything. His goal was to come and go without drawing too much attention to himself. If anyone were to find out about their past, it would be all over the newspaper and there would be no way to come and visit her like he was doing now. Most importantly, he didn't want Elsie to find out that he had been involved in her care by reading it in the front-page story of a magazine. When the time was right, he wanted to be the one to tell her. His phone buzzed again. This time he pulled out his phone, checked the time, and turned off his alarm. He let out a slight, audible sigh. His brief time with Elsie had come to an end.

"I could never find the words to tell you how sorry I am for leaving you the way I did. I never stopped loving you, and I never will," he whispered. "Please, please keep fighting," he pleaded, then turned and walked out the door.

FIVE YEARS AGO

Love left me broken without reason,
Shattered and disbelieving
There's any good left in a man.
Is there any good left in a man?

I've thrown in the towel
Tired of dating in this town
Full of heartbreak by lies
Um, yeah, I've seen my share of cheating eyes

I heard your new girl she's real pretty
Yeah, her smile won't make ya miss me

Moving on to something shiny 'n' new

She's everything you never saw in me.
She's everything I dream to be.

— *"Left"* by Elsie McCormick

Chapter 19

Her entire life had been taken away from her, stolen more quickly than the blink of an eye. The life she had planned to live with Auggie was no longer a reality for her; now it was just a dream—a dream of what could have been, a dream that haunted her at night.

Olive always said, "If you've hit rock bottom, things can only get better from there." She had two months left before she'd be moving and starting her new life in Nashville. A life that, up until two weeks ago, she had envisioned as her and Auggie starting together. They had a plan, or so she'd thought. She had been under the impression that he'd accepted the job at Vanderbilt University Medical Center and she'd be working on her songwriting career at Country Rock Studios. Now she realized that the life she thought she'd be living was not going to happen and it left her reconsidering her future. How was she to follow her dreams and start a new career when she felt more broken than she'd ever felt before? Not only did she feel broken, she felt alone and couldn't imagine how she'd feel in a big new city all by herself.

It was moments like these when Elsie really missed her parents. These were the types of decisions parents helped their children make; however, Elsie didn't have parents to go to ask for advice and guidance; she only had Marie and Olive. Marie wanted nothing but the best for Elsie and reassured her that she could make it in Nashville, but she was also her best friend, so Elsie considered Marie to be extremely biased when it came to her musical talent. And as much as she wanted Olive's advice, that meant she'd have to tell her about what had happened with Auggie, and that was something Elsie hadn't found the courage to do just yet.

Over the last two weeks, Elsie had called Olive several times, pretending to be sick with a cold so that if Olive did see her, it would explain her weight loss, the dark circles under her eyes, and her stuffy nose and hoarse throat from crying so much. She felt guilty for having missed last Sunday night dinner with Olive because of her pretend cold but she didn't have the strength to tell Olive about Auggie leaving her.

Today was Sunday, and she knew she needed to find the strength to go home for family dinner because if she missed two weeks in a row, it would only be a matter of days before Olive showed up at her apartment's front door concerned about her. Today would be the first day she would leave her apartment and face the outside world since Auggie's leaving.

Elsie had finished getting ready and looked at herself in the full-length mirror hanging behind her bedroom door. She was pleased with the girl staring back at her. Although she didn't look completely like her old self, she looked more like herself than she had two weeks ago. Her eyes still looked lost, but her face looked more determined, and her new haircut was starting to grow on her.

She thought back to the first week after Auggie left. That entire week was a blur. Elsie's daily routine consisted of crying—lying in bed crying, lying on the couch crying, trying to sleep but waking up crying. Through it all, Marie was right by her side—every minute of every day. That first week, she didn't remember eating or drinking. Marie would bring her comfort food. Elsie would pick at it, take a bite or two, and then set it aside. She didn't have an appetite; she was too depressed to eat.

Towards the end of the week, Marie was buying Elsie large bottles of Gatorade and practically forcing fluids down her throat. Elsie was dehydrating. She was at the point at which she'd try to cry but couldn't; no tears would come. The only time she'd say his name was when she'd wake up in the middle of the night calling for him and crying hysterically. Marie would run into her room and comfort her.

Marie and Elsie would go most of the day without speaking. Marie knew what Elsie needed because she had been there for Elsie when her father passed. She knew that for now, she needed to deal with this by herself. All she needed was for Marie to stay close by her side in case she wanted to talk. Marie would be there whenever Elsie was ready.

By the start of week two, Marie had to do something to make Elsie realize she needed to drink and eat, or she'd end up in the hospital. Marie dragged her into the bathroom, put her on the scale in front of the mirror, and said, "I know you're going through hell right now, but look at yourself, Els."

She didn't want to look at herself. She'd grieved before, and she knew she wouldn't like the way she looked right now. She knew she'd see a lost soul hiding behind puffy, swollen, bloodshot eyes and a red, tearstained face.

"Look at yourself!" This time Marie was a little firmer with Elsie. She grabbed her face and turned it straight towards the mirror.

It only took Elsie one glance in the mirror to witness the frail, lost girl staring back at her. She was ghostly pale in appearance with wild, untamed hair and baggy clothes that looked like they were falling down off her waist.

Elsie had seen enough. She started to turn her head away

but instead looked down at the scale. She'd lost six pounds in a week. She turned her attention to the girl looking back at her in the mirror. She looked her straight in the eyes and was suddenly filled with anger—anger that she looked so awful over a boy—a boy too cowardly to end things face to face. Angry at herself for letting her guard down and falling in love with someone who would do something so cruel to her. Angry for letting herself fall apart when her life was starting to become everything she'd hoped for, ever worked towards. Most of all, though, she was angry at *him*. She couldn't even think his name for fear it would hurt too much. She was angry at him for leaving her the way he did, with so many unanswered questions. For being so selfish and stealing all evidence of their time together and trying to take her memories too. For not letting her have any say in the way their relationship ended. And suddenly she couldn't take it anymore. She couldn't stand to look at that pathetic, weak-looking girl in the mirror for another second. That couldn't be her! She would not let herself become that girl in the mirror.

She slowly backed off the scale and turned around to look through the bathroom drawer. She took out a pair of scissors Marie always used to trim her bangs and turned back around to face Marie.

"Els, what are you going to do with those scissors?" Marie asked with a hint of fear in her voice.

She saw the concern in Marie's face. "Don't worry. I'm not going to hurt myself, if that's what you're thinking."

Marie let out a little sigh of relief.

"But it's time for a change," Elsie said as she grabbed a big chunk of her long hair and started to cut it to her shoulders.

Surprised, Marie let out a small gasp. "Are you sure about this, Els?" Marie asked. "I've never seen you with short hair."

But it was too late. A huge, long chunk of wavy hair had already hit the ground.

"Well, okay then," Marie said with a shrug. "Guess that settles that. Let me get some spray and a brush," she said, moving quickly to find some more haircutting supplies.

An hour later, Elsie looked in the mirror and could hardly recognize herself. She examined the girl staring back at her and was pleased with what she saw. Marie always had a knack for all things girly such as makeup, fashion, and nails, and now hairstylist could be added to that list as well. Marie had cut Elsie's hair to her chin in a somewhat jagged, edgy look. She was surprised to see that her short hair made her look a little older and even a bit more mature.

Now when she looked in the mirror, she didn't see a young, pathetic version of herself. She saw an older, more experienced person. For the first time in her life, her hair was cut short enough to expose the scar on the left side of her neck, and she didn't care. Growing up she always thought that it was hideous and embarrassing and felt like it stuck out like a sore thumb. She hardly pulled her hair back in fear of being teased about it by other kids. Now, however, exposing her scar to the world just felt right. The scar was a good representation of her past—painful, imperfect, and rough around the edges—exactly the way she was feeling now.

"Do you like it?" Marie asked as she was examining her hair in the mirror.

"It suits me well," she replied. "I think I'll keep it this way for a while," she said as she walked over to her friend and gave her a hug. "Thank you." Elsie squeezed Marie a little harder. "Thank you for always being there for me when I need you the most."

"Always and forever, my little friend," Marie responded as she squeezed her back. They let go of one another and looked down at the mess of hair that covered the bathroom floor. "Looks like we have a new bathroom mat," Marie joked. And for the first time in what felt like forever, Elsie let out a small laugh.

Elsie and Marie talked as they cleaned up all the hair lying on the bathroom floor.

"What that man did to you was evil," Marie said. "He doesn't even deserve to be thought of or to have his name spoken," she continued. "From now on, let's just refer to him as 'he who shall not be named.' " Marie laughed.

"Like Voldemort in *Harry Potter*," Elsie laughed along. They continued to laugh as they cleaned all the hair from the floor.

"That didn't take as long as I thought it would take," Marie said as she dropped the final wad of hair into the bathroom trash can. "Feeling a little better? I'll meet you downstairs," Marie said as she patted Elsie on the back.

Elsie nodded at her friend. "Yes. I'll be down in a few." After Marie left the bathroom, Elsie stood there looking at all her old hair clumped together in the trash can. Moments ago, it had looked like such a bigger mess when it was scattered all over the bathroom floor. Now it was just one big, messy glob.

If only it were that easy to pick up all the broken pieces of a person, she thought to herself as she turned out the bathroom light.

Now, thinking back on the week and looking at herself in the mirror, she let out a sigh and told herself, *You can do this! You will go to dinner and enjoy your time with your loving grandma, and you will not let him ruin any more of your time.* She grabbed her purse and headed home.

She pulled into the long gravel driveway and parked behind Olive's Focus. She smiled a faint smile as she parked her car. There was always something so comforting about coming home, especially when she felt lost—and Elsie had felt lost for weeks—ever since "he who shall not be named" had done what he did. She smiled, remembering her and Marie laughing and coming up with that nickname. She couldn't imagine where she'd be without Marie.

She jumped out of her Jeep and walked towards the front door. Spring was one of her favorite times of the year. All the flowers Olive and Elsie had planted in the gardens all around the perimeter of the house were in full bloom. She could smell lilies of the valley, roses, and sunflowers as she approached the door. She smiled at the memory of planting all these flowers throughout the years with Olive. Suddenly the guilt returned for having canceled on Olive for family dinner last Sunday. Elsie had smiled more in the last few minutes just from pulling into the driveway than she had in a long time. She made a mental note to tell Olive how good it felt to come home—especially after a hard couple of weeks.

She opened the front door. "Grandma!" she called into the house. "I'm home!" she said as she placed her keys on the side table to the right of the entryway. As she set her keys down, she noticed the vase of flowers sitting on the table. The vase was filled with assorted flowers that Olive had picked from the front of the house. Elsie noticed that half of the flowers in the vase were dead.

Hmm, that's strange, she thought to herself. *Olive normally doesn't leave flowers in vases after they're dead.* Elsie picked up the vase and headed towards the kitchen.

She tossed out the old flowers and began to rinse the vase. "Olive!" she called out again, this time a little louder than the first time. Over the past couple of years, Olive's hearing had been getting worse, but she was too stubborn to admit that she needed hearing aids. Elsie knew if Olive was downstairs or in the back of the house, she wouldn't be able to hear her.

She ran her fingers through her short hair and wondered if Olive would like her new haircut. She finished rinsing the vase and set it on the counter, then headed down the hallway to see if Olive was in the back room.

As Elsie passed the bathroom, she noticed that Olive's

bedroom door was partially shut. She found this to be strange since Olive always left all the doors open. She pushed the door open and immediately froze in place. Olive was lying peacefully in bed. Her eyes were open, and she was staring up at the ceiling. Olive never napped—not unless she was sick.

Her heart began to quicken. "Grandma!" Elsie said in a panic. She waited—for what felt like forever but was really only a couple of seconds—for Olive to answer, or move, or both. Instead of answering her, Olive lay perfectly still. "Grandma!" Elsie screamed this time. And she could feel the tears starting to build up in her eyes and her throat tighten in fear. The gut-wrenching feeling that was building inside of Elsie was far too familiar.

She took her hand off the doorknob and began to slowly back away from Olive's bedroom. Her legs were shaking. She felt weak, as if she could collapse at any moment. She put her back up against the wall and let herself quickly fall to the floor.

With shaking hands and blurry vision, she reached for the cell phone in her jacket pocket. Her hands were shaking so badly, she almost dropped the phone several times. She used both hands to steady her phone and let the tears fall without wiping them from her face as she managed to press the "9," then the "1," and finally the last "1."

"911. What is your emergency?" a concerned voice on the other end of the phone said.

She tried to talk but for some reason couldn't speak.

"Hello?" the lady's voice said. "911. What is your emergency? Are you injured or in trouble?" The woman's voice grew more intense.

Elsie cleared her throat, willing her voice to answer the lady. "It's . . ." she said in a shaky, weak voice she didn't recognize as her own. "It's my grandma," she said. She paused, afraid to say what she needed to say out loud. "She's . . ." Elsie paused. "I think she's . . ." and paused again. "I think she's . . . dead." Elsie's voice was weak and soft. The only way she could get those words out of her mouth was in a whisper. And as soon as they escaped her lips, somewhere deep within her, she knew they were true. There would be no going back to the way life used to be. At that moment, whatever had been holding the last pieces of Elsie together broke—shattered into nothingness. Already crushed from having lost Auggie, Elsie had known that with Marie and Olive's love and support she would eventually heal. But now, without Olive, there was nothing left of Elsie's inner being. She was a hollow, lonely girl. All these years, Olive had held Elsie together, loved her, and raised her. She was Elsie's only family. And now, a life without Olive, a life without family, wasn't a life worth living.

Chapter 20

Losing someone you love was never easy, but for Elsie, losing Olive was more than saying goodbye to her grandmother; she was saying goodbye to her entire family. All the stories Olive would tell Elsie had helped to keep her parents' memory alive. Now that Olive was gone, Elsie would never hear stories about her parents or about her childhood; no more memories of her family from a time when she was too little to remember; no more details of her parents' childhood and the years they had shared together before they had Elsie; no more stories about Olive's life growing up during the Depression. Elsie had lost her last relative, the last link to her family, and that meant parting with all the unanswered questions about her family that she'd never thought to ask but was certainly thinking of now.

As the priest said his blessing and the bagpipes played, Elsie just stared down at the grave in a daze. As she stared at the fresh dirt that covered her grandma's grave, she realized that if ever she were to marry, there would be no one to give her away. Whatever she accomplished in life, there would be no family with whom to share. At holidays she'd have no family with whom to celebrate. Elsie was the last living

McCormick. She had never felt more alone in her life. In three short weeks, she had been left by the only man, besides her father, that she'd ever loved, and now she would never see, hug, or talk to Olive again. Olive. Just the thought of her name made her chest clench in pain. The sweetest, most caring woman Elsie had ever known.

Olive had dedicated her life to looking out for Elsie, and now—even after she had passed—she was continuing to look out for her. Olive had prepared for this day. She had known the dreadful day would come when her only granddaughter would have to lay her to rest. Elsie had already been through so much heartache in her young life that Olive didn't want her to have to worry about funeral details. Olive had taken care of everything from the casket, to the flowers, to the priest, to her outfit, her prayer cards, the obituary, every detail. She had the arrangements and money stored away in her safe. Years earlier, she had told Elsie that when the time came, she was to open the safe before making any arrangements. All Elsie had to do was make a few phone calls, show up, and mourn. Elsie was both grateful and heartbroken that Olive had taken on all this by herself. She thought about what a strong person it took to make all her own funeral arrangements. Olive had always been a strong, independent woman, and Elsie aspired to be like her.

As the priest said his final words, the small crowd began to walk past Elsie, whispering a gentle "We're sorry," "She will be missed," and "She was loved" before they left the gravesite. Soon everyone had offered their condolences, and only Elsie and Marie remained. Marie gave Elsie her space and waited a few feet away.

Elsie couldn't take her eyes off the ground. There at her feet was a headstone bearing the names of everyone she'd ever known and loved as family. As she traced the names over and over again with her eyes, loneliness was eating away at her, consuming her. Elsie was envious of her family, knowing they were all somewhere else together—in a place she could neither see nor touch but knew existed. Wherever this place was, they were all there—all except her—and a small part of her wished to be with them. She felt she had nothing to live for. Elsie always knew this time would come, but she never imagined that it would come at a time in her life when she felt completely torn apart, lost, and empty inside. Everyone around her was continuing with their daily routine, but she was living in a fog. How would she continue living without any of them in her life?

She stood there staring at the three graves at her feet for what seemed like hours before she felt a gentle hand rest upon her shoulder. She didn't need to look back to know that it was Marie. Elsie knew it was time to go and was grateful that Marie had postponed her moving date to New York in order to be here for her. She wiped her eyes, turned around, leaned into Marie's side, and allowed her friend to mostly carry her back to the car. Neither one of them spoke. The two friends sat in silence as Marie drove Elsie home.

Although Olive had left Elsie with little work to do before the funeral, Elsie's body just would not shut off. In the few hours that she forced herself to sleep each night, her dreams would reopen a different chapter in her life, a chapter that her conscious mind fought to keep closed and tucked away in a mental box labeled "Do not open." Her conscious mind knew that even if she did finally manage to move on, Auggie would always torment her mind and emotions as an unfinished chapter in her life. Then there was her subconscious mind. Each night she was haunted by a love that had seemed so perfect but had ended so abruptly and heartlessly. This part of her wanted nothing more than to hold on to the unrealistic possibility that none of this was really happening—that she would wake up the next morning and find him lying in bed beside her as if nothing had changed.

In her dreams everything was so real—the sound of his voice, the smell of his cologne, the taste of his ChapStick when they kissed, the sound of his laughter, the way he could make her smile until her face hurt. Some nights she'd relive moments they had spent together right down to the last detail—what she was wearing on that day; the feeling of his fingers brushing against her cheek as he would gently push her long, brown hair out of her face and tuck it behind her right ear; the way her hands felt so small and protected inside of his; how he'd open the car door for her and say "My lady" in a British accent. Other nights she'd dream about getting married, buying their first house, and traveling together. These broken, unfulfilled dreams about a charmed life she would never live seemed to hurt the most. They were the ones she'd been cheated out of.

If it wasn't Auggie haunting her dreams, then it was guilt from having not seen Olive the week before she passed. Instead of facing Olive, Elsie had been a broken coward staying inside to mourn Auggie's disappearing act. She should have gone over for family dinner instead of pretending to be sick. She should have just told Olive what Auggie did instead of hiding from the world. Elsie would dream of her usual family dinner with Olive, only when she'd go to give Olive a hug and kiss goodbye, Olive would vanish and she would be left hugging nothing but air. Her dreams would then take her to the hallway on the day she found Olive's lifeless body. Elsie would watch from a distance as the Elsie in her dreams would curl up in the fetal position in the hallway and sob hysterically. "You should have been there for her!" she'd scream at the crying Elsie on the floor. But the crying Elsie couldn't hear her and continued to cry.

It didn't matter if Elsie was dreaming about Auggie or about Olive. Either way, she'd wake up in a cold, sticky sweat and with a tearstained face, gasping as she'd try to catch her breath. She would feel her heart pounding inside her chest so fast she felt it would explode. She would bury her face in her hands and cry until she had no tears left. Every night as her head hit the pillow she would force herself to mentally close the unfinished chapter of Auggie and Elsie and would will herself to believe that Olive knew she loved her and had forgiven her for not visiting. Elsie couldn't bring herself to think of happy times her family had shared together because her heart was in deep mourning, but she would continue to get through life in the same way she always had—one song at a time.

A long and agonizing week had passed since Elsie had laid Olive to rest. She had hardly eaten, hardly slept, and found herself sitting in her studio staring at all her equipment and at the blank piece of paper in front of her. In the past, Elsie had always found a sense of peace and excitement when she sat down with a blank notebook and a blue pen to let her thoughts take over. Something magical would happen when she started to hear a new rhythm in her mind and words started to flow onto the paper. Now when she looked at the blank piece of paper sitting on the table in front of her, she didn't see a new adventure waiting to be told. Now what she saw was a plain white piece of paper with blue horizontal lines taunting her. She didn't feel the urge or excitement to fill those lines with inspiration. Instead, she felt exactly like that piece of paper—blank. No new thoughts came to mind, no desire to tell any stories. No inspiration lived within her. She was numb, void of all emotions, lifeless, heavy, alone. The only word she could think of was a simple, six-letter word: FAMILY. She wrote that simple but emotionally complex word on the blank piece of paper, and as soon as she finished writing it, she scrawled an angry line right through the center of the word. Everyone she had ever loved was gone. Even Marie was no longer a few blocks away. She was now in New York pursuing her dreams. Elsie had no real family to turn to for support, love, advice, or help; no one to remind her that all things pass.

When Elsie's mother died, her father and grandma told stories of what a kind woman she was and what a loving mother; how she would dance around the house swinging Elsie in her arms making up silly songs; and how when her dad would come home, her mom would sing him the silly songs. After dinner, he'd get out his guitar and come up with the music to go with her mom's lyrics. Together on the covered back porch, Dad would play guitar, Mom would sing, and Elsie would laugh and dance.

Once her father died, Grandma Olive would remind Elsie how lucky she was to have had such loving parents. Even if their time together was short-lived, some children would never experience their parents' love the way Elsie had. Some parents were too caught up in their work to put their children first like her parents did. Grandma Olive always kept her parents' memory alive. Sometimes the stories she would tell during Sunday dinners seemed so real, it was as if both her parents were still there with them. Sometimes Elsie would tear up during the stories, sad that they weren't there in the flesh to celebrate her accomplishments and to watch her transform from a teenager into a young woman. Mostly though, she was just grateful that the memory of her parents' lives hadn't died when they were laid to rest.

Elsie couldn't stand sitting there any longer just staring at the blank page that had become her life. She pushed her chair backwards and worked her way to the kitchen. She opened the kitchen cabinet and saw a half-eaten box of Oreos. Immediately she was reminded of when she was a little girl sitting on her dad's lap, the two of them untwisting an Oreo and laughing about who got more of the creamy middle. Elsie would try to lick the cream off her dad's side before he'd put it in his mouth. Then he'd tickle her to try to get her side. After Elsie's dad passed, Olive made sure to have Elsie's favorite cookies in the pantry at all times, a comfort food. Sometimes Elsie would go to the kitchen, open the cupboard to see the Oreos there, smile, and then shut the cupboard and walk away. Elsie reached for the cookies, grabbed her Jeep keys, and hit the road. She needed to visit her family.

The cemetery had become a place Elsie visited frequently. After big achievements, she'd come to tell her parents how proud they would be of her. When she was sad, she'd sit next to their graves and trace their names on the headstone with her fingers, a reminder of the people who had raised and loved her.

Elsie pulled into Gate of Heaven Cemetery, turned right, and worked her way back to section seven in the far-right corner. Elsie knew this area well. Her entire family was buried here in one of the most peaceful places she'd ever known. Here, the grass was the softest she'd ever sat in. Flowers bloomed all along the sidewalks. In the left corner of the cemetery stood an old but elegant bell tower that would chime a beautiful hymn every hour on the hour.

She parked her Jeep, grabbed her cookies, and got out of her car. Although she had been here just one week ago, things already looked different. She noticed more flowers of different colors blooming all around, making the cemetery more peaceful than before. Her body was set on autopilot as she walked a familiar brick pathway, then turned left and walked through the grass directly to where her family rested only a few steps off the pathway.

She stopped and sat down on the concrete bench at the head of their graves, a bench her dad had bought many years ago for Elsie. Whenever he'd bring her to visit her mom, she'd sit in the grass next to her grave. Sometimes she'd lie in the grass looking at the sky and talking quietly to her mother. In the winter, or after it had rained, Elsie would have nowhere to sit, and her dad wanted to make sure she'd always be comfortable while visiting her mom. He bought a small concrete bench with the words, "Find Your Peace" inscribed on the backrest and had it placed at the head of her grave. Elsie looked down at the three graves before her. Her mom's and dad's were covered with thick, green grass; Olive's, with fresh dirt. Tears began to slowly trickle down her face at the thought of Olive no longer being with her.

It had only been one week. Seven days. One hundred sixty-eight hours of being without Olive, but the weight it placed on Elsie's heart, mind, and well-being made it feel like months. As selfish as it sounded, she tried not to think about losing Olive. Memories of smiles, laughter, hugs, kisses, and happy moments the two had shared flooded Elsie's mind. She reached down in her lap, grabbed an Oreo cookie, twisted it, and put the side with more cream onto her dad's headstone. She took one bite of her half of the cookie and began to talk quietly to her family.

"I'm lost," she started as small, steady tears began trickling down her cheeks. "I thought I had my life all planned out," her voice trailed off behind her sobs, "but now everything's falling apart, and I have no one." The tears came faster now. "Please, please help me figure out what to do. I'm lost without you all." She put her head down into her hands and lost herself in her tears. She stayed there until it was too dark to see the names on the gravestone that sat at her feet.

On the drive home from the cemetery, Elsie's mind was

racing with decisions. Keep the house or sell it? Move to Nashville and start a new life on her own or stay in Cincinnati? What was she going to do with all of Olive's belongings that she and Marie had spent the last week packing? Sell them, donate them? She shivered at the thought of all of Olive's belongings just sitting there in a box. Is that all we are after we're gone—a box of things to be donated?

Marie was the only person Elsie had to turn to now for help, advice, and suggestions. But Marie was miles away, where she had started her new life as a fashion designer. Elsie had never felt more alone in her life. As she turned onto Plainfield Lane, her thoughts were interrupted by a heart-stopping sight. She slowed to take it all in. Both sides of her street were lined with candles in clear jugs, a Christmas tradition her town had held for years. The townspeople would save their milk and pop jugs, cut them in half, fill the bottom with sand, and then place a small candle inside. Then at night, they would light the candles in hopes that they would guide St. Nicholas to their houses. She drove slowly, looking from side to side at the breathtakingly beautiful, candlelit street. The candles led right down her street, up the driveway to her house, and all the way to her front door. Occasionally, when someone had experienced a great loss, neighbors would light a path up to the doorstep of the bereaved to help lead the spirit of the one who had passed back home to check on their loved ones during their time of grieving. It was a heartwarming symbol reminding Elsie that the town was there for her, that they too were grieving, that she was not alone. Growing up, the bad thing about living in a small town was everyone knew everything about you. Your secrets were never a secret. Now as an adult, Elsie realized the best thing about living in a small town was that everyone knew everything about you. The town knew she no longer had a family to call her own, and they were reaching out to her, reminding her that this neighborhood knew and loved her family. She wasn't as alone as she thought she was.

She parked her car in the driveway and got out and looked back at the candlelit road, admiring the beauty, and was reminded of something her grandmother used to tell her when she was feeling down. "Ah, Elsie," she'd say, "things are never as bad as they seem. If you look hard enough, even during the darkest moments of your life, you'll always find something to be grateful for. Just remember, darkness can't exist without light. Be strong. Soon enough all of this will be in the past."

This time when Elsie's eyes filled with tears, there was a weak smile on her face. She knew this was her family's way of comforting her when she needed it most. This was her sign, the inspiration she'd been waiting for. For the first time in what felt like an eternity, she could feel the faintest glimmer of hope. She looked to the stars in the dark June sky and whispered, "Thank you." She now knew what she needed to do to get through this difficult time.

Chapter 21

What do you do when you feel like you have no one to live for, no one to disappoint but yourself? There are several choices. You can throw in the towel and say, "Forget it, I'm done," and go on living life depressed and miserable, or you can let go of all inhibitions and begin living like you've never lived before. You could live as if there is no tomorrow, as if all you have is today and the moment you are currently living. Elsie had no one else to live for and no one else to lose but herself, and she wasn't ready to give up on herself. She had lost more than enough in her lifetime, and now it was time to cash in on what life owed her, on what she'd never been given—happiness without consequence. She had everything to gain. She needed to fill the empty void inside her heart the best way she knew how—through her music. Suddenly her fear of following her dream on her own seemed obsolete. Now was the time to set all fears aside and do what she had always wanted to do— connect with as many people as possible through her music.

Immediately upon entering her house, she went straight downstairs to her studio, grabbed her guitar, a pencil, and her notebook, and began to work. New song lyrics and story ideas were flowing so quickly through her mind that her fingers could hardly keep up. Giving up on writing, she grabbed her handheld recorder and began singing her ideas. Once she felt like all her thoughts were recorded, she replayed them, taking notes and grouping her thoughts together.

To her, music was so much more than a collection of notes, chords, and lyrics. Music could tell a story, make a statement, teach an important life lesson, help her grieve, and be her only friend when she felt alone. Music had always been there to comfort her whenever she needed it. She'd listen to country when she felt sad or depressed, rock when she was stressed, and classical when she needed inspiration. She loved all genres of music, and nothing felt better than composing her own. Until recently, if Elsie had a guitar in hand, she could work through any emotion, problem, or issue. That is, until she lost Auggie and then Olive. Since then, she hadn't had the urge or motivation to write or play music. But tonight . . .

There was something about the feeling of her guitar strings under the tips of her fingers, the way the strings gently vibrated when she strummed her favorite chords. She was taken back to a time that was foggy in her memory but was still there. It was the way her mom would rock her on sleepless nights in her white wooden rocking chair that sat in the corner of her room. She heard laughter as her mom and dad chased her around the house. She smiled watching her father teach her to play guitar.

Talking about her feelings was always awkward for Elsie, but her mom knew what each of Elsie's cries meant. That always impressed Elsie's dad. When she realized her mom wasn't coming back, Elsie didn't talk much. Her father took her to a support group and counselor, but even there, Elsie sat quietly, not saying much. The counselor suggested that Elsie keep a journal, but she showed little interest in writing about her feelings. And then one day, about a year after her mom died, Elsie picked up her daddy's guitar, which had collected dust in the corner of his bedroom for more than a year, and brought it to him to play for her. Elsie found her voice through music.

"What do you want to hear, sweetie?" he asked his daughter.

"Our song," she said.

He knew what she wanted to hear. It was the song he used to sing to both his girls, his loves. He started to play and sing "Brown-Eyed Girl," and Elsie stood up and danced around the room. He hadn't seen her this happy in a while.

In the years that followed, this would be the way Elsie and her father learned to communicate. It was what they both loved and had a passion for. He would teach her how to play guitar and piano. She would make up songs just as her mom once did. He always knew what kind of day she had by what kind of music she was listening to or what kind of music she was playing. Sad songs, fast songs, angry songs . . . The days were filled with different types of music. As she grew and changed, so did her taste and style of music until she learned to find her own voice, discovering who she was through the music she'd compose.

Elsie didn't sleep that night; nor did she stop to take a break. She worked right up until sunrise. Her fingers hurt, her voice was hoarse, and she was exhausted, but in a good way. Little did she know that somewhere in those wee morning hours, fueled by heartache, loss, and confusion, a star songwriter was born.

She continued working like crazy for days, hardly stopping to eat or rest. She wouldn't, couldn't stop until she had several songs written. She was unsure of how many days had passed, but she finally came to a stopping point. With several pieces completed, she was ready to email them to the studio. Since she had missed her start date, she hoped this would prove she had been worth the wait.

After she emailed her hard work to Country Rock Studios, she turned on her phone and found about fifty missed calls from Marie. She didn't even listen to her voice mail. She just hit "2" on her speed dial and called Marie.

"You bitch!" a frazzled Marie yelled into the phone after the third ring.

"Well, hello to you too," Elsie laughed.

"Where have you been? I've been calling you for almost a week now, and you wouldn't answer!" Marie wasn't laughing; she sounded annoyed.

"A week?" Elsie was shocked.

"Yes, Elsie." Marie never used her real name unless she was mad. "I thought something had happened to you!" Marie's voice was changing from upset to concerned.

"I'm sorry, Marie. I really had no idea that it had been that long." She felt awful. She never wanted to worry Marie.

"You should be sorry!" Marie snapped. "And you owe me for a plane ticket. I'll be at your house in twenty."

"What?" Elsie was momentarily annoyed. "You flew in from New York just to check on me?"

"Yes, Els. You weren't answering phone calls or emails," Marie said. "The first week I was gone, you checked in. The second week you were completely silent. Why wouldn't I fly home?" she said, annoyed.

"Well, I hate checking both. You know that," Elsie said, trying to defend herself.

"Well, what about your landline?" Marie asked.

"Oh, yeah. Sorry, I forgot to tell you; I disconnected it," Elsie said

"And why haven't you answered your door?" Marie inquired.

"My door?!"

"Yes, your front door. I sent my mom over to check on you and you didn't answer."

"I'm sorry, I didn't hear Carol, I've been in my studio all week. And why are you so worried, Mom?" Elsie said.

"Well, you know how the saying goes: 'One flew east, one flew west, Elsie flew over the cuckoo's nest.' " Even over the phone, Elsie could tell Marie was smiling and feeling very clever for having come up with that one.

"Ha, ha, aren't you clever!" Elsie laughed.

"Well, things haven't exactly been easy for you lately." Marie's tone changed from annoyed to sympathetic. "I'll be there soon," she said as she hung up the phone.

Elsie put the phone down. Had it really been a week? Had she not showered or had a real meal in over a week? She lifted up her armpit and sniffed, then shrugged her shoulders. She didn't smell . . . all that bad. Then suddenly her stomach let out a loud, achy growl. She hadn't realized how hungry she was until now. She'd been craving junk food the entire time she'd worked in her studio. Now that she had come to a good stopping point in her work, she was going to make an attempt at cooking and eating actual meals, not granola bars, fries, or other snacks. She'd worry about going to the grocery store later; for now, she had to get ready for Marie. Elsie jumped in the shower to clean herself up before Marie barged in. If she saw her like this, she would probably hire her a nanny before going back to New York.

Twenty minutes later, Elsie was fully dressed, deodorized, and was in the kitchen trying to find a snack before Marie arrived. Her hair was still a little wet, but she didn't care. She had tried to dry her hair but felt lightheaded and shaky and had to stop. This was nothing new to Elsie. Auggie always said that one day she'd be diabetic. *Auggie.* She stopped what she was doing and grasped her hand towards her heart. Just thinking his name physically hurt her. She cursed herself for letting herself think of him. She had done so well until just now.

Elsie was snacking on some spreadable cheese and crackers when Marie barged through the front door.

"Honey, I'm home!" she hollered.

"Marie!" Elsie ran towards her with a huge smile on her face. "My amazing friend who came all this way to check on me!" she said in an over-the-top cheesy voice.

"Yeah, yeah. Quit trying to suck up to me. I'm going to be upset with you for a while." She leaned down and hugged her small friend then asked, "Hungry?"

"Starved!" Elsie answered.

"The usual?" Marie asked.

"You know it!" Elsie said.

She grabbed her purse and they headed out the door to Skyline Chili. Nothing tasted more like home than what Cincinnatians have come to know and love as a Skyline Chili Cheese Coney—beanless chili on top of a hotdog and served with onion and mustard on a bun. As usual, Skyline was packed. Elsie and Marie were too hungry to wait for a table, so they ordered take-out and headed back to Elsie's house.

Back at Elsie's, girl talk was in full swing. Marie had left for New York a day after Olive's funeral, so she and Elsie had some catching up to do. Although Marie hadn't been there long, she was already adjusting well in the Big Apple and at her new job. She loved her loft apartment and was already settled in, mostly because it was small and Marie didn't have very much stuff. Marie couldn't stop talking about how much she loved her new job and how well she was fitting in. She loved the fast pace of the city and the nightlife. Elsie laughed as Marie told her about all the interesting nightclubs and some of the people she'd met. She was surprised to hear that Marie wasn't yet dating anyone.

Even if it was only for a quick visit, it was nice having Marie home. As usual, Marie made Elsie feel alive again. When she was around, Elsie didn't think of Dr. Dream Smasher or losing Olive. The best friends had gone through some major life changes over the past six weeks, but Elsie knew their friendship was strong enough to survive any change. They would always be able to pick up wherever they left off, and Marie would always have the ability to make Elsie momentarily forget about her troubles. When Marie's stories seemed to finally be coming to an end, Elsie couldn't help herself. She had been biting her tongue for far too long.

"So, what's his name?" Elsie inquired eagerly with a huge smile on her face.

"I don't know what you're talking about, Els . . ." Marie was blushing.

"Marie! You never blush, and you never go more than a few months without a new love interest. So, what's his name?!" Elsie was intrigued.

"Well, he's not my boyfriend, if that's what you're implying. He's actually a little older than I am, and he lives in my building." She was smiling ear to ear.

"What? Not your boyfriend?!" Elsie was very curious. This was very unlike the Marie she knew. Whenever Marie liked someone, he would become her boyfriend within days, and if not, he wasn't worth her time. "Tell me more!" Elsie begged.

"Well, we met in the elevator. He lives on level ten, where all the rich people live. He is single, very cute, and is a lawyer." Marie was gushing.

"A lawyer?!? That doesn't sound like your type," Elsie said. "I like him already!"

"I know; I do too. He's different from any of the other guys I've dated, Els. He's, well, he's . . ." Marie's voice trailed off as she tried to put her thumb on it.

"A keeper," Elsie offered. "And you've never dated a keeper

before."

"Yes, he's a keeper." Marie sighed and then added, "If I were to date him, I know that just dating wouldn't be enough, and I don't know if I'm ready for that yet." Marie had never been this honest about a man before, not even to Elsie.

"So, what's this cute lawyer's name, and why haven't I heard about him before now?" Elsie asked.

"His name is Kyle Conway, but I just call him Sexy." She winked at Elsie and laughed. "And you would have already heard about him if you'd have answered your damn phone!" she snarled at her friend in between bites of food.

"Man, I'm full," Marie groaned, trying to change the topic. She stood up and walked over to the garbage can. Elsie was right behind her. "Bet they don't have Skyline in New York!" Elsie teased Marie as they threw away their trash "Nope, they sure don't. But they do have thousands and thousands of sexy Kyles." Marie moved her eyebrows up and down and laughed.

"Oh, I'm sure they do!" Elsie laughed along with Marie.

"You should come and visit, Els," Marie began. "You know, once things get settled here." Marie gave her a sympathetic smile.

"Don't worry, you can't get rid of me just by moving to the Big Apple!" Elsie smiled.

They were walking out of the kitchen towards the living room when Marie turned to her friend and said, "So, what were you so busy working on that you couldn't answer your best friend's phone calls?" And she began walking towards the stairs that led to the basement studio.

"Marie—" Elsie began but was cut off.

"Come on, if you're going to share with the world, you can share with your best friend!" she yelled up the stairs to Elsie.

"Don't mess with my stuff!" She chased after her.

"Play me your new songs," Marie insisted as soon as Elsie walked into the studio.

"Only if you agree to be brutally honest and not give me that oh-my-friend's-so-talented bull crap!" Elsie instructed.

"I may be partial, but you do have skills!" Marie debated.

Elsie grabbed her guitar off its stand in the corner, sat down on her stool, and started with her first song, "Crazy Girl." After she finished singing and playing several songs, Marie just stared at her, speechless. Elsie was used to having Marie interrupt her during her songs to give her input, but this time she had just sat quietly and listened. Elsie's stomach felt queasy, and her palms and forehead began to sweat. She wasn't sure what to make of Marie's silence. Elsie was used to playing for Marie and Olive, so playing for Marie wasn't anything new, but these songs were different from songs she'd written in the past. These songs had already been submitted to the recording studio for a possible job. These songs could make or break the start of her career.

Finally, Elsie broke the silence. "Dammit!" she exclaimed, "They're awful, aren't they? Go ahead; you can tell me."

"Actually, Els," Marie began, "those are the best songs I've ever heard you come up with."

"Seriously?" Elsie was shocked. "Come on, Marie, I'm a big girl; I can take it." Elsie got up from her stool and placed her guitar back on the stand. "Tell me what you really think."

"I'm serious, Els, I know we tease and give each other a hard time, but this—" she paused and gestured towards the sheet of music on the desk where Elsie was just sitting. "This is different. These songs—they're radio-worthy. They could be big!" Marie said, wide-eyed.

"Seriously, Marie?" Elsie was still shocked.

"Seriously, Els. And I'm not even a country fan!" Marie's voice was serious, and her face reflected complete awe of her friend's creative mind.

She could tell by the way Marie was acting that she wasn't just telling her they were good to make her feel better about herself. She was being truthful. She realized that her songs had been submitted to her producer, and by now he had listened to them. Her fate was in his hands. Suddenly, she was completely overwhelmed. She started to feel shaky, and her stomach was churning like she was going to be sick.

Something inside her didn't feel right. Then it hit her. "I think I'm going to be sick!" she said as she ran to the bathroom.

"What?!" Marie was confused. "That must have been some adrenaline rush!"

"It's not!" Elsie called from inside the bathroom. Marie rushed into the bathroom. It only took one look at Elsie to know something wasn't right. Her face was pale white, and her hands were shaking as she tried to brace herself upright while leaning over the toilet seat.

"Geez, Els," Marie ran to her side. "You're white as a ghost."

"Something's seriously wrong, Marie," Elsie said in between puking. "My stomach has never hurt this bad. And, I—I can't stop shaking," she said in a weak voice. Panicked, Elsie begged Marie, "Take me to the hospital—now!"

Marie grabbed a puke bucket, Elsie's wallet, and keys, and headed out to the car. After she put everything into the car, she went back downstairs to her friend. This was when the extra height she had on Elsie came into good use. She gently picked up Elsie, carried her upstairs, opened the car door, and laid her in the backseat of her car. Luckily, Cincinnati Central Hospital was only ten minutes away. Marie pulled into the circular entrance of the emergency room and helped Elsie out of the car and into the waiting room while a man valet-parked the car. After an IV bag of fluid, Elsie was re-hydrated. Dr. Isaac explained to Elsie that her blood work had come back and all tests were pointing to her having early diabetes. Elsie wasn't surprised. She knew that it was going to take time to learn to control her sugar levels through what she ate and exercise, but she had watched Olive manage hers for years. She knew if her grandmother could do it, then so could she. Several hours later, Marie dropped off Elsie at home.

"You sure you're going to be okay?" Marie asked before pulling away.

"Eventually I will be," she said, shrugging her shoulders, then added, "Please don't feel bad for me. I've been mentally preparing myself for this for years, everyone else in my family had it, so why wouldn't I?" she shrugged, but she could tell her friend was worried. "You heard the doctor," she tried to reassure her. "I'm young and overall in good shape. She said she thinks I'll be okay through managing my diet and exercise. I will be fine. I'll go see a specialist and I will do what they tell me to do, I promise."

The two friends hugged and said their goodbyes, and Elsie walked inside as Marie drove away. Elsie woke up the next morning feeling surprisingly rested. She was grateful that for once, she had been able to turn off all her thoughts and actually sleep. Of course, she chalked it up to all the medicines she'd been given in the ER the night before. She rolled over to her side and looked at the clock sitting on the nightstand. It was almost noon. She wasn't surprised since by the time she had gotten out of the shower and into bed it was close to two a.m.

She stretched and was glad to feel that the cramping in her lower abdomen was gone. The stress that the cramping had put on her lower back was feeling better too.

She saw that the message light was flashing on her phone. Normally, she'd ignore it, but she remembered her promise to Marie. She picked up her iPhone and saw three messages from Marie and two missed calls. She sighed and checked her messages first.

"Just checking in . . ." from Marie at one a.m.; then another message from Marie at ten a.m.: "Still feeling okay?" with an emoji face with a mask on; and from ten minutes ago: "I'm not boarding this plane till I hear from you."

Elsie quickly typed: "Get on that plane before I de-friend you . . . lol xoxox," and hit send. Marie sent her back a thumbs-up with an airplane and then, "Check in with you later," and a heart.

Elsie looked at her missed calls. No surprise, one was from Marie. There was another missed call, though, and it was from Johnny from Country Rock Studios. She quickly sat up in bed and hit play to listen to his voice mail.

"Elsie McCormick? Johnny here. Just wanted to let you know I got your songs, and I think you're really onto something, kiddo. I have some ideas I want to run by you. Give me a call and we can talk some more." Elsie was speechless as she continued listening to the message. Johnny was interrupted by a female voice in the background. Elsie could faintly hear something along the lines of, "Are you talking to Elsie? I want to say something," and Johnny protesting, but the female voice was talking over him. "Elsie, this is Kate, Kate McCord. You might not know me, but I'm someone you're going to want to get to know. I heard your demo yesterday in Johnny's office, and I know a good song when I hear one. I want to work with you! Call Johnny back, please and thank you!"

After Kate finished, Johnny's voice came back on. "Sorry. That was Kate. As you can tell, we are all very excited to hear back from you. Talk soon!"

Elsie couldn't believe what she had heard. She needed to listen again. She hit replay and listened to Johnny and Kate's message again in its entirety. After she listened for the second time and fully processed the message, she sprang from her bed and jumped up and down in excitement. A famous country music producer and manager liked her music! A combination of excitement, disbelief, worry, and relief were consuming her body. She wasn't sure what would come of this, but she didn't really care. The fact that Johnny Scott liked her music was an accomplishment in and of itself. She flopped back down on her bed and replayed the message again as she stared up at the ceiling and envisioned her future working in the music industry.

Two weeks had passed since her phone conversation with Johnny and Kate. Since then, Elsie had been busy getting everything lined up. She wasn't ready to let her childhood home and all its memories go, so she asked Marie's mom, Carol, to stop by periodically and check in on everything. Since she had been newly diagnosed with diabetes, before she left she had to attend a few health classes on how to properly manage her blood sugar levels and modify her eating habits.

She stayed occupied during the day, keeping busy getting the house ready, running errands, and doing as much research as she possibly could on Kate McCord and Johnny at Country Rock Studios. She used the computer in her studio to investigate. She typed in "Kate McCord" and hit search. Several images and articles came up. Elsie clicked on the first image. It looked like a Glamour Shot. At first glance, Kate McCord was quite pretty. She had long, curly brown hair filled with a mixture of caramel and blonde highlights, greenish-blue eyes, flawless tan skin, and straight, almost too-white teeth. Elsie clicked on the next picture. It was of Kate in a bikini on the beach, and it looked like a professional picture. She had long, slender legs, a tiny waist, and was very busty. Kate McCord looked like a supermodel.

She clicked on the first article with Kate's name in it. It was an article from a local Alabama hometown newspaper. She began skimming the article. To Elsie's surprise, Katherine

"Kate" McCord was only seventeen years old and had just graduated from high school in May! She had won homecoming and prom queen, had several leads in the drama club, was captain of the cheer squad, and had been voted by her class as "Most Likely to Succeed." Elsie continued scrolling through the article. Kate had started modeling when she was only fourteen years old.

Well, that explains the bikini pic, Elsie said to herself as she continued to read.

Kate was the youngest of five children—four older brothers, all of whom were successful or were on a successful career path. Her parents were the owners of several businesses and restaurants in their hometown. Kate's oldest brother played football for the Texans. The second oldest had already started his own finance business. The third and fourth oldest were twin brothers, sophomores in college, and had full-ride scholarships.

Elsie thought to herself, *Geez! What did their parents feed those kids to make them all so successful?* She continued reading.

When Kate was asked about her plans for the future, she said she'd like to pursue a career in acting, singing, and modeling—*all three*! Elsie clicked on a YouTube video of Kate singing the national anthem at Madeira High School's last home football game and watched in awe. Kate dazzled the crowd. Her voice was powerful, yet graceful. Elsie could tell Kate was right at home being the center of attention and had a natural ability to captivate those around her. When she finished, the crowd went wild, standing and cheering and chanting her name. Kate just stood there smiling, waving, and blowing kisses to the crowd. The look on Kate's face was the same look Elsie had whenever she finished writing and singing her own songs—a look of pride, joy, and a natural high. Elsie stared at the screen. Kate was good at everything. Elsie had a feeling she was going to get to know this Kate McCord very well, very soon.

Within the next five months, Elsie would move to Nashville and become more successful than she had planned. She and Kate hit it off instantly. Kate reminded her of Marie—energetic, free-spirited, good at everything she put her mind to, and easy to love. Elsie agreed to write music for Kate and to be a backup singer and guitar player, but Elsie's role would quickly change. One day in the studio, Kate was having a hard time singing "Crazy Girl." No matter how many times they recorded, Kate just didn't have enough passion and anger in her voice. She was too young and too naive. She hadn't experienced enough pain, loss, and suffering in life to sing the words with authenticity. No matter how many times Elsie worked with Kate to try and make her feel the passion behind the song, when it boiled down to it, Kate McCord's life experiences were just too good to allow her to convey the rawness and pain one could hear in Elsie's voice on the demo tape. After days of recording and re-recording "Crazy Girl," the song just wasn't right. Finally, out of pure exhaustion, Kate asked Elsie to sing it in the studio to show her how to do it.

All the pent-up anger from the way Auggie had left her came pouring out through the song lyrics. The overwhelming heartache of Olive's death and the realization that all her loved ones were gone transported Elsie to another place—a place where all that she saw was ugly and painful and dark. She sang as if she was trapped in a room full of people moving in every direction, and she was standing still screaming for someone to stop and notice how much pain she was in. In only one recording, Elsie nailed the song.

Heard she got a tattoo of his name
In her mind, oh everything's still the same
Yeah, she thinks he's hers to be claimed

Well, crazy girl, I'm tired of your head games
They're not okay
'Cause it's been two years of him and me
When's that crazy ex gonna see
He left her to be with me
He's blocked her number
Changed his locks
Come by again
We're calling the cops
Well now it's time you deal with me
Crazy girl, get a life
Dun, Dun, Dun, Dun
Crazy girl, get a life . . .

She finished singing, and everyone exploded with applause. It took her several moments to remember where she was and what she'd been doing. Without realizing it, Elsie McCormick had just determined her fate, and she did it with one recording.

PRESENT DAY

Chapter 22

Six months had passed and Elsie was recovering incredibly well. After six weeks in the ICU, she was moved to the long-term rehabilitation unit. There, she received daily physical and occupational therapy. Auggie had been right; from the nurse's notes in Elsie's chart, ever since Marie arrived at the hospital, she practically never left Elsie's side. She was still her pushy self, and most nights she found a way to convince the nurses to let her stay long past visiting hours.

His way of keeping his distance, but still knowing that Elsie was recovering well, was through checking the notes in her chart, sometimes multiple times a day. Half of him felt guilty for reading her progress notes, like he was invading her privacy, but the other half of him was convinced that it was his responsibility to double-check all her doctors' work to ensure she was receiving the best care possible.

Months of not seeing her in person were eating away at him. He was so close to her, yet still so far away from where he wanted to be; right by her side, helping her recover and, of course, apologizing to her every moment he could.

He didn't know how much longer he could stay away from her, until one day he checked her chart and felt as if his heart had stopped beating as he read the following progress note: "The patient has been cleared for discharge." A sentence he'd been simultaneously eagerly awaiting but also dreading. He wanted her to be healthy enough to leave the hospital, but selfishly he wasn't ready to let her go again.

After reading her discharge instructions, he knew his time was now or never. He grabbed the letter, a letter long overdue, explaining everything, from why he had left her the way he did to his involvement in her care the night she came into the ER, shoved it in his lab coat pocket, and rushed out of his office. He had thought he'd have more notification before her discharge and had planned on leaving the letter in her room along with a vase full of calla lilies. He had been monitoring her daily routine. Every night after dinner, Marie would leave to spend time with her husband and Elsie would go to the gym before heading back to her room for the evening. He planned to wait for Elsie to go to the gym, then he could quickly sneak into her room and leave the letter. He wanted to ensure that she received his apology alone, without Marie around.

He waited until 5:25 p.m. and, from the second floor, peered down at the cafeteria to see Elsie hugging Marie at the door. After parting ways, Marie approached the front door while Elsie turned the opposite way and walked towards the patients' elevators.

From the nurse's notes, Elsie went to the gym from 6:30 p.m. until 7:30 p.m. Nurse change was at 7:30. He planned to wait until 7:00 p.m., when the night shift nurses began to arrive. During that time the unit would be chaotic as the night shift nurses were updated by the day shift nurses. They'd be occupied and less likely to notice Auggie coming into the unit and going into her room.

His plan worked perfectly. By 7:15 p.m., all the nurses were too busy with shift change to even notice him. He briskly walked into Elsie's room and set the letter down on her nightstand. As he was turning to leave, he heard the bathroom door open behind him and a voice from his past say, "Good evening, Doctor, everything still on track for my discharge tomorrow?" she asked in a hopeful tone.

This isn't going to go well, Auggie thought to himself. He took a deep breath and tried to brace himself for what was about to come.

"Doctor?" the woman asked a second time.

"Please don't freak out," he said as he turned around to face Elsie.

A look of confusion, shock, and then pure rage spread across her face. "What are you doing here!" she yelled as she stood, shocked, frozen in place, not knowing what to do.

"Els," Auggie said calmly. "Please let me explain," he quickly pleaded with his hands out in front of his body in a defensive position.

"Explain?" she snorted. "You're about seven years too late for an explanation, Dr. Owens." She yelled louder this time. "And don't call me 'Els' and get the hell out of my room!" she commanded.

"Miss McCormick," Angela, her nurse, said, running into her room. "What's the matter?" she asked, confused.

"I want this man out of here, and I never want him to step foot in my room again!" Elsie furiously pointed her finger at Auggie as she demanded that Angela have him removed.

"Elsie, please," Auggie pleaded, "please just give me a chance to explain." He wanted nothing more than the chance to finally apologize and talk to her.

"Miss McCormick," Angela said. "This is Dr. Owens," she began to explain, only to be interrupted.

"Oh, believe me, I know who he is!" she snapped as she glared at him.

"No, I'm not sure you understand," Angela said, approaching her and placing her hand on her shoulder. "Dr. Gus is a very, very talented doctor. He was the trauma specialist working in the ER the night of your accident. He took care of you," she clarified.

Elsie briefly made eye contact with Auggie long enough for her to see his deep blue eyes swimming in the sea of painful memories of her unrecognizable body. Then she looked to Angela, urging her to continue.

"Without Dr. Gus, well, frankly, you wouldn't be alive today. He's the doctor who brought you back to life, Miss. He saved you." Angela said as she gently patted Elsie on the back reassuringly.

Elsie was in shock. After a moment of silence, she looked at Auggie, threw her hands in the air, and said, "Of course you did! Un-freaking-believable!" and then stormed out of the room.

Angela looked at Dr. Owens and asked, "Anything you wanna explain, Doctor?"

"We're, um, old friends," he said. "I'm sure once I talk to her I will be able to calm her down. Just give me a few minutes."

Angela nodded and said sternly, "You better go get your affairs in order, Dr. Gus, so I don't have to call security."

"Will do," he said, racing out of the room.

Elsie was already out of the unit and walking down the long main hallway before he caught up to her. He pleaded, "Elsie, please stop so we can talk."

She threw her hands up in the air, implying that she had heard him, but wasn't going to stop to listen to him. She continued to walk angrily down the hall.

"Elsie," he said again, this time with a little more authority in his voice, "You're still recovering and shouldn't be walking this fast, you could hurt yourself. Please, stop!" he said as he quickened his pace and was only a few steps behind her.

Before he knew what was coming, she stopped walking,

turned around, and slapped him square in the face. Caught off guard, he stumbled and braced himself against the wall.

"You have some nerve, Auggie!" she yelled as she furiously shook her finger in his face.

"I deserved that," he said, rubbing his freshly slapped pink cheek. Then he asked, "You feel better now?"

"No!" she shouted. "That's nothing, and I mean nothing, compared to what you deserve!"

"Everything alright here, Dr. Owens?" another doctor asked as he passed them in the hallway.

"Yes, everything is fine. Miss McCormick and I were just heading to the conference room to discuss her, um, plan of care," he looked at Elsie with pleading eyes, willing her to go along with his story.

She folded her arms across her chest and continued to stare him dead in the eyes. "Thank you for your concern, sir, but believe me, I know better than to try to argue with Dr. Owens. In the end he always gets what he wants, no matter the cost," she snarled as she moved to the side and flipped her long brown hair towards Auggie. "After you, DOC-TOR," she pronounced doctor as if she were addressing His Royal Highness and gestured for him to lead the way.

Auggie led them to a private conference room across the hall, shut the door, and closed the shade in order to keep anyone from seeing the wrath of Elsie he was about to endure.

"Go ahead, get it all out of your system," he said, sitting down, knowing he'd be there for a while. He remained silent as he stared straight at her. For twenty-three minutes, with bright red cheeks and flaring nostrils, she let out years of pent-up anger.

Finally, she stopped. Emotionally exhausted, she sat down in a chair on the opposite side of the table, looked across at him, and said, "Now I feel a little, and I mean only a little bit better."

"I deserved every bit of that," he said as he folded his hands together and rested them on the table.

"Well, at least we can agree on something!" she sassed as she rolled her eyes.

"What I did to you," his voice cracked a little as he thought back to the night he left her, "was beyond awful," he said, too ashamed to look her in the face.

"You have no idea!" She shook her head and looked up towards the ceiling, willing herself not to cry.

"I know that you will most likely never forgive me for what I did," he looked back at Elsie, then added, "and that's a cross I'll have to bear."

"You're right, I won't," she said as she shook her head, still in disbelief that he was not only sitting across the table from her, but that this conversation was actually happening.

"Will you please give me five minutes to apologize and explain why I left the way that I did?" he pleaded. "I know now it wasn't the right thing to do."

She sat quietly for a few minutes, debating. She had waited seven years for an explanation but now that she saw him begging her to listen, she felt he didn't deserve five minutes of her time. However, deep down she knew she needed to hear what he had to say to officially give her the closure she'd longed for.

"Five minutes and not a second more. Then I walk out that door and I never, and I mean never, want to see or hear from you again. Are we clear?" she said sternly.

"Understood." He nodded and quickly continued on before she had a chance to change her mind. "I'm not asking you for forgiveness because I know I don't deserve it," he said. "Looking back now, I know what I did was horrible. I know I handled the entire situation poorly, and if I could take it back, I would. I would redo it all, and I would make it right. I wouldn't have left you the way I did. I wouldn't have left you at all . . ."

"Stop right there!" She stood up and began walking towards the door. "You don't get to say shit like you wouldn't have left me, because YOU DID LEAVE ME! And not only did you leave me, you ghosted me in every possible way with NO explanation!" she screamed, as tears began to stream down her face.

"You're right, you're right. I'm sorry. Please don't go, please let me finish explaining," he said, jumping out of his chair and beating her to the door, blocking her only way out.

Watching him race her to the door reminded her of their first date, when he had been late and she assumed he had stood her up. Needing to blow off steam, she had grabbed her guitar and walked out the apartment door, planning to head home to her studio. The next thing she knew, he had pulled into her driveway and run to her truck. He'd placed his hand on her truck's door and pleaded for her to listen to his explanation. Thinking back to how their relationship began made her cry harder. She turned her back to him, knowing that she couldn't bear to look at him any longer without completely breaking down.

"You might not believe anything I'm about to tell you, but seven years of carrying this guilt has practically made me dead inside. So, I'm going to continue," he said, stepping away from the door and moving to the other side of the room to try to see her face.

"I didn't get the job at Vanderbilt. I thought I was going to get it but I didn't," he explained.

"Wait, what? You didn't get the job?" she asked, wiping the tears from her face, still unable to look at him.

"No, I was planning on telling you—"

"What, did your pride get in the way?" she snarled. "So, you decided to just leave me instead of admitting you actually failed at something in your life," she said, lashing out in anger.

"Yes, I was embarrassed, but I planned on telling you. There's so much more to the story if you'd please just let me finish explaining," he begged.

She glanced at him and said, "I'll give you three more minutes. Talk fast."

Not wanting to waste any time, he quickly said, "When Vanderbilt called me and told me I didn't get the job, I was shocked but quickly turned angry when they told me who got the job over me. It was Bobbie. They gave my job to Bobbie," he said.

She looked at him, confused.

"You were right about Bobbie. She was jealous of what we had and told me that she was still in love with me. She applied for the Vanderbilt just to try to keep us apart."

"That bitch!" she exclaimed and quickly looked him in the face to confirm he was telling the truth. From her experience, his expression appeared honest; however, she wasn't sure what to believe anymore.

"You're telling me, she fooled me for ten years!" he retorted. "I'm sorry I didn't listen to you." He was sincere in his apology. "There's more though. The night I went to confront her, she practically backed me into a corner and kissed me."

"You cheated on me!" Elsie screamed with angry tears refilling her eyes.

"No, she kissed me and I told her to stop! I was in love with you, not her. What she did was unforgivable and I haven't talked to her since. I swear."

"Right," she mocked him. Feeling defeated, she sat down, not knowing what to believe or say.

"The next day, I came to your house to tell you everything about Bobbie and the job, but you weren't there, you were out running errands." Auggie paused, taking the time to choose his words carefully, knowing what he was about to tell her was a sensitive topic.

"Olive could tell something wasn't right, she asked me, and well, you know Olive," he said with a chuckle, trying to lighten the mood. "She was determined to get the truth out of me, so I told her I didn't get the job in Nashville and I was scared of disappointing you. But the worst was yet to come." He swallowed hard.

"Olive told me that it was good that I didn't get the job and encouraged me to let you go."

"Stop lying," she interrupted him as she stood up and began pacing. "There's no way you told Olive all of that and she didn't tell me anything." Elsie's cheeks were flushed with frustration. "She knew how much I loved you. She would never tell you to leave me."

"I understand why you would feel that way, but I have absolutely no reason to lie to you anymore. I already lost you, so I have nothing else to lose," he said, standing up and walking towards her. "Believe me, none of this is easy for me to admit!"

"Olive and I didn't keep secrets from each other. She loved me!" Elsie's voice began to crack at the thought of Olive.

"She did love you and was extremely protective of you. So protective that she wanted you to have everything in life and thought that I'd only hold you back from advancing in your career."

"She'd never tell you to leave and break my heart the way you did," she said with a cold, straight face.

"She told me that she never had a chance to follow her dreams and was going to do everything in her power to help yours come true. She encouraged me to leave you."

"No, she'd never do that!" she said, shaking her head in denial.

"I know you wish that what I'm saying is all a lie, but it's not. It's the truth," he defended himself. "Think about it. Seven years ago, if I would have told you what Olive said to me, you wouldn't have believed me just like you don't believe me now. And then what? You would have asked Olive and I have no idea what she would have told you. She could have told you the truth or just said that I was lying. Who knows? Either way, I knew she didn't want me in your way. She knew I loved you but she also knew how hard you've worked to make it in the music industry. And she wouldn't let you throw away your chance at a career for anyone, not even me. I didn't want to cause any drama with the only relative you have." Auggie said. "So, what was I supposed to do?"

"You should have told me the truth and let me figure it out for myself, Auggie! Instead, you decided our future for the both of us!" She was crying now.

"I know that now and I am so incredibly sorry."

"Don't! Don't apologize anymore. The way you left me . . ." she was crying so hard she could hardly talk as the memories of a broken and lost Elsie from years ago came to life in her memory.

"A part of me died the day you left!" She was having trouble catching her breath as she added, "Before I could even begin to heal, I went home and found Olive dead. She died, and I," she sobbed, "I wasn't there for her because I was too busy crying over you!"

"I am so sorry," he apologized, walking towards her, wanting more than anything in the world to hold and comfort her. His eyes welled with tears at the thought of broken-hearted Elsie finding Olive dead.

"You should be!" she screamed, wiping her tears and snot on her hands. "And now," she gasped for air, "I want nothing to do with you anymore! Stay out of my life!" she sobbed as she stormed out of the door.

He followed behind her but stopped a few steps down the hallway. He wanted nothing more than to run after her, take her into his arms, and tell her how much he still loved her, but he knew he'd caused her a lifetime of pain. As he watched her storm away, he cried quietly to himself, "Goodbye, Elsie."

FIVE YEARS AGO

Chapter 23

So just where had Augustus Owens disappeared to all those years ago? Although he didn't care for his father, this was the one time in his life that having the last name of Owens, son of the Doctor Bruce Owens of the LA Plastic Surgery Center, had worked to his advantage. He moved to LA, mentioned his father, and immediately had his choice of working at any hospital in the city. No, he was not proud of getting his job by name-dropping, but he needed a place for a fresh start, and here he knew that's what he could get.

Deleting himself from her world was easier than he had anticipated. A quick click of a button and his profile was erased from the internet. A quick click of the mouse and all their pictures were deleted from her computer and saved onto his personal memory device. And with a swipe of his finger, all of his messages were permanently deleted from her phone. As far as the cyber world was concerned, just a simple click and Auggie Owens no longer existed.

Moving without Elsie knowing was much more challenging. A week before he left, he began packing up his apartment. He found time while Elsie was asleep, visiting Olive, or with Marie. Gathering his belongings from her room and all the things he had given her was much harder to do. He waited until after she had fallen asleep the night of the concert and then quietly put all those things in a box while tears streamed down his face. A suitcase of his clothes and that box were the only two things in his car with him that night when he drove off. He couldn't bring himself to throw those things away. It may have been wrong for him to keep those things and all of their photos, but he knew that if he left them for Elsie, she'd cling to the possibility of the life she so desperately wanted them to have. He wanted the best for her. He wanted her to find someone who could be there for her every night, every weekend, every holiday, to celebrate the small things and big things that life was about to bring her. A clean break would be easier for her to deal with, to erase his existence from her life. She would have memories, but eventually they would fade. He, however, wanted to hold onto those possessions for as long as he could so he could torture himself with them and remind himself that he was never good enough for her. He didn't deserve her. To look at that shoebox of treasured memories would be a constant reminder to him that if you really loved someone, sometimes the best thing you could do for them was let them go.

Auggie arrived in LA an empty, hollow shell of a man. The months to follow were the most difficult months of his life, only comparable to the months after his mother died. Emptiness, anger, confusion, and bitterness consumed every ounce of his body, and the only person he could blame was himself. After settling in LA, Auggie couldn't control the urge to call her or to look at her picture he still had on his phone. He began to doubt everything he had done and hated himself. He tried to release his frustrations by working. He'd pick up extra shifts to cover when his coworkers needed off. He'd work a double shift and sleep in the on-call room for a couple of hours only to wake up and do it all again. Having his mind constantly focused on work helped to keep his thoughts off of Elsie and his loneliness at bay until sickness and pure exhaustion would overtake his body. After a couple days off work to catch up on sleep, thoughts of Elsie would consume him. She was everywhere he looked. He tried to distract himself by working out. If he wasn't running, he was lifting weights at the gym. Every time he turned on music on his phone and began to run, his thoughts would drift to one of the many concerts they had been to together and her beautiful voice. Elsie's voice, talent, smile, and laugh were in every song he heard. He couldn't take it anymore. He ripped the headphones out of his phone and threw them in the trash. On the drive home, he turned off his radio and drove in complete silence. At home, he couldn't even turn on his TV. Every show he watched reminded him of a movie or show they had watched together. He found himself reading anything medical he could get his hands on—journals, his old anatomy books. After months of living in silence at home and concentrating solely on work, he hated himself even more and wanted to run to Elsie and beg for forgiveness. He knew if he explained to her why he had done what he did and explained that he was wrong, she'd forgive him, and they'd find some way to work it out. And that was the problem. Elsie was far too selfless. She had, and always would, put his needs and wants before her own.

Auggie knew what he needed to do to make himself move on from Elsie McCormick. Late one night, after one of his shifts had ended, he headed to a bar several blocks away from his apartment. It had been a long, hard, unsuccessful day in the ER. He had lost several patients that night in a freak roofing accident. All he wanted to do was pick up the phone and call his Elsie just to hear her voice. And that's what he planned on doing, but first he had to get drunk enough to go back on what he had spent the last several months trying to convince himself was the right thing to do. He pounded several beers as he sat by himself and looked at pictures of her on his phone. He punched her number into his phone several times only to hit clear instead of call. As he struggled, a nurse from work named Stephanie sat down next to him and ordered him another beer. There they sat, drinking beer after beer and carrying on with small talk until the bartender announced last call. They both drunkenly stumbled back to Auggie's apartment. The next morning Auggie woke up feeling sick with regret as he looked over to see Stephanie lying in bed next to him. At that moment he knew that even if he wanted to go back to Elsie, now he couldn't. He was no longer good enough to exist in Elsie McCormick's world. Before Stephanie, he could have begged and pleaded for Elsie to forgive him and take him back, but he knew she'd never forgive him for a one-night stand.

He was no longer the good guy she fell in love with. Auggie had purposefully sabotaged his own life thinking he was doing what was best for her life—even though it was her choice to make, not his. All those months of trying to convince himself that a clean break was what was best for Elsie was really what he needed, not her. Elsie would have wanted to try. She would have wanted them to make the move together and try to make their worlds co-exist. Even if Auggie knew it wouldn't work, Elsie needed to see it to believe it. Leaving her the way he had was more for him, not her. He quietly rolled out of bed, turned on the shower in the bathroom so Stephanie couldn't hear, and sat on the floor and cried.

Sometimes love makes you do things you never knew you were capable of doing. Auggie loved Elsie, and he needed to let her go in such a way that he'd never be able to return. Some would argue that this was not how you show love. Auggie was repeating the actions his father had shown him when he was just a kid. His father loved his mother, and after her death he tried to forget her by throwing himself into one meaningless relationship after another. And just like that—after all the years of trying to be nothing like his father—Auggie suddenly realized that he was following precisely in his father's footsteps, and he hated himself even more. But it was too late; there was no turning back. He would never be Auggie to anyone ever again. From that day on, Auggie no longer existed, only Dr. Gus.

. . . Until one day when he woke up at four thirty in the morning as he always did. He showered, made his cup of coffee to go, hopped in his car, and headed to work. Normally he listened to a news channel while driving in, but on this particular day, he decided to do something he had been avoiding for years. He decided to listen to the country channel. The announcer was talking about a new single having just been released. The artist was just getting around to releasing some songs she'd composed towards the start of her career.

"Here's Elsie McCormick with her new single, 'Pieces,' " the announcer said. Auggie's mouth dropped open as he braced himself to hear her voice, the voice of his first love. Over the years he had randomly Googled her name just to confirm that he had made the right decision and that she was making it in the music industry, but he had never listened to her music. She had one of the most amazing voices he'd ever heard. Listening to her music was like reopening a jagged scar that had never completely healed. As his car was filled with Elsie's voice, he was filled with conflicting emotions. His mind was racing, his eyes began to water, and he willed himself to move his hand to change the station, but he couldn't. Hearing her voice on the radio filled him with pride. He had always wanted her to succeed, for her talents to be exposed, and for her to follow her dreams.

You're the missing piece to the puzzle
That I used to call my life

Blue eyes, who knew I'd find you
When gray skies were all I'd seen
And nighttime had been so lonely
Year after year

Well, Blue Eyes were my summer skies
On a rainy September night

You stood there at the entrance
Holding an umbrella meant for two
One smile and I was taken
To a future, me and you

Blue Eyes, who knew you'd save me
From a lifetime full of hate
Well, Blue Eyes were my summer skies
On a rainy September night.

When the song ended and her sweet voice was gone, he panicked, not knowing when he'd ever hear her again. In that moment he realized that he'd been wrong in trying to convince himself that what he did was best for her; in reality, what he did was easiest for him. It had been easy to leave and start a new life somewhere else. In leaving her, he was leaving the old Auggie behind—the Auggie who couldn't find a balance between love and a career. He believed he could forget Elsie's existence and erase her memory, but this was just a cowardly way of running from his issues, just like his dad had done. Auggie couldn't balance his personal and professional life, so he convinced himself that Elsie needed a successful professional life to be happy, just as he did. Now, with almost five years of a successful career under his belt, he realized he still wasn't happy. And he would never make peace with himself again until he stopped picking at his scar and found a way to do what he should have done years ago—give Elsie the explanation and apology she deserved. It was time to grow up, to be a real man, to stop following in his dad's footsteps and finally make his own path. Shortly after this realization, things began to fall into place. A job opened up in Cincinnati, and a little voice in his head told him that it was time to return to where it had all started.

PRESENT DAY

Chapter 24

Flowers were blooming, and the woods behind Elsie's house were full of vibrant spring colors. Nearly eight months had passed since Elsie's accident. Her months had been filled with physical therapy, follow-up doctor's appointments, neurological tests, and more appointments and tests than she could recall. Her ribs had completely healed as well as her arm and leg. Every time she looked in the mirror and saw her reflection staring back at her, she couldn't help but think of how grateful she was that *he who shall not be named* had called in a favor to his dad. Dr. Bruce Owens's work was impeccable. Her face looked nearly identical to how it had looked before the accident. Without makeup, Elsie could still make out several small scars, and certain areas around her eye felt harder than the surrounding bone, but no one besides her could tell the difference.

She had several large scars on her abdomen, but scars were a small price to pay for surviving. She would be eternally grateful for all the doctor's gifted ability to help her look and feel as good as new.

Since her accident, she hadn't returned to Nashville. After the argument she had in the hospital with Auggie, she went back to her room and called Marie, who immediately came to the hospital and demanded that the doctor release her that evening. Within an hour, Elsie was home and Marie was sitting at the kitchen table with an open bottle of wine, rereading Auggie's letter over and over again. She continued to ask Elsie questions about their argument until she practically knew it word for word. After a few hours of processing all the information had passed, for the first time in Marie's life she was speechless.

Eventually the two of them came to an agreement that it was best for Elsie to stay in Cincinnati and continue to heal physically, mentally, and emotionally. With the help of a therapist, week by week Elsie slowly began to work through all her emotional trauma from her accident, losing her family, and the complexity of her relationship with Auggie.

Although she was taking a break from composing music with her band, every night she found herself in her basement studio. There was something nostalgic, healing, and peaceful about working alone, by herself, like she had all those years before her career took off. After everything Auggie admitted to her, she had many complex emotions to work through, and playing music was her way of coping.

Every time she picked up her guitar she was not only filled with loving memories of her family, but also with a new appreciation for all the talented medical professionals who helped her regain her strength and mobility. Without them, she wouldn't be able to do the thing she loved most in life, play her guitar. However, thinking about her time in the hospital quickly turned her thoughts to Auggie; how challenging it must have been for him to work on her in the ER that dreadful night, and then finding out the truth about his involvement in her care and why he had left her. When it came to Auggie, she couldn't so much as utter his name without enduring an emotional roller coaster ride. Her gratitude would turn to anger and regret, only to be transformed into confusion and love and then back to gratitude then anger again. Sometimes she'd stay on this ride for minutes at a time, whereas other days she'd struggle for hours.

Elsie's birthday came and went. Instead of having a big, extravagant party like she used to have with her bandmates and friends, she celebrated quietly with Marie's family by watching the fireworks in downtown Cincinnati. The display reminded her of all the times she'd enjoyed them from her father's shoulders and the year she watched the display with Auggie on the beach in Hawaii. She sighed with the thought of him. It seemed no matter what she did or how hard she tried not to think of him, her thoughts always circled back to him.

The day before the year anniversary of Elsie's accident, she received an unexpected knock on her front door. She opened it to see a delivery man holding a stunning bouquet of white calla lilies and a letter. She thanked him, shut the door, set the flowers on the table, and eagerly opened the letter. It read:

> *Elsie,*
> *I know you said you never wanted to hear from me again but what can I say, in my opinion, I've stayed away from you for far too long.*
> *I needed you to know I'm no longer in Cincinnati. Believe it or not, I'm living in Nashville and working at Vanderbilt. I know this job, just as my apology and explanation, has come a day late and a dollar short but I couldn't help myself. I needed to be as close to you as possible. Even if you might never acknowledge my presence again.*

You may think it was me who brought you back to life,
but the truth be told, the only time I've ever felt alive was
during our time together.
   I know it's naïve of me to think you'd ever consider
giving me another chance but you have to know that I will
wait for you for the rest of my life. I will never love another.
It has always been you and will always be you.
   Yours,
   Auggie

After reading his letter, it was as if everything they had been through now finally made perfect sense. The stars had aligned the night they met at a party, bringing him to life. And the stars aligned once more the night Auggie met Elsie in his trauma bay and brought her back to life. For the longest time, Elsie had looked for meaning in why they had fallen in love only to fall apart. She now knew that her relationship with Auggie was bigger and far more complex than she ever could comprehend. Their paths were destined to cross, and there was no stopping destiny.

With that realization, it was as if her body was set on autopilot. She found herself packing her bags, jumping in her car, and driving to Nashville.

"Am I crazy?" she asked Marie over the phone as she drove.

"Yes, but that's never stopped you before." Marie laughed.

Elsie chuckled. "Seriously though, am I making a mistake?"

"I think one way or the other, you owe it to yourself to find out," Marie said encouragingly.

Four hours later she arrived in Nashville. She didn't even go to her apartment to drop her bags off; she drove straight to the hospital and parked in the ER parking lot.

She walked into the ER and eagerly approached the lady working at the desk, saying, "Excuse me, can you please let Dr.

Owens know Elsie McCormick is here to see him?"

"Is he expecting you?" she questioned.

Elsie smiled, then said, "I believe he's waiting for me."

Author's Note

Dear Reader,

   As a young reader, I always wondered how authors would get into character. Any time I'm starting a new chapter, it's important for me to connect to my characters through their emotions. I do this through music. After outlining the chapter, I know how the character is feeling and I pick a song that helps me feel the same way. While listening to the song, I go for a walk or bike ride. When I return home, I feel "in character". Only then am I able to make my characters come alive.

   You'll notice throughout *When Stars Align* that music is a common theme. This is a tribute to all the artists that have helped inspire me to write this story.

   To help enhance your reading experience, I have created a *When Stars Align* Soundtrack available on Spotify. These are songs I listened to bring my characters to life. I also envision these songs playing on the big screen when *When Stars Align* becomes a major motion picture. Cheers to making that day a reality!

Chapter 1
Elsie: "Videotape" by Radiohead

Chapter 2
Auggie: "The Night We Met" by Lord Huron
ft. Phoebe Bridgers

Chapter 3
Elsie: "Paradise" by Coldplay
Auggie: "Campus" by Vampire Weekend
The Force: "Electric Feel" by MGMT

Chapter 4
"The Middle" by Jimmy Eat World

Chapter 5
"Fire for You" by Cannons

Chapter 6
Auggie & Elsie: "Someone To You" by BANNERS

Chapter 7
Elsie: "Let Me Down Slowly" by Alec Benjamin
ft. Alessia Cara
Auggie: "Make You Mine" by PUBLIC
Car Ride: "Keep the Car Running" by Arcade Fire
Ault Park Dance: "Bright" by Echosmith

Chapter 8
"Just Like Heaven" by The Lumineers (The Cure Cover)

Chapter 9
Dating: "Electric Love" by BORNS
Halloween Night: "Existentialism On Prom Night"
by Straylight Run

Chapter 10
"Christmas Time is Here" by Vince Guaraldi Trio
Elsie's Studio: "Bright" by Echosmith
New Year's Eve: "Lover" by Taylor Swift ft. Shawn Mendes

Chapter 11
"BRIGHTSIDE" by The Lumineers

Chapter 12
Elsie: "Somewhere Over The Rainbow" by Israel
Kamakawiwoʻole

"Three Little Birds" by Bob Marley & The Wailers
Elsie and Auggie: "Black" by Dierks Bentley

Chapter 13
"Sign of the Times" by Harry Styles

Chapter 14
Elsie watching Auggie talk to Bobbie: "Maps"
by Yeah Yeah Yeahs
Elsie and Auggie in Limo: "Ocean Eyes" by Billie Eilish

Chapter 15
"All I Want" by Kodaline

Chapter 16
Elsie: "Girl on Fire" by Alicia Keys

Chapter 17
Concert: "Read My Mind" by The Killers
Auggie: "when the party's over" by Billie Eilish
Elsie: "The Night We Met" by Lord Huron ft. Phoebe Bridgers

Chapter 18
Auggie talks to Bobbie: "My Body Is a Cage" by Arcade Fire
Auggie talks to Olive: "The Funeral" by Band of Horses

Chapter 19
Elsie: "You're Somebody Else" by Flora Cash
Returning Home: "Lovely" by Billie Eilish ft. Kahlid

Chapter 20
Funeral: "Danny Boy" by Bing Crosby
Haunted Dreams: "Possibility" by Lykke Li
Coming Home: "Thunder" by Leona Lewis

Chapter 21
Studio: "Yellow Flicker Beat" by Lorde
A Star is Born: "Believer" by Imagine Dragons

Chapter 22
Auggie : "The Scientist" by Coldplay
Elsie: "Arcade" by Duncan Laurence

Chapter 23
Auggie: "Cringe" by Matt Maeson
"You're Somebody Else" by Flora Cash

Chapter 24
Elsie: "Heat Waves" by Glass Animals
"Shake It Out" by Florence + The Machine
Auggie: "All I Need" by AWOLNATION

End
"Bright" by Echosmith

About Atmosphere Press

Atmosphere Press is an independent, full-service publisher for excellent books in all genres and for all audiences. Learn more about what we do at atmospherepress.com.

We encourage you to check out some of Atmosphere's latest releases, which are available at Amazon.com and via order from your local bookstore:

Dancing with David, a novel by Siegfried Johnson

The Friendship Quilts, a novel by June Calender

My Significant Nobody, a novel by Stevie D. Parker

Nine Days, a novel by Judy Lannon

Shining New Testament: The Cloning of Jay Christ, a novel by Cliff Williamson

Shadows of Robyst, a novel by K. E. Maroudas

Home Within a Landscape, a novel by Alexey L. Kovalev

Motherhood, a novel by Siamak Vakili

Death, The Pharmacist, a novel by D. Ike Horst

Mystery of the Lost Years, a novel by Bobby J. Bixler

Bone Deep Bonds, a novel by B. G. Arnold

Terriers in the Jungle, a novel by Georja Umano

Into the Emerald Dream, a novel by Autumn Allen

His Name Was Ellis, a novel by Joseph Libonati

The Cup, a novel by D. P. Hardwick

The Empathy Academy, a novel by Dustin Grinnell

Tholocco's Wake, a novel by W. W. VanOverbeke

Dying to Live, a novel by Barbara Macpherson Reyelts

Looking for Lawson, a novel by Mark Kirby

Yosef's Path: Lessons from my Father, a novel by Jane Leclere Doyle

About the Author

E.K. McCoy is a Cincinnati, Ohio native who currently resides in Hawaii. At the age of ten, she fell in love with the magic she created, using a simple spell that consisted of a pen, a composition book, a flashlight, and her imagination. She spent fourteen years as a medical professional before she decided it was time to cast a new spell and trade in her scrubs for a MacBook. She and her husband, Kyle, enjoy traveling and spending time with their two fun-loving daughters, Ellie and Ava.

CPSIA information can be obtained
at www.ICGtesting.com
Printed in the USA
LVHW111152211022
731219LV00003B/370